"Who are you and why are you here?"

He frowned and released her hand. "What do you mean, who am I?"

"While we're at it, how do you know my name?"

"Why shouldn't I know your name? I am Nathan Rutledge and you are Kate—"

"O'Brien," she finished. "Yes, I know that—"

"Rutledge," he reminded her.

"What?"

"Rutledge."

"Why do you keep saying that?"

He looked at her for a second. "You mean to tell me that you, Kathleen O'Brien, have never even heard my name before today?"

"That's exactly what I mean."

He began to speak then shook his head and strode over to where his saddlebag rested near his horse's stall. "I suppose you'd better have a look at this."

She took the piece of paper he extended to her. "What is this?"

"It's our marriage certificate," he replied quietly.

"What?" Her gaze held his before she stared down at the certificate. "You don't mean—"

"I mean," he interrupted with quiet authority, "that you, Kate O'Brien Rutledge, are my wife."

NOELLE MARCHAND

Her love of literature began as a child, when she would spend hours reading beneath the covers long after she was supposed to be asleep. Over the years, God began prompting her to write by placing ideas for stories in her head. Eventually, those stories became like "fire shut up in her bones," leading her to complete her first novel by her sixteenth birthday. Now, at the age of twenty-two, that fire of inspiration continues to burn.

Noelle is a Houston native and a student at Houston Baptist University, where she is pursuing a double major in mass communication with a focus in journalism and speech communication. Though life as a college student keeps her busy, God continues to use her talent for writing as a way to deepen her spiritual life and draw her closer to Him.

NOELLE MARCHAND

Unlawfully Wedded Bride

Love Inspired

Recycling programs
for this product may
not exist in your area.

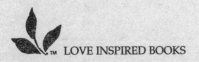 ™ LOVE INSPIRED BOOKS

ISBN-13: 978-0-373-82890-6

UNLAWFULLY WEDDED BRIDE

Copyright © 2011 by Noelle Marchand

www.LoveInspiredBooks.com

Printed in U.S.A.

The righteous shall live by his faith.
—*Habakkuk* 2:4

To God for completing this good work in me.

Acknowledgments

Thanks to my family for fostering a spirit of creativity. Special thanks to Mom for being my first and most avid reader. To my sister, for believing I actually could write a novel, thus allowing me to believe it, too. Thanks to the Butterfly Sisterhood for being you and allowing me to be me.

God bless you, Elizabeth Mazer, for all of your encouragement, advice, patience and expertise! I am so proud of what we accomplished together.

Prologue

August 1877
Peppin, Texas

"We ordered a husband for you."

At the sound of her little brother's voice, Kate O'Brien's finger froze on its trek down the page of her financial ledger. Her gaze shot to the kitchen doorway where twelve-year-old Sean stood next to their ten-year-old sister, Ellie. She met their serious stares blankly. Surely, she'd heard wrong. "I'm sorry. You did what?"

Sean exchanged a look with Ellie, then met Kate's gaze before carefully repeating himself. Kate's heart began to beat faster in her chest. She placed the ledger on the kitchen table and tried to swallow the sense of foreboding that skittered down her backbone. "What exactly does that mean?"

"Something wonderful," Ellie exclaimed with a smile before slipping into a chair across from Kate. "I heard Mr. Johansen talking about mail-order brides at his mercantile. I knew that was what we needed so we put an advertisement for a mail-order groom in a few newspapers."

She glanced from Ellie to Sean, hoping for some indication that they were joking. They both looked perfectly serious.

"We received a lot of responses," Sean said as he pulled a small pack of letters from behind his back and placed it on the table in front of her. She spared the packet a brief glance before meeting her little brother's sincere green eyes. "One response was special. We knew he was perfect for us so we wrote back."

"Oh, Sean," she breathed in dismay.

His gaze faltered for an instant before he continued. "I knew he wouldn't respond if we told him we were children so we just told him all about you and took a few passages from Ma and Pa's love letters to make it sound more grown-up."

Her heart froze in her chest. "You forged letters from me? That's against the law."

His eyes widened and he shook his head adamantly. "We didn't forge letters. We just never said which Miss O'Brien was doing the writing."

"Why did you do this?"

"We wanted to help," he insisted quietly.

She widened her eyes imploringly. "How does this help?"

"You do a lot, Kate," Sean said. "We don't always say thank you for it, but when we stop to think about it we know."

"I do what has to be done."

He nodded. "That's just it. Ma's and Pa's deaths were just as hard on you as they were on us but you were strong. You had to be. We wanted you to have someone who would do for you what you do for us."

Kate was astounded at the maturity in his voice but

still shook her head in disbelief at their actions. "I appreciate that, Sean, but what you two did was wrong."

Ellie leaned forward earnestly. "We knew what you needed and that you would never get it for yourself. You're too shy around handsome men."

She gaped at her younger sister. "Oh, Ellie, really."

"Well, it's true," the girl declared obstinately. "You never let men court you. It's all that awful Mr. Stolvins's fault. Ever since he—"

"Ellie, bringing *that* man into this conversation *really* isn't going to help you."

Ellie allowed her words to stumble to a halt then lifted her brows archly. "It's true and you know it. Besides, you need someone to take care of you."

Kate slammed the ledger shut. "I do not."

"You do so, but you won't admit it," Ellie said firmly. Her small fist pounded on the table. "That's why we had to act."

Kate crossed her arms. "You were trying to marry me off without my consent."

"I know," Ellie said then lifted her chin nobly as tears gleamed in her large green eyes. "We couldn't because you have to sign a silly paper."

Kate's eyes widened. A dry laugh spilled from her lips. "Well, thank the Lord for that."

"It isn't funny," Ellie said as large tears began to roll down her cheeks. She pulled a folded-up paper from the pocket of her skirt and held it toward Kate. "Please, Kate. You just have to sign it."

"No."

"At least, read the letters," Sean urged pleadingly. "Give the man a chance."

"Absolutely not." She pushed the letters away from her as though they might bite her.

Ellie pulled the letters to her chest. The effect of her glare was slightly ruined by a large hiccup. "He's wonderful. His name—"

Kate silenced Ellie with a look. "I don't want to know anything about that man. I've heard enough from both of you on this subject. I've made my decision and the answer is no."

Sean shook his head. "You're making a mistake."

"If I am then it's my mistake to make." She pinned them both with a stare. "I don't want to hear that you two have been writing to this man again. Ever. Do you understand me?"

"Kate," Sean protested.

She cut him off with a shake of her head. "Both of you go to bed. I'll figure out a more suitable punishment for you when my head stops spinning."

Ellie met her gaze defiantly then threw the folded paper on the table before rushing from the room. Sean pulled in a deep breath. He picked up the paper and smoothed it out carefully. Meeting Kate's gaze patiently, he slid the paper across the table until it rested in front of her. With that silent urge for her to think about it, he calmly left the room.

"I don't have time for this," she muttered as she shook her head. She had more important things to think about, like how she was going to save her family's farm. She opened the ledger and continued to search the farm's financial records for some indication the situation wasn't as bad as she feared. Hours passed and she kept coming back to the same conclusion.

Somewhere between buying food for her family and the livestock, the mortgage payments would have to be made. That meant she wouldn't be able to pay the wheat harvesters, which in turn meant she wouldn't be able to sell her wheat. Without selling the wheat, she wouldn't be able to make the other mortgage payments. It was a dizzying cycle with dangerous implications.

If something didn't change soon, they were going to lose the farm. She braced her elbows on the table, then covered her face with her hands. She heaved out a quiet sigh. "Lord, what do I do?"

She'd applied for a short-term loan at the town's only bank and had been denied almost immediately. The banker, Mr. Wilkins, had kindly informed her it would not be in the best interest of either party to enter into another loan agreement when the farm was heading toward foreclosure. She'd put her pride aside long enough to ask if there was anything at all that would make him change his mind. He'd said the only way he would consider giving her a loan was if she married. A single woman in her position would have little success paying back the loan. However, if she had a husband the situation would be entirely different. Since she didn't, he couldn't help her.

Her breath stilled in her throat. Her gaze slid from the mess of papers in front of her to the official-looking document across the table. The bold font read Absentee Affidavit. The only way she could get a loan was to find a husband. Suddenly one was literally at her fingertips. Was it pure coincidence or was it something more?

She set the paper on the ledger in front of her. All she had to do was sign it and she could save the farm. She swallowed. She toyed with the pen, then pulled it carefully from the bottle of ink. Impulsively she set it against the paper. It only took a minute for her to fill in the little information that was required. She signed her name with a desperate flourish, then shoved the pen back into the bottle of ink.

Staring at her signature, dread settled in her stomach. She couldn't do it. The farm was her parents' heritage, yet she could only imagine how appalled they would be if they knew she'd given up her entire future to keep it. She let out a deep sigh, then set the paper as far away from her as possible. *I am not that desperate, but I am not giving up. There is another way. There has to be. Perhaps if I spoke to Mr. Wilkins one more time...*

Exhaustion pulled at her senses. She'd take a moment to rest her eyes, then clean up the mess she'd made and go to bed. Someone called her name and she jerked her head up. Sean stood at the end of the table watching her in concern.

"I'm awake." She pushed her hair away from her face. "What are you doing up? It must be late."

"It's almost midnight. I couldn't sleep." He settled into the chair opposite her.

She closed her drowsy eyes and leaned back in her chair. "You worry too much."

She heard the smile in his voice as he responded. "I promise not to worry anymore."

"Good."

"I know what Ellie and I did was wrong, but I think you made the right decision about everything in the end."

It took a moment for her sleep-fogged mind to catch up. When it did, she felt relief fill her being. She forced her eyes open. "Good. I'm glad you think so."

His gaze flickered to the table then back up to meet hers. "Do you want me to take care of this for you?"

"Would you? That would be wonderful." She glanced at the table strewn with papers and shook her head. "If you could just stack the papers for me, I'll put them away in the morning."

"Sure," he agreed.

She carefully pushed back from the chair then reached out to touch his dark blond hair as she passed. "Good night, Sean."

Satisfaction filled his voice. "Good night."

Chapter One

Three weeks later

Kate felt Ellie's side of the bed dip, then rise. She listened to her sister's small feet pad against the wooden floor of the farmhouse loft. She turned on her side to watch Ellie drag a chair to the window. The soft blue light of morning spilled through the glass as Ellie pushed back the curtains for a better view. Kate sighed then sat up in sleepy curiosity. "What are you doing?"

"I can see the road from here," Ellie said, then jumped down from the chair with a decided thump. She ran to kneel in front of the bed and lifted her sparkling green eyes to meet Kate's. "Do you have a feeling that today will be a very special day?"

"No, not particularly," she said. Seeing Ellie's crestfallen expression, she amended, "I suppose that every day can be a very special day if we let it."

Ellie gave her a half smile seemingly more out of politeness than anything else. Kate hid her bemusement as she turned away from Ellie and quickly dressed. Her siblings seemed to have made a concerted effort to behave since she'd managed to stop their plan to marry her off. While she was relieved to see such an improvement in their behavior, she found it unnerving. How could they possibly not be up to something?

Kate smoothed her hair into an upturned twist as she watched her sister suspiciously. The girl had gone back to her post at the window. "Are you looking for something, Ellie?"

"Hmm? Oh, no," she said absently.

"Then please get ready for school."

"Yes, Kate."

Sean and Ellie stepped into the kitchen just as she set the food on the table. Kate packed their lunch pails and set them in the usual place, then turned to survey their progress and was satisfied to find them nearly done eating. "Do you both have your slates and your homework?"

"Yes." They answered as they deposited their empty plates in the sink.

"Don't lollygag on the way or you'll be late again," she warned, then sank into an empty chair and sent them a smile. "Be good and have fun."

Sean grabbed the lunch pails and slates before hurrying out of the kitchen. Ellie began to follow him then paused to look at Kate. She met the girl's measuring stare. "Yes, Ellie?"

"Are you going to wear that the rest of the day?"

She looked down at her serviceable blue dress. "Why? Is something wrong with it?"

Ellie stepped farther into the room. "Wouldn't it be nice to get dressed up this once?"

"I'll be doing the wash all day. Why would I dress up for that?" she asked in confusion.

Ellie shrugged. "If someone stopped by, you would want to look presentable. Don't you think—"

Sean appeared at the door and frowned at Ellie. "Let's go. We're going to be late."

Ellie nodded then sent Kate a hopeful smile. "Perhaps just your hair—"

"Bye, Kate." Sean grabbed Ellie's arm and pulled her toward the door. As they left Kate heard him whisper, "What are you trying to do, anyway?"

The door slammed shut behind them leaving Kate in perplexed silence. She shook her head in frustration even as her lips curved in an amused smile. It looked like things were finally back to normal. She grabbed a biscuit for breakfast, then went about the chores with her usual determination.

She gathered their laundry and carried the large basket through the forest to the small creek that ran through the property. She washed clothes until her fingers became wrinkled from the cool water, then took a break to let the sun warm her freezing hands. She carefully stretched the kinks from her back. The waterfall that pooled into the small creek provided a drumming rhythm that lulled her senses into disarming relaxation.

A gunshot reverberated through the still morning air. Kate started, then spun toward the sound. Stunned, it took her a moment to realize she was staring into the forest toward her family's farm. She picked up her skirts and ran. She dashed through the trees, her bare feet creating a quick rhythm on the path she'd traveled only an hour ago.

The edge of her petticoat caught on a fallen branch but she refused to slow down as she neared the large clearing where her father had built their farm. The curious sound of masculine voices made her pause. She cautiously moved around the side of the barn toward them. The voices grew louder. With one last step, she cleared the barn and found herself in the middle of a standoff.

Kate froze. Her gaze traveled from the tall cowboy on her left whose gun was drawn toward the house, to the young man standing just outside her doorway. He was struggling to keep his grip on his pistol and control the haphazard pile of possessions in his arms. She narrowed her eyes as she recognized the items, then gasped as realization tumbled over her. She stepped forward. "What do you think you're doing with my things? Put those down!"

He jumped and turned to stare at her with panic in his gaze.

Her eyes widened as she realized he was just a boy. She lifted her chin and her tone turned imperious. "I said, put those down. Just you wait until—"

A wild shot flew from the boy's gun.

She jumped, then stared at him in surprise.

"Get down!" The deep unyielding command from the cowboy made her obey without question. Another shot broke out, this time from her side.

"Of all the foolish things to do…" The cowboy let out a volley of shots. The boy ran for the horse waiting in the barnyard and somehow managed to mount with his armful of goods.

A shot from beside her sent the boy's hat flying from his head. Kate caught her breath then pushed the man's gun away from its target. "Don't do that. You'll hit him!"

She watched as his aggravation seemed to flare along with the golden ring outlining his deep brown eyes. "Woman, don't touch my gun."

She gasped at his harsh tone. "I was trying to keep you from killing a child!"

"If I had meant to hit him, I would have." He stood then caught her elbow to help her to her feet. "As it is, he got away with my horse."

"Not to mention his life," she delivered testily.

He frowned at her.

She glared back.

His frown slipped, then pulled into an amused half smile. "I wondered if you'd have a temper to match your hair."

She let out a confused breath, then caught an escaping lock of her rich strawberry-blond hair and vainly tried to tuck it into place. "What do you mean?"

"Not a thing I didn't say," he said seriously, but his eyes held hers teasingly.

Kate found herself momentarily distracted by him as she suddenly became aware of his strong yet dangerously handsome features. She took a small step back, feeling a telltale warmth spill across her cheeks. He eyed her for a long moment, then gave his gun a small spin before tucking it safely into the holster. He tipped his Stetson to introduce himself, "I'm Nathan Rutledge."

She lifted her chin. "Miss O'Brien."

"Rutledge," he reminded with a nod.

Didn't he just say that? she wondered. "Yes, I know."

Unnerved by the friendly grin her statement caused, Kate glanced away. "Thank you for your help. Unfortunately he still got away with everything."

"Oh, he hasn't gotten away with anything yet."

She glanced up to survey the determined glint in his eye. "You're going after him."

"Of course I am," he said. "Delilah's been with me more than three years. I'm not letting some little thief get away with a horse of that stock."

"Delilah?" she asked, unsuccessfully denying her curiosity.

The man nodded. "Yes. Delilah."

Uncomfortable with his warm gaze, she glanced down at her dress. "That's an interesting name for a horse."

"One of a kind," he admitted.

Kate frowned.

He stepped closer.

Surprised, she looked up and couldn't seem to look away. She closed her eyes against the searching, his and her own. *What is going on here? This is not normal. No one should have this sort of rapport with a total stranger. I may spend most of my time alone on the farm when Sean and Ellie are in school, but I can't be that lonely. Can I?*

"Kate," he said, and her eyes flew open at the sound of her name. Snapped from whatever spell held her, she lifted her chin and stared at him. She hadn't given him her Christian name. Perhaps she'd met him before and forgotten? She allowed her gaze to sweep from his dark brown eyes and past his blue checkered shirt. His dark gray pants fit loosely against his long legs, and the dark metal of his gun rested against his thigh while his low-slung gun belt stretched across his hips. Meeting his gaze, she shook her head. If she'd met him, she would have remembered.

She opened her mouth to question him but he was already speaking. "I have to go after him. May I use your horse?"

She managed to nod, then watched him hurry toward the barn. A few minutes later, he reappeared on her horse and went in pursuit of the thief without a backward glance. Kate watched him disappear into the distance and vainly tried to sort out what just happened.

An hour later, back on Delilah and with the thief secured on Kate's horse, Nathan Rutledge rode down Main Street, noting the curious stares from the citizens of Peppin, Texas. He had been on the receiving end of a town's stares before, only they hadn't been so friendly. But this was his new beginning—the fresh start he'd prayed for. He tipped his hat toward the young women who watched him shyly, then nodded at the older man sitting on the feed store steps.

The man narrowed his eyes suspiciously, then sat up in his chair to spit a stream of brown chewing tobacco juice on the ground in Nathan's direction. He smiled wryly. Now, that was more like what he was used to. He was ready to put that life behind him as sure as he was breathing.

A "howdy" broke into his thoughts. He glanced down to find a man with graying hair and a belly that overlapped his belt watching him suspiciously.

"Can I help you with something?" the man asked.

Nathan eyed the star on the man's chest and nodded. "I'm looking for the sheriff. Is that you?"

The man gave a single nod. "That's me."

He dismounted. Tipping his hat back, he nodded toward the person who had really been drawing all the attention. The young thief sent him scathing glares from where he sat with his hands bound and tied to the saddle horn of Kate's horse. "I found him trying to steal from the O'Brien place this morning. He took off with my horse when I tried to stop him. He's just a boy so I'm not sure what's to be done about it."

The sheriff's suspicious gaze went from him to the

boy and back again as the man obviously tried to discern who was guilty of what crime. "Is that so? What were you doing out at the O'Brien's in the first place?"

"With all due respect, sir, I reckon that's my business." He wasn't sure how much Kate had told the town about him, but he wasn't about to announce his presence to strangers without even a proper first meeting with the woman.

The sheriff's eyes narrowed for a moment. Nathan held the man's gaze, looking him straight in the eye without shifting or backing down. Finally, the sheriff nodded. "Let's get him down from there and we'll sort all this out."

Nathan cut the boy free, then waited for him to slide off the horse. The boy looked as if he might try to bolt but the sheriff put a hand on his shoulder and steered him toward the jail. Though his stomach tightened in dread, Nathan had no choice but to follow. The sheriff directed the boy to a chair in front of the desk, then sat across from him.

Nathan's gaze nonchalantly surveyed the walls of the office until he found the "wanted" posters. He was relieved when only the grizzled faces of strangers stared back at him. Movement to his right caught his eye. He nodded at the young-looking deputy who rose from that side of the room to watch the proceedings curiously.

"This man says you tried to steal from the O'Brien place. What do you have to say about that?" the sheriff asked.

The boy glared at them defiantly. "I gave it all back. Let me go!"

The sheriff sighed. "You know I can't do that. Are your parents around here?"

"No."

"Who's taking care of you?"

"I am."

The sheriff grunted. "Deputy Stone, take him in the back for now."

"What's going to happen to him?" Nathan asked after the boy was led away.

"I don't rightly know. He isn't from around here and it doesn't look like he has any family." The sheriff eyed him carefully. "You aren't from around here, either, are you?"

Nathan tensed but played it off with a shrug and an easy smile. "You can tell that easy?"

"You sure don't look familiar. In a town this small, that's clue enough." The sheriff narrowed his gaze. "I guess I won't get a chance to know you much if you're just passing through."

"I guess not," he said, hearing the sheriff's message clearly. He'd just been told to get his business done and move on. Apparently, Peppin didn't tolerate strangers coming through and causing trouble. Nathan wasn't looking to cause trouble and he certainly wasn't planning to leave Peppin anytime soon. He had too much to stick around for, like that red-headed woman he'd promised to return to. When he stepped outside, Delilah's whinny was just the distraction he needed after visiting the jail. He stepped close to the large black mare to tenderly stroke her nose.

"You knew I'd come for you, didn't you, girl?"

She blew out a puff of air onto his hand. Then with a final wary glance toward the town jail, he stepped into the saddle and turned the mare toward the O'Brien place.

Kate leaned on the kitchen table with her elbow while she placed her chin in her palm. As she turned the next page of the family Bible, she realized she'd barely skimmed the past few verses. Dissatisfied, she closed the large book and sank despondently into the chair. She had already finished the laundry. Most of their clothes were flapping in the wind outside while she waited inside for the stranger to return. *If* he returned.

She was beginning to wonder if the whole thing had just been a big ruse between the pair of strangers. They were probably both thieves. Now not only had she lost a number of her family's few valuable possessions but she'd also lost Pa's horse. She groaned. What had made her think she could trust that man?

The sound of horse hooves in the barnyard drew her gaze toward the kitchen doorway. Rising from her chair, she hurried to the living room window to peer out. The stranger rode into the barnyard on his large black horse with her bay trailing after it. Relief poured from her lips in a heavy sigh.

Her relief did not change the resolve that filled her being. She was going to get some answers from this man. Her determination did not fade as she opened the door and marched toward the barn. It did not falter when she caught up to him or while she watched him loop the horses' reins around his hands to walk them into the barn. It was only when his friendly gaze met hers that it wavered.

"I found him, but he can't be more than fourteen," he said as they stepped into the relative coolness of the barn. "The sheriff isn't sure what to do with him. He isn't from around here and doesn't claim to have any family."

Take your time, she reminded herself as he guided the horses to their stalls. She waited as he removed the saddle from her horse to place it back where it belonged. He repeated the process with the reins and bridle, then glanced up questioningly. She opened her mouth to speak but he was already asking, "Where's the brush?"

She blinked. "It's on the shelf near the bridles. I'll get it."

She moved toward the hooks, then glanced up at the shelf trying to see over its edge. Her father had been much taller than her and, as a result, everything was nearly out of her reach. It took a moment for her to spot it. "There it is."

"I see it," Nathan said at the same time.

Her hand reached it a moment before his did. She stilled as his hand covered hers. She pulled the brush down half expecting him to release it, half hoping he wouldn't. He didn't. She turned toward him and slowly glanced up past his blue checkered shirt to his face. His gaze solemnly slipped over her features. She swallowed. "There's something I have to ask you."

His gaze met hers.

She lifted her chin. "Who are you and why are you here?"

He frowned and released her hand. "What do you mean, who am I?"

"While we're at it, how do you know my name?"

"Why shouldn't I know your name? I am Nathan Rutledge and you are Kate—"

"O'Brien," she finished. "Yes, I know that."

"Rutledge," he reminded.

"What?"

"Rutledge."

"Why do you keep saying that?"

"Because your name used to be—" He paused and looked at her for a second. "You mean to tell me that you, Kathleen 'O'Brien,' have never even heard my name before today?"

"That's exactly what I mean."

He began to speak, then shook his head and strode over to where his saddlebag rested near Delilah's stall. "I suppose you'd better have a look at this."

She took the piece of paper he extended to her. She glanced up as she unfolded it. "What is this?"

"It's our marriage certificate," he replied quietly.

"What?" Her gaze held his before she stared down at the certificate. "You don't mean—"

"I mean," he interrupted with quiet authority, "that you, Kate O'Brien Rutledge, are my wife."

Chapter Two

"I don't understand how you could marry me without my consent," Kate said as she handed him a glass of water, then settled onto the dark green settee in the living room a few minutes later.

He sat at the other end of the settee, then turned toward her. "What are you talking about? You signed the affidavit."

"I signed it but I never intended to send it," she admitted.

A confused frown marred his face. "I don't understand."

She bit her lip. "Mr. Rutledge, I'm afraid my family owes you an apology."

"An apology?"

She pulled in a deep breath. "Let me explain how this started."

She watched a myriad of emotions flit across his face as she carefully explained what her siblings had done. Shock, confusion and disappointment battled for dominance before a bemused, disbelieving smile settled upon his lips. Once she finished, his gaze strayed to the saddle bag he'd set on the low walnut table in front of them. "So your little brother and sister are the ones who wrote the letters."

"I'm afraid so."

He watched her carefully. "Were they also the ones who sent the affidavit?"

"They must have because I certainly didn't."

He nodded, then looked as though he didn't know what else to say. An uncomfortable silence filled the living room. What was she supposed to do now? She shrugged. "You're welcome to stay and help me sort this out when they get home."

"Thank you."

Silence again. She glanced around the room for something to do and her gaze landed on his saddle bag. Meeting his gaze, she asked, "Is there any chance I could see one of those letters?"

"Of course," he said, then pulled out several letters from the saddlebag and handed them to her.

She looked at the curved letters written in a formal script. "This isn't Ellie's handwriting."

"Then whose is it?"

"It looks like Ms. Lettie's. She must have helped them." The young widow would do whatever she could to support Kate and her family. Still, if not for seeing her familiar handwriting, Kate would never have suspected the woman of doing anything this drastic.

She continued to read the contents of a letter and frowned. "This is something I told Ellie about Ma's wedding dress. It was destroyed in a fire when I was eight. Nothing was left but—"

"A small strip of the Irish lace that trimmed the hem of the dress," he continued. "Your mother brought it with you on your journey here from Illinois and just a week before she died she sewed it into your own wedding dress. You keep it in your small wooden hope chest."

"Yes, that's right," she said quietly. "That was all—"

"In the letter?" he asked. "Yes, it was all there."

Her eyes narrowed as she softly queried, "What else was written in there?"

"Oh, just the generalities."

"Such as?"

He grinned. "Such as your name, birth date and other general information."

Her lips curved into a slightly amused smile. "How helpful."

"I thought so."

"Right," she breathed, looking at the letter in her hand, realizing this man whom she knew nothing about could probably recite her entire life story. "You know so much about me yet I know nothing about you."

"You could ask," he said with an inviting lift of his brow.

Curiosity begged to accept his invitation but wouldn't it be best to let the man remain a mystery? The more she knew, the harder it would be to forget this ever happened. She planned to do that as sure as she planned to send him away. Until then, there was only one thing she really wanted to know. "Why would you even agree to something like this in the first place?"

Nathan should have known that would be the first question she asked. "I explained the best I could in the letters but I guess you didn't read those, did you?"

She shook her head.

He was quiet for a long moment as he searched for the right words. Finally, he asked, "Have you ever felt like God took your plans for the future, crumpled them up in his hands and scattered the pieces?

"That's what happened to me," he said gravely. "Then I saw the advertisement. I scoffed at it at first, don't get me wrong. Still, try as I might, I couldn't get it out of my head. I finally just broke down and wrote to you. I didn't expect anything to come of it, but you responded and the more I learned about you the more I felt God leading me to continue."

Her blue eyes filled with doubt and skepticism. "Then why didn't you just try to meet me first? All of this could have been avoided."

He shrugged. "The letters insisted on a proxy marriage. They said you wanted to cause as little disruption to the farm and your family as possible. I'm not saying it didn't seem a little odd but at that point I believed God wanted me to do it. I wasn't about to go against that."

She smiled sympathetically then lifted her shoulders in a shrug. "We all make mistakes. I've certainly made my share. Thankfully, this shouldn't be too hard to fix."

"I never said I was mistaken."

Her eyes lit with surprise. "Oh." Her gaze faltered for a moment then shot toward the large window. "I think I hear the barn door."

As she went to the window, he carefully refolded the letter she'd read, then slid it back into his saddle bag with the rest of them. He was in trouble if Kate's last statement was a hint of what was to come.

He'd questioned his sanity for taking on a proxy bride but that advertisement had sparked more hope in him than he'd had in a long time. He hadn't fooled himself into thinking their marriage was a love match. That would surely have been impossible. He had hoped that within a relatively short time that would change.

Now, if he wasn't careful, it would all slip through his fingers.

Suddenly Kate turned with a frown marring her delicate features. "They're here."

Kate forced herself to sit calmly on the settee as she waited for her siblings to come inside. She couldn't stop herself from peeking at the man sitting next to her. He nearly caught her sideways glance so she pulled her eyes away to let them land on the front door.

"Kate, calm down. We'll figure this out." His deep voice startled her but she covered her reaction to it.

"I know. It's just—"

Childish voices approached. The wooden door creaked open and Ellie appeared. Kate watched as the girl's gaze skimmed deliberately over her before moving on to the stranger. "Oh, Mr. Rutledge, I see you've made it. That's wonderful!"

Sean entered the room but paused at the doorway to cautiously take in the scene before him. Ellie glanced at her brother, seemingly for support, then smiled brightly. "What's for supper?"

Kate glanced at Nathan hoping to convey a message and he seemed to receive it for they both sat in silence. The silence drew all eyes to her. Once she had her siblings' attention she quietly commanded, "Sean, Ellie, sit down."

They moved to their seats, placing their lunch pails and slates on the side table. Neither would meet her gaze. Sean stared at the floor while Ellie looked off into a corner.

"Explain this," she commanded with a sweeping gesture toward Nathan.

Sean finally met her gaze. "It all started out as a misunderstanding. I thought you changed your mind when I saw the filled-out form. I asked if you wanted me to take care of it. You said yes. I mailed it the next morning before school. I didn't realize you just wanted me to stack those papers until much later."

She groaned. "Why didn't you tell me?"

"You told us never to mention it again," Ellie reminded, giving Kate a pointed look.

"I also told you not to send him any more letters."

"We didn't," Sean interjected. "We just sent that paper. He sent something telling us when he was coming. That was all."

She glanced up to find Ellie surveying her carefully. Her sister shot a glance at Nathan. "Did she try the ring?"

He lifted his eyebrows as an amused smile teased his mouth. "Somehow we haven't quite gotten to that part."

"That's too bad. Do you still think it will fit?"

He discreetly glanced at her ring finger. "It probably would."

Ellie nodded. "Can I see it?"

"May I," Kate automatically corrected, then frowned. "Ellie, don't you think there are more important things to discuss?"

"I was wondering." Ellie glanced between them. "Did you fall in love at first sight like Jacob and Rachel did in the Bible?"

Kate's mouth fell open. "Ellie, that's enough! This is serious. You've tampered not only with two people's lives but also with one man's emotions. He came all the way from who knows where—"

"Noches, Texas," he supplied.

"He shows up and defends me and our house, all the

while thinking I'm his wife. A wife created by a ten-
and a twelve-year-old."

Sean lifted his hand to speak. "Remember we just
told him about you. We didn't make you up."

"And we didn't do it on purpose," Ellie interjected,
then blushed. "Well, not this time."

Ignoring those statements, Kate continued firmly,
"I want you to apologize to Mr. Rutledge for lying and
interfering in his life before doing the same to me."

They looked properly ashamed, and humbly apologized before they went outside for their evening chores.
Kate rose to heat up the food for supper. The clamor of
the pans hitting the stove seemed jarring in the silence.
Clearing her throat, Kate apologized, "Mr. Rutledge, I
don't know what to say."

"It's Nathan," he said, his voice sounding closer than
she anticipated.

She turned to look up into his dark brown eyes and
persisted. "Mr. Rut—"

He smiled knowingly, then shook his head. "Nathan."

Frowning, she yielded. "Nathan, I guess the only way
to get out of this would be to get an annulment."

He leaned back against the table. "Should we want
to get out of it?"

"Of course we should." Her eyes widened. "Why?
Don't you?"

His gaze slid thoughtfully over her face. "I don't
know."

She placed her hands on her hips. "How can you not
know? It's the only sensible thing to do."

"Sensible to me is this. You need a husband, I need
a wife, and we're already married. Why not stay that
way?"

She laughed. "You can't mean that."

His jaw tightened. "Just why can't I?"

"Because…" She wavered and he seemed to sense it. Why couldn't she stay married to him? It was too dangerous. He was too dangerous. She wasn't ready. She'd never even met him before today. It simply wasn't plausible. Yet she looked into his eyes and reason began to melt, along with her resistance.

"We can make this work," Nathan insisted. "I'm already fond of you and I have nowhere else to go."

She slowly shook her head. "I won't do this. It isn't fair to expect me to honor a commitment I never made."

He stepped closer. "You were willing to honor that commitment when you signed the affidavit."

"That was different."

"How?"

She bit her lip then admitted, "I needed a loan from the bank. The banker said he would only give it to me if I was married."

His gaze filled with a concern that strengthened into compassion. "I'm sorry to hear that."

"I never intended to send the affidavit because I decided to look for some other way—any other way. I pleaded with Mr. Wilkins to let me postpone the payments until after harvest. He agreed, with the understanding that if I don't make a payment after the harvest, the farm will immediately go into foreclosure. I planted more wheat than usual so I'm sure the harvest will be enough to keep the farm safe."

"In other words, you don't need me anymore and you'll risk everything you own to keep it that way." He paused, looking at her searchingly. "Why put yourself through that when it would be so much easier to go through with your original plan?"

She stiffened. "You're right. I don't need you. I have

a plan and it's going to work. It may be hard, but I'm going to make it the same way I have for two years. That means without you or any other man getting in the way."

"So that's it? I sold my property back in Noches because you said you wanted the children to grow up here. All of that was for nothing?"

"I'm sorry, but I hope you realize that I never said any such thing."

"No, I guess you didn't." He took his Stetson from the table. Holding it in his hands, he nodded. "Sorry for the trouble, Ms. O'Brien. You'll get your annulment. I'll make sure of it."

Nathan slid the bridle onto Delilah's head, then glanced at the two children who watched him in disappointment.

"You're leaving," Sean said, more as a statement than a question.

"I'm afraid so."

The boy looked down. "You aren't coming back."

"I doubt it."

Ellie climbed onto the short wall that sectioned off Delilah's stall to stare at him with imploring green eyes. "Why don't you win her back?"

"You can't win something back you never had, Ellie."

She crossed her arms. "You didn't even try."

He *had* tried but Kate wasn't willing to do the same. If Ellie thought he was the problem, then so be it. He'd caused enough strife in his own family to know better than to start it in someone else's. Besides, Kate was probably right. He'd thought God was leading him to a new life, but this seemed to be just as much of a mistake as everything else he'd done lately—everything he was trying so desperately to forget.

He did his best not to let Ellie's glower bother him as he finished saddling his mare. He led Delilah from her stall. The children followed him in silence until Sean asked, "What are you going to do now?"

He glanced back and was surprised to see deep concern in the boy's eyes. Ellie seemed to have lost most of her defiance, because while her chin still tilted upward, her eyes looked suspiciously moist. He realized that even though he was nothing more than a stranger to Kate, her siblings probably felt they knew him well. In truth, they probably knew him better than anyone else in his life right now.

Impulsively he knelt to put himself on their level. "Hey, I hope you two aren't worrying about me. I'll figure something out. I always do."

Ellie's chin quivered. "We want you to stay."

"I know you do." He guessed he didn't have to tell them that things didn't always turn out the way you wanted. He figured they'd been through enough in their short lives to know that better than most. "I'm sorry I can't do that, but you two have each other and Kate. You'll be all right. Just remember to mind your sister. No more of this kind of stuff, you hear?"

They both nodded.

He stood and didn't bother to knock the dust from his britches before he swung onto Delilah. He glanced down to offer the pair parting smiles. "Goodbye, now."

A few minutes later he turned Delilah so that he could get one last look at the O'Brien's farm. The children had gone inside, so all he could see was the house and its fields. He swallowed against the unexpected emotion in his throat. He'd failed just like he always did when it came to chasing down his dream.

Hadn't his Pa told him this would happen? He tried to push away the memory of his father's parting words. He heard them anyway. "You're going to fail. You're going to come crawling back. Stay at the ranch and take your place like your brother. This is where you're supposed to be."

Turning Delilah back toward the main road, he urged her into a canter. It looked like his Pa had been right about him all along. It had just taken him five years to figure it out.

Kate swayed in her seat as the wagon jolted over a bump on the road to town the next morning. They were nearly to Peppin before anyone dared to bring up the subject foremost on their minds.

"I think you should ask him to come back," Ellie said, over the groaning wagon wheels.

"I'm sure I know what you think, Ellie." Kate's grip tightened on the reigns. "I've already made my decision."

"I liked him," Sean said.

"So did I," Ellie chimed in with a slight lift of her chin. "Didn't you like him, Kate?"

"I'm sure he's a nice man." She was sure because she'd seen the way he'd knelt in the dirty barnyard to talk to her siblings before he left. The sight had touched her more than she cared to admit.

"And handsome?"

Kate glanced at her sister in interest. "Since when do you care about handsome?"

"I don't." Ellie recoiled then sent Sean a mischievous

glance. "That's just what Lorelei Wilkins always says about Sean."

"Really?" Kate asked as Sean's face lit up like a red beacon.

"It is not," he protested.

"It is, too. I heard her at recess. She told all the girls how much you like her and how you'll get married one day."

"That's just because she's a dumb girl."

Kate arched a brow. "I hope you didn't tell her that."

"No, but I'd sure like to," Sean growled.

"I'm sure you would. Don't worry, Sean. She'll move on soon enough. In the meantime, try not to let it bother you."

He looked over at her. "I thought we were talking about you, Kate."

She feigned disinterest. "Not anymore."

He frowned as he surveyed the row of businesses on either side of Main Street. "Are you really going to get a whatever-it's-called?"

"An annulment? Yes. That's why I'm driving you to town to today."

That put a damper on the conversation until the children jumped off the wagon and called goodbye as they headed to the schoolhouse. Kate pulled the horses to a stop across the street from the town's small courthouse. She stared at the gray wooden building and frowned. *Exactly how does one get an annulment?*

She didn't know but she was certainly going to find out. Filled with resolve, she discreetly swung her legs over the side of the wagon and hopped down. Her forward momentum suddenly stopped when her dress caught on the wagon wheel and caused her to stumble. She managed to catch her balance just as she heard shouts sound farther down Main Street. Curious to step over and see what the commotion was about, she worked to release her skirt from the splintery clutches of the wagon's axle. She pulled at the dark green fabric until she heard the sound of pounding hooves and a wild neigh behind her.

She glanced up to find a startled horse and struggling rider almost upon her. The man on the horse looked down. She took in the detail of his eyes widening before he yelled, "Get out the way!"

She gasped, then suddenly a strong arm snaked around her waist and she was slammed against the wood of the wagon. The force of a hard body pressing against her own knocked the wind out of her. Her breath came in ragged gasps. She heard the horse scream and a loud thump, then found herself struggling to hold up a limp and heavy body. Losing the battle, she sank to the ground along with the man.

She glanced up in time to see the terrified horse give one last turn and a swift kick in the air before galloping away, its rider also thrown to the ground. Her gaze flew back to the man whose body pinned her arm to the ground beneath him. Her sharp gasp rent the air as she looked into the handsome features of Nathan Rutledge.

She was close enough to see the golden flecks lighting his mahogany eyes when they fluttered open. He murmured her name, then his eyes drifted shut. His face went pale. She stared at him in disbelief. Surely he wasn't dead!

She cradled his head in her hand, then pulled her arm from beneath him to place her other hand over his heart. Though she couldn't feel its beat, she detected the slight rise and fall of his chest. Kate heard someone calling for help and realized it was her own strangled voice. Then arms were pulling her away and setting her aside as Doc Williams attended to Nathan.

She stared at the pale face and large form of the man sprawled in the middle of the street. A comforting arm came around her. She clasped her hands beneath her chin. Feeling something wet on them, she looked at her hands to see one mottled with blood. She stared at the traces, realizing it was Nathan's. Her body went cold and she began to tremble. Everything flashed black for a moment.

A voice she absently identified as Mrs. Greene's chided, "Now, don't you swoon, child. We already have one out let's not have another."

Gathering her courage Kate locked her knees, forcing the darkness away by the sheer power of her will. Then she fainted.

Chapter Three

Kate pulled in a cleansing breath as she stood at the window in Doc's waiting room. Her nose twitched as she remembered awakening to the acrid scent of smelling salts ten minutes ago. She heard gasps sound behind her. She whirled to find the sheriff and Mrs. Greene staring at her in astonishment. She looked from their faces to Ms. Lettie's pleased one and groaned. She never should have whispered the truth about Nathan's identity to the woman after waking up. "Oh, Ms. Lettie, you told them, didn't you?"

Ms. Lettie's eyes widened. "Don't tell me you wanted to keep the marriage a secret."

Mrs. Greene frowned. "You mean to tell me Kate is really married to that man?"

"I suppose I shouldn't have told you anything, but yes, she is."

"Goodness," the other woman breathed, placing a dainty hand over her heart.

Sheriff Hawkins frowned. "Wait just a minute. He acted like he was just passing through. Why didn't he tell me you two were married?"

"He is just passing through," Kate said, smoothing

her green dress calmly. "And we're not staying married for long. Mr. Rutledge and I are getting an annulment."

Ms. Lettie gasped. "You're getting an annulment? Kate, whatever for?"

"Surely you didn't expect me to agree to this crazy scheme?"

"Why not? The man is nice, he's a Christian and he's half in love with you already," Ms. Lettie stated.

"He's a stranger! Even if he was completely in love with me, it wouldn't change anything. I don't need a husband. We are getting an annulment," she said with determination as she leaned her shoulder against the window sill.

"No. She's right, Lettie," Mrs. Greene said. "She's trying protect herself from getting hurt, as well she should. We all know what happened with that Stolvins fellow down at the saloon."

Kate glanced out the window hoping to hide the flush spreading across her cheeks. "That was before he sold the hotel to open the saloon."

"To think, he tried to convince you to marry him even after you found out he was only after the pittance your parents left. I'm sure he broke your heart straight to pieces."

"Hardly," she breathed in disdain. Perhaps it was a little true, but she'd never let on; especially not to Mrs. Greene. She lifted her chin and met the woman's prying gaze. "That was a long time ago."

The woman arched her brow. "Andrew Stolvins doesn't seem to think so."

"I'm sure I don't care what he thinks, but that has nothing to do with me getting an annulment."

"I was only complimenting you on keeping a level head in the matter." Mrs. Greene lifted a hand as though to ward off Kate's anger. "Really, you're a nice enough girl, I suppose, but your siblings are a handful. Especially Ellie. Why, every time I'm around that girl, she causes trouble. Sometimes I wonder if she does it specifically to annoy me. You can't really believe the man would stay once he's met them." She shook her head. "Why frankly, I don't think you'll ever be able to marry."

Kate's breath caught at the woman's rudeness. Her temper rose with the color in her cheeks but Ms. Lettie came to her defense. "Amelia, that's a horrible thing to say!"

"We've all thought it, haven't we?"

"No, we haven't," Sheriff Hawkins said.

"Certainly, we have. The girl is no great beauty and has a temper hotter than the Fourth of July. To make matters worse, she's saddled with two young children who aren't even her own. Why, her chances are slim to say the least. Now that she is married, it's really no great surprise to me that her husband is eager to leave."

Kate lifted her chin defiantly. "I'm the one who wanted the annulment. Not him. He wanted to stay."

"But he wouldn't stay long."

She shook her head incredulously. "How can you know that?"

"I know you and your family," Mrs. Greene said with a nod.

Kate felt her temper soar. "Please, don't talk about my family."

"Don't get angry, child. I'm agreeing with you. You're doing the wise thing and it's better now than when an annulment isn't possible."

"Mrs. Greene, I could keep that man as long as I

want," she said with more confidence than she felt. "The problem is I don't want him."

Mrs. Greene stood. "I saw that man and he's too much for you. Now, my Emily would be a right fine match for him in looks and temperament."

"Good. She can have him. Though there might be a small problem in the fact that he's still married to *me*."

"As you've said, that will soon be rectified."

"Kate, give the man a chance," Ms. Lettie insisted.

"I am not going to discuss this."

Doc Williams appeared at the door and cleared his throat loudly. "Kate, I need you to come with me."

Grateful for the interruption, she immediately stood to follow him but glanced back at the others with a beseeching look. "Please, don't tell anyone else about the marriage. He'll be gone soon and I'd rather not have everyone know."

Mrs. Greene nodded staunchly. "I wouldn't say a word about it. It certainly wouldn't do Emily any favors for everyone to know."

Somewhat comforted by their agreement, she followed Doc to Nathan's room. She stepped inside and immediately noticed Nathan's prone body stretching from one end of the bed to the other. He was still pale, though some color was beginning to return to his face.

"I think he'll be fine if we can bring him back to consciousness," Doc Williams said.

She frowned slightly. "We? But what can I do?"

"I'm hoping the sound of your voice might bring him back."

She looked at him in suspicion. "Why should it?"

"You're the only one he knows in town—the only voice that will sound familiar. And even though he's not awake, you're probably in his thoughts. He was hurt protecting you."

Kate stiffened. "That isn't my fault. I could have taken care of myself."

Doc sighed. "Kate, I didn't agree with what Lettie was planning at first but she convinced me it was the best thing for you." He shook his head. "I know you can take care of yourself. We all do. But you shouldn't always have to. That's what marriage is for."

Kate sent him a knowing look. "Speaking of marriage, when are you going to get around to popping the question to Ms. Lettie? You've been courting over a year now. I'd say it's about time."

"I've been busy." Kate knew that was the truth. Doc Williams had devoted himself to their town since his arrival fifteen years before. But now that the man had entered his forties, everyone was ready to see him nicely settled.

"She could help you with that. She is an expert in natural remedies and would be a good nurse."

He frowned at her, though his eyes continued to twinkle. "I doubt even Lettie could find a natural remedy for busyness."

"I didn't mean—"

"You meant to distract me, but it won't work." He ignored her exasperated protest, to continue, "My marital status is not what matters at the moment. What matters is that however you became this man's wife, you are exactly that—his wife. Regardless of what happens in the future, he needs you right now."

Kate bit her lip as she gazed back at the doctor, then with a sigh she relented. "What do you want me to do?"

Doc smiled. "Just call to him, talk to him, anything for him to hear the sound of your voice."

Kate looked at Nathan a moment then moved to the side of the bed. "Nathan."

He didn't respond.

"Nathan." Her heart jumped. Did his eyelid twitch just the littlest bit? She glanced at the doctor who nodded encouragingly. She frowned thoughtfully. *If the doctor thinks there is a chance he might regain consciousness, then shouldn't I give it a real try?*

Wishing she knew his middle name, she commanded in a stern voice, "Nathan Rutledge, open your eyes this minute!"

She narrowed her eyes. Did he blink or had she?

Determined, she sank to her knees beside his bed. An idea hit her and she reached for Nathan's hand, feeling the rough calluses on his hard palm. She glanced at Doc Williams. He was watching her intently if not with some amusement. Glancing back to Nathan, she called in a helpless voice, "Nathan, save me. Oh, save me, Nathan."

His eyelashes drifted upward then closed again.

She looked at the doctor triumphantly. He smiled in return. Kate looked toward the closed door before lending an air of desperation to her voice. "Nathan, please help me. Help me, Nathan."

Caught in the throes of her theatrics, she threw her head back dramatically before dropping it on the bed beside his pillow. She let out a puff of air. There. She'd given it all she had and the man still wouldn't come out of his state. No one could say she hadn't tried. Now maybe she could leave.

Kate leaned back onto her heels to look at Doc Williams. "Doc, I really don't think this is going to work. Have you tried the smelling salts they used on me? I—"

She paused realizing the large hand in hers was

squeezing back. Her eyes widened as she slowly turned to meet Nathan's gaze. Eyes more golden than brown stared back at her as his dark brows lowered into a frown. His voice was strong and clear as he responded to her cries for help. "You said you didn't want me, so why are you in my bedroom?"

She gasped, pulling her hands from his grasp.

He wasn't finished. "And what do you need saving from this time? Honestly, I can't seem to turn around without having to get you out of trouble."

"Never mind," she said as her gaze darted to the doctor whose lip twitched with suppressed laughter.

"Where am I?" he asked as he tried to sit up.

Doc stepped forward. "No sudden movements. That's good. Lie back down. Now, tell me. Does your head hurt?"

Nathan grunted. "Yeah, it hurts."

Kate slowly edged toward the door.

"How would you rate the pain?"

"Bad enough."

"That's to be expected since you were—" the doctor faltered as though trying to find the right words "—hit in the head by a horse about twenty minutes ago."

Nathan looked at the doctor in surprise. "I've been out for twenty minutes?"

More than ready to leave, Kate used their distraction to sneak quietly out the door.

Nathan's head pounded like the ground after a stampede. Actually, he felt as if *he'd* been the ground during a stampede, which wasn't too far from the truth. He'd never felt as much panic as when he'd seen that horse barreling toward Kate. Thankfully, that panic had turned into action so he'd been able to keep Kate from getting injured.

Where did Kate go? he wondered, glancing toward the door. It sure had been nice to wake up finding his hand in hers with her wide blue eyes watching him in astonishment. He frowned. Why was it that he always ended up snapping at the woman?

His mother would be ashamed. Snapping at a person was never allowed no matter how irritable, tired or in pain someone was. Heaven forbid if that snapping was directed at the more delicate one of Adam's ribs.

He wished the doctor would stop asking annoying questions and let him go. He'd only been awake a few minutes and he already had cabin fever.

The distinguished-looking doctor broke into his thought. "I'd like to observe you for a few days before I let you go."

Nathan grimaced. "Do you have to?"

The doctor frowned thoughtfully. "Well, you certainly can't be alone—someone will need to keep an eye on your condition. But I suppose I could tell Kate what signs to look for regarding the concussion."

Nathan waited as hope began to rise within him. Surely Kate wouldn't mind letting him stay in the barn a few days. The barn would be a much better place to rest than this tiny room in the doctor's house where he'd be poked and prodded and bored. The farm would have something for him to do. He might have to sneak around to do it but there would be something, anyway.

Doc nodded at some unsaid thought. "I just might let you go with Kate. I'll write down some instructions for caring for the wounds you have on your back and head. Make sure you show them to Kate. You'll need her help to change the dressing."

He frowned. "What type of wound did you say I have on my back?"

Doc didn't look up from his tablet and continued to write as he said, "You have some heavy bruising and a laceration. I think the hoof must have scraped you on the way down. The cut is long but thin. I think it will heal without stitches, but you'll have to be careful."

Doc ripped the page from the tablet and handed it to Nathan. "Make sure you change the dressing every day. I'll give you something to ward off infection but it won't be effective unless you keep everything clean."

"I'll be careful," Nathan promised as he tucked the paper into his right pocket. Now he only had to pray Kate would be like the Lord and extend mercy to help him in his time of need.

Two hours later Kate paused in the entrance of the barn, watching in disbelief as Nathan raked a pile of new hay into the stalls. "What do you think you're doing?"

He froze, then looked up guiltily. "The stalls needed fresh hay and I was in the barn anyway…"

She took the rake from him. Holding it in front of her threateningly, she said, "You are supposed to be resting not pushing hay around my barn."

"Yes, but—"

"Doc Williams gave me orders and I mean to follow them even if you won't."

He carefully took the rake from her as though afraid she'd wield it against him. Then leaning on it, he gave her a smooth half smile and drawled, "You get the prettiest little lilt of an accent when you're angry. Irish, isn't it?"

Kate narrowed her eyes. "Your charm doesn't work

on me, Nathan Rutledge, so you'd better get into the house before I resort to speaking Gaelic."

"Yes, ma'am." He tipped his Stetson with a rakish grin and started toward the house, then turned to face her with a curious glint in his eye. "Did you tell Doc we were married?"

"Actually, we aren't really—" She stopped when he lifted a knowing brow. Instead, she settled for, "Ms. Lettie told him."

"Ah," he said as though enlightened. "Don't think you're stuck with me forever. When I get a chance, I'll head back into town and see about the annulment."

"Good." She watched him exit the barn and go inside the house, and shook her head. "He's an interesting man that Nathan Rutledge."

She looked to Delilah for support but the horse only stared at her. "You're sort of an odd one yourself but that goes back to him. Why would anyone name a perfectly good horse Delilah? Esther I might understand, but Delilah?" Kate extended her hand to Delilah slowly and attempted to stroke the horse's nose. The horse lowered her head. Her large nostrils flared, then she sneezed directly into Kate's hands.

"Oh, gross." Kate grimaced as she stared down at her slimy palm.

"Isn't that Mr. Rutledge's horse?" a voice chirped from behind her. She whirled to find her brother and sister watching her curiously. Her clean hand covered her heart. "You scared me half to death."

Sean spoke again. "Well, isn't it his horse?"

Kate looked away from their hope-filled eyes. "Yes. It's his horse."

Ellie stepped forward. "So he's staying?"

"No, he isn't staying. Well, he is," she amended. "But

only for a short time. He was injured by a runaway horse so Doc asked me to keep an eye on him for a few days."

Sean grinned. "So he's here."

Kate nodded. "He's inside."

They whooped and took off running toward the house. Leaving her calling to the empty barn, "He won't stay long."

Kate could hardly keep up with the flow of conversation during dinner. Sean and Ellie were coming up with question after question about what it was like to be a cowboy. Nathan didn't seem to mind but his answers were becoming slower and his eyes seemed to hold the pain he disguised in his face. At the moment, he was smiling. "Of course I'll teach you to lasso."

Kate raised a hand to silence the celebration. "I hate to ruin your fun, but Nathan needs some rest. He's tired and I'm sure he's in pain. Why don't you two finish eating while I show him to the barn?"

Neither Ellie nor Sean protested, but instead looked at their newfound hero with concern. Kate lit a candle as the two said good-night to Nathan, who then stepped outside. She waited for the door to close behind them before apologizing, "I still don't feel right about you sleeping in the barn. What if you start feeling worse?"

"I'll be fine," he returned optimistically. "I've gotten over worse injuries than this."

At the barn, she turned to light a lantern hanging there. "I left a few blankets out here earlier for you. Is there anything else you need?"

He was quiet for a moment and she turned to find him staring thoughtfully at his boots with his right hand in his pocket.

"Nathan, are you all right?"

"I was thinking." He glanced up and shrugged. "I've bothered you enough. I don't need anything else."

"I'll have to bother you for a moment. Doc told me to check your eyes before you went to sleep," she explained.

He nodded and seemed amused though Kate couldn't fathom why. She simply ignored him and did as Doc had instructed her. She lifted the lantern so that it was near his eye level, then raised its wick until it was very bright. She waited as he tipped his chin down to give her a clear view of his eyes while she stared at what Doc Williams called his pupils.

They quickly grew smaller as the bright candlelight reached them. Finally, she lowered the wick to a small flame and watched his pupils widen slightly. She couldn't help noticing that he had beautiful eyes. They were coffee brown but tinged with gold with a slight ring of gold encircling his pupil. She took a quick step back.

Thankfully, he couldn't know that she'd gotten distracted by something as basic as his eyes' color. "They seem normal. How do you feel? Do you have a headache? Do you feel as though you're going to throw up or anything?"

He frowned. "I have a slight headache but my stomach is fine."

"Are you dizzy?"

"No."

She looked down. "Don't you think you should sleep inside for just this one night?"

"Kate, I'll be fine."

She frowned. "Well, if you're sure."

He nodded. "I'm sure. Thank you, Kate."

"Good night, then," she said, already stepping backward to leave.

"Good night," he returned sincerely.

She took another step backward, almost reluctant to pull from his warm gaze before she turned away. Reaching the door, she paused to glance over her shoulder at him. He smiled gently. Her lips tipped into an answering smile before she stepped into the warm night air.

She hadn't known he was coming, she hadn't wanted him to stay but somehow, oddly, it was nice to have him there.

Chapter Four

The stalks of wheat seemed to whisper to each other about the stranger she led through the paths of their uniformed rows. Kate tucked an escaping tendril behind her ear, then turned to look for Nathan. Why he cared to tour a farm he wouldn't stay at for more than a few days was beyond her.

Apparently he found it fascinating because he'd been lagging behind since they'd started. Every time she turned around he'd stopped to look at something new. If he didn't hurry up she'd be late starting lunch, which would probably put her behind on the chores for the rest of the day.

She spotted him a few yards away kneeling in the dirt to get a better look at the wheat head in his hand. She smiled at the confused frown that marred his face. "You really don't know much about wheat, do you?"

He glanced up, then slowly rose to his feet as though the movement pained him. No doubt that was a result of him throwing himself in front of the horse to save her. Maybe she should cut him some slack. She glanced up at the sky to gauge the sun and realized it was still before noon. She had more time than she thought.

"I grew up on a cattle ranch in Oklahoma so wheat and I haven't been much more than nodding neighbors," he said as stepped up beside her.

She glanced at him in surprise. "You're from Oklahoma?"

"I guess you thought I was from Texas." At her nod, he grinned. "I'll take that as a compliment. But yes, I grew up in Rutledge, Oklahoma, with an older brother and three younger sisters."

She stopped walking and turned to him with a suspicious smile. "Wait. You grew up in Rutledge. Does that mean your family owned the town?"

"That means my pa owned the land the town was built on. He was a cattle baron and he wasn't much interested in running a town." He took off his Stetson and fiddled with its brim. "He wasn't especially interested in anything else, either."

"I'm sorry," she said softly.

"For what?"

"You said 'he was.' I guess that means he passed away."

His confused frown lifted into an amused smile. "I should have said 'is.' He isn't dead. At least, he wasn't the last I heard."

"It sounds like it's been a while since then," she said as they continued walking toward the end of the field.

He put his Stetson back on. "My folks weren't pleased when I left for Texas to become a cowboy. I haven't heard much from them since then."

"That has to be hard."

He shrugged away her concern. "A man can get used to almost anything, given the chance. It helped being on the trail. You get so caught up in being busy that it's easy to forget how alone you are."

"So that's what you did before you came here? You were a cowboy?"

He shrugged. "Nothing else worked out."

He was intentionally being vague and she knew it. She figured since he was living on her farm, she had a right to a real answer. "What didn't work out?"

He was quiet for a long moment, then turned to meet her gaze. "I met two brothers while I was on the trail. We became really good friends and decided to start a horse ranch. I was in charge of training the horses. I loved it. I thought I'd found my calling. Things were great for a while, then they turned bad—real bad. We lost the ranch. There's nothing left of it now."

She bit her lip. "That's what you meant about God scattering your plans to the wind, isn't it?"

"Pretty much."

"What happened to your friends?"

He frowned then tugged his Stetson farther down. "One of them died. The other one didn't end up being such a good friend after all."

"I'm sorry to hear that," she offered softly.

He gave a short nod in acknowledgment of her sympathy. "That's why your advertisement seemed Heaven-sent. I wanted a new life and there it was."

"You thought it was God's will."

"Yes, I did," he said, then shot her a half smile. "But, as you said earlier, I guess I was wrong."

She glanced at the fields thoughtfully. "You know, I can't hear the words 'God's will' without thinking about my parents' deaths."

"Why?"

"After they died, I can't tell you the number of people who tried to comfort me by saying that. 'It's God's will.' It became almost more of a cliché than 'He needed them in Heaven.'" She swallowed, then shook her head. "I remember thinking if that was God's will then I didn't want it."

"You were grieving," he reminded gently. "People think all sorts of things they don't mean when they're grieving."

Yes, but I meant it. She pulled her gaze from the field to meet his. The sympathy there unnerved her. What had she been thinking? She'd told a stranger more than she told her close friends. There was aura of warmth about Nathan that made it easy to talk to him.

It was like the feeling she'd had when they first met: an implicit knowing. It hadn't made sense then. Now she knew it stemmed from the information he'd received through the letters. He knew enough about her without her confiding even more.

They were both quiet for a while, then Nathan tilted his head to gesture toward the field. "How do you normally bring in the harvest? I guess it's nothing like herding cattle."

She smiled. "Probably not. The harvesters are coming in about a month. They have a big machine that goes through the field and cuts the wheat. After that they use another machine to separate the wheat from the hay. They'll take fifteen percent of our wheat as payment."

Nathan glanced at her in surprise. "They take fifteen percent of a crop this small? That seems like a lot."

Kate frowned at him. "First of all, this isn't a small crop. It's even larger than the one I planted last year. Secondly, there isn't much I can do about the cost of the combine unless I want to use a scythe. It would take much longer for me to do it that way by myself. I wouldn't get it to the market on schedule."

"I see your point."

She glanced up at the sky, realizing she'd gotten distracted. "Speaking of time, I'd better get back to my chores."

"Can I help?"

"You can rest or go explore the farm by yourself." He looked frustrated by her statement but she pinned him with a look. "No working. Doctor's orders, remember?"

He caught her arm before she could turn away. "Before you leave, you should know I'm planning to go to town tomorrow to find out what needs to be done for the annulment. You might want to come with me in case there's something that can be done right away."

"That sounds fine. I have some supplies to pick up from the mercantile anyway. You can take care of the paperwork. Just come get me when I'm needed, and we might be able to finish this matter then and there." Strangely enough, she couldn't make herself smile at the thought.

As she walked away from him she realized she'd taken a dangerous step by finding out so much more about Nathan. He wasn't a stranger anymore. He was a man she could sympathize with. He had feelings, hopes and dreams that deserved respect. She was going to crush one of those dreams when she signed that annulment, but it couldn't be helped. She'd forget about the man she'd known for a few days. He'd forget about her and move on just as easily. That's all there was to it.

Nathan hit his Stetson against his leg impatiently, then leaned against the wall of the cramped waiting room of the only courthouse in a fifty-mile radius, fidgeting uncomfortably as the cut on his back started to itch. He hoped that meant it had already scarred over but he couldn't be entirely sure since he couldn't actually see the wound.

The note Doc had given him said to change the dressing every day but he hadn't done that because he couldn't reach it. He knew he was supposed to ask for Kate's help but he couldn't get himself to ask. He'd be long gone in a few hours anyway so it hardly mattered now.

He'd considered getting a job in Peppin, but that would mean seeing Kate and knowing she thought of him as nothing more than a mistake. Perhaps he should contact Davis Reynolds. The Rutledge and Reynolds families had been neighbors in Oklahoma. The Reynolds main crop had been cattle but they'd also maintained a beautiful herd of horses. As a teenager, Nathan had sneaked away to the Reynolds' farm to watch the ranch hands work with the horses. Eventually, Davis had recognized his passion, taken Nathan under his wing and taught Nathan everything he knew about raising horses.

Nathan's father had never gotten along with Davis and was chagrined to watch the man encourage what he called Nathan's goofing off. He'd begun to restrict Nathan's freedom more and more. The less freedom he had, the more he'd yearned for it. He dreamed of wandering the open plains as a cowboy. He'd longed for the chance to combine the skills he'd developed with horses with the knowledge that had been drilled into him about cattle.

When the Reynolds family had sold their ranch and decided to move to Texas, Nathan traveled with them. They parted ways not long after passing the state line. Davis made Nathan promise to send word if he ever needed anything. Now it looked as though he needed a new future—again. He'd be willing to settle for a new job.

He looked up as a small man with spectacles perched on the end of his nose stepped into the waiting room. "Who's next?"

"I am," Nathan said. He walked into the office to find shelves of books lined the wall while a large mahogany desk stood in the middle of the floor.

"Sit right down there," the man said before sitting behind the desk. "What can I help you with?"

Nathan sat, placing his hat on his knee. "I'd like to receive an—" His throat closed as he tried to get the word out. Clearing his throat, he tried again, "I'd like to find out how to receive an annul—annulment."

The man sat up in his chair. "Do you mean a marriage annulment?"

Nathan's affirmation was low.

The man took off his spectacles to clean them on his shirt. "Well, how about that? I don't remember the last time someone asked for one of those."

Nathan shifted his hat to his other knee.

Placing his spectacles back on his nose, the man peered over them. "I sure hope you aren't leaving some little lady high and dry."

He smiled ruefully. "No, it's kind of the opposite."

The man laughed in an almost cackling sort of way. "Well, how about that? Run you off, did she?"

He cleared his throat nervously. "Well, not exactly."

"I wouldn't take that from my little woman," the man said between laughs, then, taking a gasping breath, continued. "You shouldn't give up on one of those little spitfires. I've heard tell they're mighty fun to tame."

Nathan shifted in his chair, causing his hat to fall to

the ground. He picked it up and placed it back on his knee. "So do you think you can give me one?"

"One what? Annulment?"

He began to grow impatient. *Isn't that what this whole conversation is about?* "Yes, an annulment."

The man removed his spectacles to wipe away his tears of laughter. "No. I don't think I can."

Nathan shot to his feet, then wished he hadn't when a searing pain ran across his back. Had he just broken the cut open? "What do you mean you can't? Why can't you?"

"Sit down, sit down. No use getting all excited about it."

Eyes narrowed, he carefully sat in the chair, ignoring the pain.

"I told you it's been a while since we've had to give one."

"Yes."

"Well, I've plumb forgot how it's done."

Nathan looked at him incredulously. "You've what?"

The man shrugged carelessly. "I can't remember for the life of me."

"But you're a judge. You can't forget things like that," Nathan protested.

"I'm no judge. I'm just his assistant." The man leaned forward conspiratorially. "I mostly hand out forms and tell folks to come back later."

"His assistant?"

"I declare, there's an echo in here."

"If you're his assistant then where's the judge?"

"He's seeing to a case north of here, then he'll visit his family near Abilene. He has a pretty little daughter who had twins, can you imagine? Then his older son settled about ten miles from there—"

Nathan held up his hand to still the flow of words. "So how do I get my annulment?"

"Well, I don't rightly know. You see, even if I could trouble myself to remember how to do it, I'm pretty sure I wouldn't be able to make it legal. I suppose the only thing you can do is wait for Judge Hendricks."

"How long will that be?"

"Not sure."

"Any guesses?"

"I'd say about a month. He may decide to go an extra thirty miles and see his cousin. Then you're looking at two months, easy."

Nathan's jaw slackened. "Two months?"

"Maybe more. You see, there is always a chance someone else will call for a judge. There aren't many in these parts so he does a lot of traveling."

Nathan sighed. "So no one really knows when the man will be back."

"Oh, I know he'll come back. I just don't know when."

"That's what I just s—never mind. I don't suppose there a chance another judge might travel this way?"

The man paused thoughtfully, then shook his head adamantly. "Probably not, seeing as this town has a judge."

Nathan frowned as he stood. "I guess you're right. I have no choice but to wait."

"It was a pleasure doing business with you." The man shook his hand.

Nathan walked out the door, barely hearing the small man call out, "Who's next?"

What was he going to do? Two months. Two long months!

After Kate's refusal he'd been able to put aside…

well, to put aside Kate. After all, this was just one part in a long string of things that had gone terribly wrong. He'd dusted himself off from the latest fall in the dirt, literally; he fingered the sore spot on his head, and he'd told himself he'd just have to find something else.

For two whole months he would be reminded of everything that he'd thought he'd have. Every time he looked into Kate's eyes he'd have to remind himself that there must be something better or brighter waiting for him. There must be some reason that yet another dream, another hope had been deferred and had become only that—a dream.

"Rutledge, wait!"

Nathan paused and turned to find the sheriff hurrying toward him as fast as he could amble. "Sheriff Hawkins," he acknowledged in greeting.

"Rutledge, I have an idea," the man said eagerly. "Come with me."

The sheriff turned and headed toward the jail. *Not again,* Nathan thought as he followed the sheriff into the stone building. Upon entering it, his gaze was immediately drawn to the jail cells in the back of the room. He swallowed, then quickly glanced away. His eyes landed on the little thief from a few days ago, prompting a wry smile. It was almost as though the child had never moved because he sat in the same off-to-the-side chair. He still wore the same sullen look of disinterest that unsuccessfully hid his obvious curiosity about what was going on around him.

The sheriff sank into the wooden chair behind the desk and motioned Nathan to sit down. "I've been bringing the boy here during the day and home with me at night but it unnerves the missus some. I was thinking on what I could do for the boy and it hit me."

Nathan waited as the sheriff let the tension build.

"You and Kate should take the boy."

"What?" Nathan exclaimed.

"You and Kate should take the boy. He could work in the fields and sleep in the barn with you. You two would only have to feed him and steer him in the right direction."

Nathan stared at the sheriff in disbelief. "We can't do that."

"Why not?"

Nathan glanced at the boy, who tried not to appear to be listening to the conversation. "It just isn't right. The boy should have a home if he doesn't already. Surely someone will want to take him in."

"Yes, but not everyone would be a good influence on the boy. He's been a thief and a drifter. All I'm asking is that you let him work as payment for the things he tried to steal. It will be a good lesson for him."

Nathan leaned across the desk to speak in a low tone. "If he's a thief, wouldn't he be a bad influence on Sean and Ellie?"

"No, those kids are strong. Their ma raised them right. Look at it this way, the O'Briens will be three good influences. Wouldn't three good influences cancel out one bad one?"

Nathan sat back in his chair, wincing just a tad when his back made contact with the wood. *If the boy and I harvested half of the field, Kate wouldn't have to pay fifteen percent off that. That would be a fair amount of money saved. The boy needs someone to turn his life around. Who knows why he's on his own?*

Nathan glanced at the boy, who'd dropped all pretenses and was eagerly listening to the conversation about his future. He couldn't be more than a year or two older than Sean. But by God's grace, life could have dealt him such a blow.

Nathan looked at the sheriff, who waited tensely for an answer. *Two months,* Nathan reminded himself. *All I can offer is two months,* and no more. Nathan's voice was low, hopefully too low for the boy to hear, as he said, "If Kate and I take him in, it can't be forever, understand?"

"Of course," the sheriff complied. "I'm just asking you to show him how to do good, honest work. Give him some sort of skill so he'll have something to fall back on other than stealing."

"And you'll look for a real family for the boy?"

"Yes."

Nathan blew air past his lips then shook his head before he stood. "I'll try to convince Kate but if she says no..." He shook his head again.

"I understand," Sheriff Hawkins said, rising quickly to shake his hand. "Thank you."

Nathan strode toward the door then turned to look at the boy still watching from his seat. "What's your name?"

"Lawson," he responded clearly.

"Lawson what?"

The boy's hazel eyes watched him carefully. "It's just Lawson."

Nathan looked at him for a moment, then nodded. "I'll see what I can do."

Chapter Five

Kate carefully took inventory of the small pile of goods Mr. Johansen deposited on the counter. Something was missing. She checked her copy of the list. "Were you out of corn meal, Mr. Johansen?"

"No, I gave it—" The tall Norwegian lowered his thick blond eyebrows as he surveyed the counter. A grin bursted across his face. "I lost it. I will find it. When I come back, I will count the eggs you brought for me. I will be back in half a minute. Do not leave."

"Yes, sir. I'll be right here," she said then smiled when the man was quickly distracted by another customer. It looked like this was going to take a while. She placed her elbows on the counter and rested her chin on her hand as she watched Mr. Johansen conclude his business with the other customer and turn toward his storage room.

She wished the smell of those lemon drops behind the counter wasn't so strong and tempting. Her stomach let out a small rumble, reminding her she hadn't eaten since early that morning. Suddenly a tanned arm came to rest next to hers on the wooden counter. She tensed as a too-familiar voice called, "Johansen, grab me a few packs of that tobacco while you're back there."

Mr. Johansen glanced over and paused. His gaze bounced warily between Kate and the man beside her before he nodded. "I'll be right back."

Kate straightened and slid farther away from the man, hoping he'd take the hint. He didn't. "Kate O'Brien, why do you have to go around looking so pretty?"

She kept her gaze trained on her egg basket. "Andrew Stolvins, why don't you find some nice girl to settle down with and leave me alone?"

"How can I think about another girl when you're around?" He leaned sideways onto the counter to get a better look at her.

She dodged the hand that reached toward her, then turned to pin him with a cold gaze. "Don't."

He stared at her with predatory green eyes. "You're going to have to start being nice to me again."

He looked entirely too satisfied with himself. She narrowed her eyes. "What are you talking about?"

"It's amazing what you can find out in a small town if you ask the right questions," he said nonchalantly. "For instance, I heard your financial problems are so bad that you're going to lose the farm if this harvest isn't enough to stop the foreclosure."

"That's none of your business."

"I made it my business." He smiled smugly. "You see, I just bought the wheat combine and thresher from Mr. Fulsome. If you want your wheat harvested, you'll have to go through me now. I'm raising the rate three percent on each farm. I know you can't afford that so I'm willing to negotiate. What are you willing to bargain?"

Her fingers clenched the handle of the basket tightly. "I'm not bargaining with you. I'll pay the same rate as everyone else."

"How do you plan to pay me? You don't expect me to accept these, do you?" He chuckled, then snatched one of her precious eggs from the basket. He held one in the air to inspect it. "They look like they're worth a pretty penny but appearances are deceiving, aren't they?"

"Put it back."

He tossed it back and forth between his hands but his gaze never left Kate's eyes. "What's it going to be, Kate?"

The egg slipped from his clumsy grasp. Kate gasped and reached out for it but Nathan appeared from behind her to beat her to it. The egg landed safely in his cupped palm. He stepped between them to carefully deposit the egg in the basket, then turned to face Andrew Stolvins. "Is there a problem here?"

Andrew glared up at Nathan. "This doesn't involve you."

"If it involves Kate, it involves me."

Andrew shifted to stare over Nathan's shoulder at Kate. "Is that how it is now?"

Nathan answered for her. "That's how it is. From now on, you'll leave her alone. Is that clear?"

A tense moment passed in silence before Mr. Johansen emerged from the back room. The store owner apologized for taking so long. Andrew grabbed his tobacco and left. Kate let out a sigh of relief. Mr. Johansen looked perplexed but shrugged. "I guess I will add that to his account."

Kate waited while Mr. Johansen totaled her order, then applied the credit for the eggs. She paid him for the rest and was finally ready to go. Once Nathan had her purchases settled into the back of the wagon he turned to meet her gaze seriously. "Do you want to tell me what just happened in there?"

"I'd rather hear what happened at the courthouse."

He nodded. "That's fair enough. You can tell me about that fellow and I'll tell you about the judge while we eat lunch at the café."

"I'm not paying for lunch at the café when I have food at home." She covered her stomach as it growled in protest. It would take at least another half hour to get home and it was already long past one.

Nathan grinned. "It's my treat. I may not be a cattle baron but I can afford to pay for one meal in the café while I'm here."

She didn't like the idea of him paying for her but perhaps this was his farewell lunch. He'd order the food, tell her what he'd learned, they'd sign the paper he must have folded away somewhere and finish the meal. He'd make a quick exit. It would be amiable and painless. They'd go their separate ways, which was exactly what she needed.

At first Nathan did exactly as she'd planned. He ordered. After that he didn't seem inclined to talk about his meeting right away. Instead, he asked about the man in the store. Kate sent him a quelling look. "First tell me what happened at the courthouse."

He shook his head. "I'd rather wait until we get our food so we won't be overheard."

"Oh," she breathed, then took a sip of her water. She didn't need privacy for her explanation. The whole town knew the story he wanted to hear. "That was Andrew Stolvins. He courted me for a while two years ago, after my parents died."

Nathan's brows rose with interest. "He doesn't seem like the kind of man you'd want as a suitor."

"He was new in town. I was young and vulnerable. Andrew seemed like a nice, stable young man, so when he asked to court me I said yes." She shrugged. "Like you, I was convinced I was following God's will. For the first time in the six months since my parents' deaths, I was hopeful. I thought my life was finally turning around."

Nathan's gaze filled with concern. "That isn't what happened, is it?"

She shook her head. "I found out that Andrew wasn't the man I thought he was. Or, rather, Sean and Ellie spied on him enough to find out the truth. Andrew didn't want me. He wanted my inheritance."

She paused as their food arrived and waited until the waiter left, to continue. "When I found out, I broke off our relationship. It's lucky for him that I did, since my inheritance was hardly anything more than an expensive mortgage on the farm."

Nathan pulled the napkin away from his cutlery. "Why is he bothering you if you didn't have what he was really after?"

"My siblings weren't shy in telling the town what type of man Andrew really was. It hurt his reputation but it hurt his pride more. He's gone out of his way to make my life difficult since then."

"That's what I walked in on." He glanced around the café with a frown. "Why doesn't anyone stand up to this man and make him leave you alone?"

"I can handle Andrew Stolvins just like I handle everything else—on my own."

He looked at her carefully then gave a slow nod. "I think I understand."

"Good." She took in a deep breath then smiled. "Now, let's say grace, then you can tell me what happened at the courthouse."

"It seems we have run across a slight…problem," he said a few moments later.

"What kind of a problem?" she asked suspiciously.

He glanced around at the busy café. The room was loud and everyone seemed too involved in their own conversations to listen in on theirs, but he inclined his head to speak lowly. "Kate, we can't get an annulment. At least we can't for a month or two or even longer."

She stared at him in confusion. "What do you mean we can't? Why not?"

"There's no one to perform it."

"But didn't the judge—"

"He isn't here."

"I know that, but he left Mr. Potters in charge. Surely Mr. Potters can help us."

Nathan shook his head, stating dryly, "He doesn't remember how."

"I should have known," she said with a moan, then bit her lip thoughtfully as she searched for some other option. Unable to think of anything, she asked, "What do we do?"

He swallowed a piece of his chicken pot pie and shrugged. "We wait."

She pushed her green beans around on the plate, knowing he was right. "What will people think? I don't want to tell everyone we're married—it'll just make talk when you leave. But if you stay at the farm, there are sure to be questions."

"We'll tell them I'm your hired hand, but I agree. We need a chaperone."

"Where would we find a chaperone?"

"In jail."

She froze as he continued eating. "What?"

"Do you remember the little thief from a few days ago?"

"You mean the one who made off with your horse?"

"Yes, unless you know of a different one," he said with a grin. "The sheriff doesn't know what to do with him so he asked if we would consider taking him in."

"We can't! I feel for the child but I can hardly manage my brother and sister. How can I take on another child?"

"Sheriff Hawkins just wants to have him work a bit for us as a form of restitution. I was thinking, if the boy and I took on part of the harvesting, you wouldn't have to pay the harvesters for that part of the field. That would mean you get to keep more of your money."

She shook her head. "I can't let you do that."

"I'm not afraid of hard work and the boy needs a roof over his head and a new start. It'll be good for him to put in an honest day's labor."

"I couldn't just make the boy work. I would need to feed him, clothe him and get him into school. He'll have spiritual and emotional needs."

"You won't have to do it on your own. I'll take responsibility for him. He could live with me in that abandoned cabin not far from the farm. I'll pay room and board for us both."

"Well…" she wavered. How could she turn the needy boy away? What if no one else would take him in?

"I told the sheriff we couldn't take him in forever and he agreed to keep looking for a more permanent option. Besides, I'll be leaving in a few months. The boy should have a family by then."

"Fine. You convinced me." She pulled in a deep breath. "Now we'll just have to convince Ellie and Sean."

Nathan tugged his Stetson a bit farther down on his head as if that would shield him from the boy's wary stare. It didn't. He leaned back against the wood behind him and crossed his arms as he snuck a glance at the boy sitting in the back of the wagon. The boy's gaze shot away from him toward the schoolhouse where Kate talked with Sean and Ellie. Sean glanced at the wagon, then nodded soberly. Ellie crossed her arms looking less than convinced at whatever Kate was saying.

"Who are you?"

Nathan tipped his hat to look at Lawson. From the way the boy was staring at the schoolhouse, it appeared as though he hadn't even spoken. Nathan felt the hair rise on the back of his neck. "I'm Nathaniel Rutledge, but I go mostly by Nathan. You're Lawson, right?"

Lawson gave a stiff nod.

"Well, it's a pleasure to meet you, Lawson." He smiled wryly. "I mean without also meeting your friends, Smith and Wesson."

The boy didn't respond.

Nathan allowed the conversation to fall into silence for a few moments, then he couldn't help but ask, "How long have you been on your own, Lawson?"

"It's been two or three years the best I can figure."

Two or three years ago the boy would have been ten or twelve. That was certainly no age to be forced to fend for himself. "That must have been mighty hard."

Nathan glanced at him to find the boy looking in the opposite direction, seemingly intent on studying their surroundings. Nathan cleared his throat. "Do you know where we're going?"

"We're going back to the farm where you shot at me."

He raised his brow. "I shot at you? I remember you did a fair share of shooting yourself."

Lawson looked at him with a frown. "You hit my hat and busted a hole clean through it."

Though he inwardly smiled at Lawson's first real display of emotion, Nathan frowned back at him. "You stole my horse. I think we're square."

"You got it back, didn't you? 'Sides I didn't shoot him," Lawson grumbled.

"Good thing you didn't, either," he said dryly.

Lawson turned indignant. "I wouldn't shoot a horse, mister. My ma taught me right from wrong."

"I suppose that's why you went around stealing, too."

"Better stealing than begging," he said. There was a short silence before the boy spoke again. "Since you killed my hat I think you ought to give me yours. That would make it an even trade."

Nathan chuckled, then pulled the article more firmly onto his head. "No."

Lawson frowned, then looked past Nathan to where Kate was still talking with her siblings. Ellie shrugged and gave a long-suffering sigh. Kate turned to send them a victorious smile.

"Who are they?"

Nathan tensed in surprise, then turned to find Lawson sitting much closer than he had been earlier. "The young lady is Kate O' Brien. You have her to thank for letting you stay at the farm. The other two are her little brother and sister."

"Are you two sweethearts?"

He watched Lawson curiously. "Not quite. Why?"

The boy shrugged. "You've been watching her the whole time."

"I was not."

Again, the boy shrugged then settled farther away. Kate led her siblings toward the wagon and introduced them to Lawson. For a moment everyone under the age of fifteen stared at each other. Sean broke the uncertain silence with a friendly grin. "I won a new marble today. Do you want to see it?"

Lawson nodded hesitantly. Sean lifted Ellie into the back of the wagon, then climbed in after her. Ellie frowned. "You didn't show me the marble when I asked earlier."

"You know I couldn't take it out in class. I'll show it to you now." Sean settled next to Lawson and pulled Ellie down beside him.

Kate smiled as she stepped up beside him to whisper, "I'd say that went pretty well."

"Ellie didn't seem to like the idea."

She rolled her eyes. "It wasn't personal against Lawson. She just didn't want to add another boy. She said we're overrun with them now."

He laughed. After helping her into the wagon, he started down the road to what would be his temporary home. But only for the next two months, he reminded himself. This home, this growing family was only his for the next two months. He couldn't let himself get too attached, or it would hurt to leave them behind.

He ignored the sinking feeling in his gut that told him it was already too late.

The first few stars began to twinkle in the huge Texas sky as Nathan and Lawson made the short walk to the cabin that evening. Lawson trudged beside

Nathan with his head down. Occasionally he'd glance up at the woods around them and each time his face seemed to grow more troubled. "Is something on your mind, Lawson?"

The boy ducked his head again. "I was just thinking."

"About what?" Nathan prompted when it became obvious the boy wasn't going to continue without some prodding.

Lawson glanced up to survey him with a measuring stare. "How did you end up here?"

Nathan smiled wryly. "That's a pretty complicated story. It all started when I saw this advertisement in the paper—"

"No, I didn't mean here as in 'this place.' I just meant…" Lawson's words stumbled to a halt. His gaze searched the forest as if the words he needed were written in the trees. Finally he turned back to Nathan. "I've never had this before."

Nathan had never felt more confused. "Had what? Supper?"

"Yes. I've never had supper in a house with people who acted like I mattered." Lawson rubbed the furrows in his brow. "I don't usually talk to people much, but I don't know how long I'll be here and I need you to tell me something."

"I'm listening," Nathan said quietly.

"I don't know much about who you are to that family. Maybe you're just a hired hand, but you fit, Nathan. You fit it there with them and I want to know how you did it." Lawson swallowed, then continued urgently, "I want to know what made you the kind of man who can fit in a family."

Nathan met Lawson's gaze for a long moment,

then he turned to look at the farmhouse. Light danced cheerily out the windows. The house looked worn in a lived-in sort of way that made it feel like a home. A home he'd thought would be his. Lawson thought he fit there. He didn't, but telling Lawson that wouldn't really answer the question so he said the one thing that came to his mind.

"Choices." He turned back to Lawson with a helpless shrug. "I guess somewhere along the way, I made enough good choices to cancel out the bad ones."

"What kind of good choices did you make?"

"I decided not to let the mistakes I've made in the past define who I am in the present. I decided to be honorable even when those around me aren't." Nathan paused. He wondered if he should continue but Lawson's rapt attention urged him onward. He wondered if this was the first time anyone had told the boy that he could decide what kind of life he wanted to lead. Perhaps the Lord had arranged everything just to bring them to this moment. "I decided to admit that I wasn't a good man."

Lawson's rapt expression turned into pure shock. "You aren't?"

He shook his head. "We all fall short of being completely good. It's when we admit that we aren't good enough by ourselves that we can finally make the best choice of all."

"What's that?"

"We can choose to let God cleanse us of our sins by simply asking Him to do it. As soon as we allow that to happen, He makes us good and fits us into His family, joined together by faith. It's just like how members of the same family have the same blood. The same spirit that would be in you is in everyone else who has ever believed. I believe, so if you decided to do the same then that would make us brothers, in a way. Does that make sense?"

"Yeah, it does. I guess it's something to think about."

Lawson began walking away, so Nathan figured their discussion was over. Once they reached the cabin, Nathan hung his Stetson on the bed post and sat on the lone chair in the cabin to take off his boots. "That was a pretty deep discussion when I don't even know your last name," he said teasingly.

Lawson scrubbed his face, neck and arms with water from the pitcher and bowl, then blotted his face on his shirt before he deigned to respond. "My parents moved to Nebrasky Territory when I was little. Ma said it'd be best if I didn't come because she'd rather see me gone than bleeding from a beating. That's why, as far as I'm concerned, I don't have a last name."

It seemed wrong to delve into platitudes after all the things the boy must have been through so Nathan simply said, "Fair enough."

"What about you? I bet your family was nothing like mine."

"I came from a loving family, but we had our own problems."

"What kind of problems?"

Nathan placed his boots by the side of the bed then admitted, "My pa cut me off not long after I left home. I haven't heard from my family since then."

Lawson frowned. "Why did he cut you off?"

Nathan shrugged. "We both wanted to run my life. I wouldn't let him. He got mad when I tried to do it myself."

"That's it?" Lawson scoffed. "You let him cut you off from your entire family because of that?"

"I can't make them take me back. In my family, whatever Pa says, goes. The rest of us have little choice but to go along with him."

"When was the last time you tried to contact them?"

"I gave up a long time ago."

"Try again." Lawson leaned forward in his bed. "They're your family. You can't just let them walk away. You have to stop them. You have to get them back."

"I'll think about it, all right? Now, it's time to sleep. It will be an early morning for both of us." He leaned over and blew out the lantern.

Placing his hands beneath his head, he replayed Lawson's words in his mind. What was it about families that made them so hard to hold on to? He'd already lost two—the one he'd been born into and the one he'd chosen for himself. His heavy sigh turned into a silent prayer. He asked God to bless them all and maybe, if He thought it best, to let him hold on to at least one.

Chapter Six

Kate gave the pancake batter one more stir as she waited for the stove to warm up. She heard the front door fly open followed by the familiar sound of loud, clomping boots. Ellie appeared in the doorway breathless and grinning. "You have to see this."

Kate stared at her sister in amusement but shook her head. "I need to fix breakfast. Why don't you just tell me?"

Ellie's eyes widened in desperation, then she surged into the kitchen and grabbed Kate's sleeve. "Believe me, breakfast can wait."

Kate decided it was probably in her best interest to find out what Ellie was so excited about. Especially since she was out the door and being pulled toward the barn before she could protest. Sean was waiting by the door with a smile on his face. Kate frowned as she stepped inside. "What is going on?"

Ellie pointed toward the stalls. "Look." She pivoted toward the cows. "Look." She turned in a circle. "It's all done."

"What's done?"

"The chores," Sean explained from his spot near the door.

"Every single one," Ellie said as she stopped spinning and held her hands out to regain her balance.

"Almost every single one," a deep voice said behind them. Kate turned to find Nathan entering the barn with a large bucket of water in his hand. Lawson followed with another. "We needed more water for the horses."

"You did everything," Kate said more for her own benefit than anyone else's.

Sean chuckled then shot Nathan a smile. "She's a little slow in the mornings."

She flashed Sean a glare, then glanced around the barn with new eyes. She noticed the full grain bins, the fresh hay in the stalls, the curried horses, the full pails of milk covered in cheese cloth and she didn't like it. She didn't like it one bit. It gave her a strange feeling in the middle of her stomach. It felt like dependency.

Nathan handed the bucket to Lawson, then tilted his head to survey her face carefully. "You don't look happy."

Ellie bounced toward them doing a little jig. "I'm really happy. I hate chores. Thank you. Thank you."

Sean stepped forward. "What do we do now?"

"I guess we eat breakfast," Kate said, then led them all back into the kitchen. After everyone had a plate of pancakes she filled Sean's and Ellie's lunch pails. She set them aside and started pumping water into the sink. Maybe she could get a head start on the dishes.

"Kate."

She was startled to find Nathan standing beside her. The kitchen was noisier than usual so she hadn't heard him approach. "Did you need something?"

"We're waiting for you, to start eating. Where's your plate?"

She glanced over her shoulder to find the children's plates untouched. They didn't seem to care because Ellie was retelling a story of some mishap with Mrs. Greene, but Kate caught her breath. "Oh, you didn't have to do that. They need to eat. I'll eat—"

"A biscuit later?" he asked.

"How did you know?"

"It took me a while but I caught on." He sent her a knowing look. "Are you trying to save time or money by not eating breakfast? I guess it's probably a little of both, right?"

She narrowed her eyes at him. "I don't see how my eating habits are any of your business."

He smiled as though he wasn't intimidated by her bluster in the least, then he nodded toward the table. "Eat with your family, Kate. Sit down and say grace. Take my plate. I'll fix myself some more."

"Fine." She complied more for the time she'd save from not arguing than anything else. As she slid into the seat he'd vacated she said, "Please, bow your heads for grace."

Sean frowned at her. "Kate, we never say grace at breakfast."

She bit her lip but refused to allow her eyes to move guiltily toward Nathan. "I guess we'd better start then." She bowed her head. "Lord, thank You for providing this meal. We are truly grateful for another day. May this day be blessed as we live it in Your presence. Amen."

Everyone echoed her amen. The conversation lagged as they began to eat. Nathan slid into the seat across from her with a modest pile of perfectly round, perfectly golden pancakes on his plate. They almost looked better than the ones she'd made. She hid her frown by taking another bite.

Ellie slid closer to quietly say, "Kate, we're using all the chairs again."

It took a moment for Kate to realize what her sister meant. When she finally did, her entire being stilled and she glanced around the table. Ellie was right. They were using all the kitchen chairs again—even the two that had been vacant since their parents' deaths.

She swallowed a lump of pancakes, then glanced at the two men filling the seats. The one to her right could hardly be called a man. He wasn't much older than Sean but from what she had heard, he was just as much an orphan as they were. Her heart broke a little each time she saw the cautious world-weary look in his eyes. He hesitantly took a biscuit from the plate in the center of table, then glanced around to see if anyone minded. She caught his gaze and sent him an approving smile. He offered a cautious one in return before returning to his meal.

She glanced past him to the man sitting across from her. He was saying something that made the children laugh so hard they could hardly eat. Kate stared at her plate and had to bite her lip to keep from speaking out. She wanted to remind them that this situation wasn't going to last forever. They wouldn't always have someone to do their chores or teach them to lasso or give them rides on a half-wild horse.

Nathan was leaving and it would be best if they remembered that. In the meantime, she hoped he would live up to the hero worship he was receiving. They had already learned the hard way that not everyone could be trusted and villains easily masqueraded as heroes.

* * *

Nathan didn't have to look up from his plate to know Kate was seething. He could literally feel the heat of her glare from across the table. He rubbed the moisture from his forehead as he reminded himself that he was prepared for this and knew exactly what he was going to do about it. He used the last few minutes of breakfast to remind himself of what he needed to say. When Sean and Ellie grabbed their lunch pails and left for school, Nathan caught Lawson's gaze and cut his eyes toward the door. Lawson gave a short nod then murmured something about needing to do something in the barn before he slipped out.

They were alone. Kate refused to meet his gaze as she gathered the dishes and set them in the sink. He watched her pump the faucet with a bit too much force and realized it was now or never. He winced at the pain that raced across his back as he stood to carry his plate to the sink.

Oddly, the room seemed to sway so he gingerly leaned against the nearby counter. "Kate, I think we need to talk."

She whirled toward him and lifted her chin in defiance. "So do I."

"As your hired hand, I'd like to go over my job responsibilities with you. I figured it would be best for me to take over the bulk of the barn chores. I did them all today just to give everyone a nice surprise but I guess you'll probably want Sean and Ellie to retain some of their responsibilities there."

He'd managed to regain his equilibrium and he waited with baited breath to see if he'd pulled the right bee from her bonnet. She began to speak then stopped.

Her chin lowered just a tad. "Yes, that's exactly what I want."

He didn't dare give the sigh of relief he wanted to, but instead allowed himself a serious nod. "Good. Just let me know what to leave for them."

"I will," she said almost reluctantly, then turned to sprinkle soap on the dishes.

"I thought you'd also want me to take on most of the outside chores." He hid a smile at the suspicious gaze she leveled on him. "I may not know much about wheat but I'm a quick learner. I hope you won't mind teaching me."

She bit her lip. "I suppose I won't."

"While I'm here, I figure I might as well make repairs to whatever might need fixing. Why don't you make a list for me with the most important ones first? I'll take care of those, too."

She frowned and he sensed she wanted to resist but she gave him a short nod. "I'll have it ready for you tomorrow."

He swallowed, knowing that if she was going to balk it would be about this next part. "The Bible says if you don't work, you don't eat. I figured Lawson and I are working for our food."

He reached into his shirt pocket and pulled out a folded-up envelope. He handed it to her. She looked at it in confusion. "What's this?"

"That's for our rent," he said.

She frowned, then opened the flap of the envelope and looked inside. Her eyes widened. "Nathan, you don't have to do this. You're already paying by working for me."

"You didn't think I expected to stay here for free, did you?" He placed his hands in his pockets when she tried to give the envelope back. "Count it. Make sure it's enough for the first month."

"Nathan, you really don't have to do this."

"I already did. Now, why don't you tell me what's on your schedule today? Lawson and I will need to know what you want us to do."

He waited through the long moment of silence, then watched as Kate slipped the envelope into her apron pocket. "I've never had a hired hand before."

He smiled but tried not to show his relief as she went over the day's schedule and told him what she needed him to do. Keeping the farm was obviously important to her. All of her hard work was meant to take care of her siblings and preserve her parents' legacy. He might not have gotten the future he'd hoped for, but maybe he'd be able to help Kate get hers.

The next day, Kate stilled at the sound of someone shouting her name. She slipped the potato seedling into the ground and covered it with soil before shifting on her knees toward the sound. Lawson stood near the edge of the field waving at her. She waved back in confusion for a moment before she realized he wasn't really waving. He was beckoning her.

She set her garden trowel on the ground and wiped her hands on her apron as she stood and hurried toward him. "What's wrong?"

Fear etched across his features as he led her into the field. "Something is wrong with Nathan. We were working and he suddenly knelt down and now he can't seem to get back up. I think he must be sick."

Kate spotted Nathan a few yard ahead of them. He sat on his knees with one hand braced on the ground in front of him while the other rubbed his forehead. "Nathan."

He glanced up at her and grimaced. "I told Lawson I'd be fine in a minute. It's just a headache."

Lawson placed a hand on Nathan's shoulder. "Did you throw up like you said you might?"

Kate let out a frustrated breath. "Obviously it isn't just a headache." She knelt beside him. She was close enough to notice he was sweating profusely. Narrowing her eyes, she gently moved his hand out the way to feel his forehead. "You're burning up with fever."

He groaned. "I don't know what's wrong. I was fine earlier, but now I feel too weak to even stand up."

"We'll help you," she said then glanced over Nathan's bent head to Lawson. "We need to get him into the house. You take one side and I'll take the other."

He nodded then slipped his arm around Nathan's back. She did the same. On the count of three they helped Nathan to his feet. He immediately let out a cry of pain. Her worried eyes lifted to his pain-filled gaze. "Is it your head?"

"No, it's my back," he bit out as he walked between them. "Doc said it would heal on its own but it hurts."

"Wait. What's supposed to heal on its own? I thought you just had a concussion."

He grimaced guiltily. "I didn't tell you. When the horse reared…one of its hooves…hit my back. It cut the skin."

"Why didn't Doc tell me?"

"I was supposed to…but I didn't want to bother you. I thought I was leaving. I tried to clean it on my own." He swallowed harshly. "If I keep talking I might get sick."

She glanced at Lawson in time to see the boy's eyes widen. "Then don't talk."

They helped him into the house, then into Sean's bed. Lawson pulled off Nathan's shirt while Kate prepared a cool cloth for his head. When she stepped into the room again Nathan was under the covers but his back lay exposed. She took one look at the cut and grimaced before meeting Lawson's gaze. He frowned. "It's infected, isn't it? That's why he's sick."

She nodded then pulled a chair close to the head of Sean's bed. "I need you to go in to town and bring Doc. If you can't find him, bring Ms. Lettie."

"I think I know how to get to town but I don't know who those people are."

"Oh," she breathed. "You know who the sheriff is, right? Ask him to help you. Take one of the horses."

"You can take Delilah. She's faster," Nathan muttered, then passed his hand over his forehead again. "Tell her I sent you."

Kate and Lawson exchanged a confused glance before he hurried out the door. Kate laid the cool cloth over his head. She knew Doc would want to clean the wound so she decided not to mess with it. There was really nothing she could do but wait and try to make Nathan as comfortable as possible. He groaned. "I'm sorry, Kate."

"You don't have to apologize to me. Why don't you just close your eyes and rest until Doc gets here?" She watched as he smiled faintly then closed his eyes. She began to pray.

Nathan strained toward the voices edging in and out of his consciousness. Every so often they called to him but he could never reach them. The heat engulfing his

body stood in stark contrast to the streaks of cool relief
that intermittently traveled from his brow to his chest or
back. He slowly slipped further away from the sweet familiar voices as the whisper of haunted memories filled
his mind.

Nathan. Nathan.

Eli, he breathed then spun to face the desperate whisper.

Eli backed away. His were eyes filled with panic. His
appearance was disheveled. His hand crept toward his
holster. *Let me go, Nathan.*

You know I can't do that. Stay, Eli. Stay.

A struggle, then the room exploded in sound. He
dropped to Eli's side but it was too late. Blood spilled on
the floor and covered Nathan's hands. He couldn't get it
off. It spread until it was everywhere. There were traces
of it on his arm, streaks of it in his hair. The smell of it
sickened him. *Get it off,* he demanded.

He heard a gasp and the heat increased. Pale faces
stared back at him in disbelief, then condemnation. *You
did this,* they whispered. *Murderer. Murderer.*

"No." They wouldn't listen. They were trying to restrain him. They were trying to lock him up. He had to
get out. "Let me go. I didn't. I didn't do it."

"I believe you."

He stilled. He turned toward the voice. It was out of
place. He knew this nightmare well. That wasn't what
happened next.

He suddenly became aware of his labored breathing. He turned toward the cool hand on his cheek, then
forced his eyes open. Deep blue eyes stared back at him
from the prettiest face he'd ever seen.

"Say it again," a young voice whispered from
behind him.

"I believe you," Kate said.

Calm enfolded him and he closed his eyes but braced himself. The nightmares would return. There was nothing he could do to stop them.

Chapter Seven

Kate watched as Nathan's face relaxed into more peaceful sleep. Her gaze lifted to the children who stood at attention on the other side of the bed. Lawson and Sean had tried to help restrain Nathan's wild thrashings but nothing had calmed him until she'd said those words. Sean watched Nathan soberly. "What do you think he didn't do?"

"When people are delirious they say a lot of things that don't make sense," she said. "I'm sure it's nothing to worry about."

They nodded as though they accepted that as fact. She wasn't so sure. He'd mentioned something about a man named Eli and muttered something about blood before she'd had to call for reinforcements. He might have just been having a random nightmare. He also might have been reliving some event in his past—but she couldn't tell the children that without scaring them.

Ellie leaned against Sean while tears of concern filled her eyes. "You should hold his hand. When I'm sick, I always feel better when you hold my hand."

Kate reluctantly covered Nathan's hand with hers to make Ellie feel better. To her surprise, his hand tightened around hers. She looked at him more closely but he still seemed to be sleeping so she left her hand in his. "It must be after ten o'clock. Ellie and Sean, you need to go to sleep so you can be ready for school in the morning. Sean, you can bunk with Ellie. Lawson—"

"I'd like to stay in here with you, ma'am. I can help keep watch." He pulled a chair to the side of the bed and took his seat when she nodded her approval.

"I think he's starting to get better," Sean said as he guided Ellie toward the door.

Kate nodded. "He might be over the worst of it. You two try not to worry. Get some sleep."

Nathan turned his face away from the warm sunlight and opened his eyes. Ellie sat in a chair beside the bed, toying with her hair as she read the book in her lap. A sound from the other side of the room caught his attention and he turned to see Sean showing Lawson how to carve small figures out of wood. Sean met Nathan's gaze and his eyes widened. "Look. He's awake."

Nathan watched the three children crowd around the bed. "What happened?"

"You almost died," Ellie whispered cautiously as though saying the words might somehow change his fate.

Lawson leaned closer. "I rode to town and brought Doc back. He took a long time cleaning your wound. He gave you medicine, too."

"How long have I been lying here?" he asked groggily as he tried to sit up on his side.

Sean placed a restraining hand on his shoulder. "Since yesterday and Kate says you aren't allowed to get up. She and Lawson stayed with you all night so she's taking a nap right now. We're supposed to tell her if you wake up."

"I'll do it." Ellie set the book she'd been clinging to aside, then patted his cheek. "I know you'll do the right thing."

Nathan watched in confusion as she sent the boys a meaningful look then slipped out the door. "What's she talking about?"

"We think you should write to your family," Lawson said.

Nathan's head started to pound. He was trying to figure out what his family had to do with this but he couldn't. Unless… "You think I'm still going to die."

Sean looked startled. "No, that's not it at all."

"Kate mentioned that she wouldn't know how to notify your family if anything worse had happened," Lawson said. "Sean and I decided that when you woke up he should tell you something." He prodded Sean forward. "Go on."

Sean gave a nod then pulled in a deep breath before he began. "I don't talk about my parents much. I reckon you know they died in an accident when I was ten. One day they were here. The next day they were gone and there was nothing I could do to bring them back." He swallowed then gestured to the bed. "You still have a chance to make things better with your family but you never know when something like this will happen to take that chance away."

Sean ducked his head then lifted his gaze to Nathan's. "That's why I couldn't hold my peace until you got better. You ought to send a letter to them. It's important." His gaze slid from Nathan's to the doorway. "It's so important I risked Kate's wrath to say it."

Nathan followed Sean's gaze to where Kate stood in

the doorway. She didn't look angry. Instead her eyes glittered with unshed tears. She lowered her gaze for a moment, then met his to see how he would respond to Sean's speech. He almost sighed but it turned into a cough. Ellie slid past Kate to hand him a cup of water. He thanked her with a smile, then pulled in a deep breath. "I guess if you can risk Kate's wrath, I can risk my pa's."

"You should do it because you want to, not because you feel pressured," Kate gently cautioned.

He shook his head. "No, they're right. There's no harm in trying again. Maybe this time will be different."

He wanted to believe it would be different. He didn't see how it could but glancing around at the children's young hope-filled smiles he knew he had to try. He prayed this time that it would be enough.

An eerie howl pierced the night and Kate almost shivered at the sound of it. It was a week after Nathan agreed to send the letter to his parents. During that time he'd managed to gain back most of his strength and grow closer to the children. So much so that Sean had begged to spend the night roughing it in the cabin with Nathan and Lawson.

Another howl split the night. If they didn't settle down soon she might just go out to the cabin and put a stop to their antics. *You have ten minutes, boys. Make the most of it.*

She pulled the bed covers closer to her chin and snuggled into the pillow as a satisfied smile curved her lips. She was sure one of those howls belonged to Sean. It was good to hear him having fun and acting like the child he still was. The same went for Lawson. He'd told her a bit about what he'd been through before he'd shown up on her doorstep. Survival had been his aim and having fun probably hadn't been anywhere on his agenda.

She couldn't speculate about Nathan. He hadn't mentioned anything about the delusions he'd experienced during his fever. She'd be tempted to believe that the words he'd mumbled were meaningless if he hadn't seemed so shaken after his sickness. Every once in a while she'd catch a haunted look in his eyes that she hadn't noticed before. Maybe it had been there all along and she just hadn't been looking.

She sighed. Her original resolve to forget Nathan as soon as he left now seemed ridiculously naive. He'd only been at the farm for two weeks but he'd managed to become almost like family to her little brother and sister. It was obvious they were craving male attention. The same attention she'd tried so hard to avoid since her run-in with Andrew Stolvins.

Her fist clenched the edges of the pillowcase. That romance had ended in complete disaster, yet the whole time she'd been so sure she was following God's will. Either she had been mistaken the entire time or God had led her down the wrong path on purpose. She wasn't sure which it was but both options were frightening.

That was why she needed to be careful when it came to Nathan. She was attracted to him, she could admit that. She just couldn't allow her feelings to go any further. She didn't want to end up in the same mess she'd gotten out of with Andrew Stolvins.

Just then another howl sounded through the air. She pushed her troublesome thoughts from her mind. Maybe she couldn't howl at the moon, but she didn't want to lie in bed agonizing about the past when she should be sleeping. The mattress dipped on Ellie's side and Kate heard footsteps. She turned over to see Ellie walking quietly toward the stairs.

"Where do you think you're going, young lady?" she asked.

Her sister froze. The room was silent until another howl pierced the air. As if that released Ellie from her spell, the girl turned to face Kate. "It isn't fair. They're having all the fun."

Kate stared at her sister. "What do you suppose we do? Go trooping through the weeds at nearly ten at night?"

"Yes." Ellie's eyes grew larger and more pleading.

"Ellie, you know we can't do that. The cabin is too far away."

Ellie hung her head. "I knew you'd say that."

Kate felt guilt creep up and overtake her. Since her parents' deaths she'd been so focused on surviving that she hadn't really thought about fun. Was that why Ellie felt the need to create her own fun even at the expense of others like Mrs. Greene? She sat up, then slid to the side of the bed and met Ellie's gaze. "How did you know I'd say that?"

"You're really serious most of the time."

"What's wrong with that?"

"Nothing," Ellie said, then fiddled with the folds of her nightgown. "It's just that since Nathan came, we all laugh more. You know, like we did when Ma and Pa were here."

"I know," Kate admitted.

Ellie lifted her shoulders in a shrug. "I like that and I want to go howl but I'm supposed to mind you, so…"

Ellie stepped toward the bed but her gaze slid toward the stairs. Kate bit her lip for a moment, then glanced toward the moonlit window thoughtfully. "Oh, what would it hurt?"

Kate pushed the covers away and grabbed her sister's hand.

"Where are we going?" Ellie asked.

"Just follow me." After they made their way down-stairs, Kate took a lantern and led Ellie outside. The two ran in the direction of the old cabin where Nathan, Sean and Lawson were, until Kate brought them to a panting stop about thirty yards away from the farmhouse.

Ellie was watching her suspiciously but Kate met her sister's look with a daring one of her own. Throwing her head back, she let out a strange howling yodel that carried well on the still night air. In the dim light of the lantern Kate saw her sister's mouth drop open then curve into a grin. Ellie let out a howl more convincing then Kate's. The two waited a moment. A chorus of answering howls filled the air just as Kate expected.

Ellie giggled. Kate howled again. When was the last time she'd done something just to be silly? When was the last time she'd tossed her cares aside and howled at the moon? It had been a while, at least the tossing cares aside part; she'd never howled at the moon before.

Ellie let out a mournful yipping sound so loud Kate had to cover her ears. The answering call was so real it was almost eerie. Somehow she knew it came from Nathan. Kate gave an answering *aroo* and the same yowl sounded in cadence. She took a breath and they all howled in unison, each one with its strange man-made sound except for one that sounded almost real.

There was silence for a breath, then one voice lifted in a kind of growling sound. She and Ellie spun to face the same direction. They exchanged glances.

"Nathan, is that you?" Kate asked.

The bushes moved just beyond the lantern's reach.

"Sean," Ellie called. "This isn't funny. Come out so I can see you."

Three howls sounded from the direction of the old cabin one after another, rising to a different key as if harmonizing. Then that strange sound lifted from a different direction.

"Kate?" Ellie moved closer to press against her side. "Something is in there."

Something definitely was. Kate swallowed. Placing an arm around Ellie, she lifted the lantern higher. "What was I thinking bringing you out here?"

"Oh, Kate, I had fun. I'm glad I laughed before I cross the river Jordan."

"Cross the river—Ellie don't talk like that. You aren't crossing any river. I won't let you. You're staying right here, do you understand? I don't want to think of losing you, too."

Ellie glanced up at her. "This is very sweet and I'm glad you care, but could we focus on the problem here?"

"I wish I had a gun."

"Howooool," Ellie called in the air.

"Now who isn't focusing on the problem?"

The animal let out its strange call again and Ellie looked up smugly. "Now we know where it is. It's right in that bush over there."

Kate stared at the bush that seemed to quiver from the inside out. "Let's just walk back home slowly and calmly."

"What if it attacks us?"

"Don't you know you aren't supposed to ask questions like that?"

"Don't you know you're supposed to question something when it might kill you?"

Kate looked at her in exasperation. "I'll bash it with the lantern if it attacks us."

"Let me bash it."

"No. I'm stronger."

"I'm smarter."

"Ellie O'Brien, I've had more than enough sass from you for one night. Contain it. I'm trying to get us to safety."

Ellie grumbled something Kate couldn't quite understand. Ignoring her, Kate reasoned, "We have to pass it if we walk home. If we go to the cabin then we walk away from it but it's a much longer walk. Then again, the closer we get to the cabin, the easier Nathan can hear us if we call for help."

"What's your decision?"

"Thataway." Kate pointed toward the cabin. "Walk calmly. Do not run or it might chase you."

"Wonderful thoughts."

They walked calmly but lengthened their strides to cover more ground. Ellie kept looking behind them, so Kate figured she could watch ahead of them. Minutes later, Ellie asked, "You do know where you're going, don't you?"

"Yes, I do."

"I think it's following us."

"Why?"

"Just a feeling. Plus, when we're quiet I can sometimes hear panting."

She spotted the cabin and barely resisted the urge to run to its shelter. Kate banged on the door while watching furtively behind them. There was no response. She banged again. Suddenly the door flew open. She stared down the length of a rifle then up into Nathan's eyes.

"It's Kate," Nathan announced as they moved past

him into the cabin. Kate closed the door firmly behind her then glanced up. She found herself in a room with two boys who seemed not the least bit drowsy and one overgrown boy who looked very sleepy.

Ellie sat on Nathan's vacated cot. "Something was following us. It was big and I heard it growl."

Kate was leveled with Nathan's questioning glance. She nodded. "Our howling must have attracted it. I came here because it seemed the safest route. I think it's still out there."

As if on cue, scratching sounded across the door followed by a whine. Sean and Lawson jumped from their cots. Ellie followed more sedately, then snuggled into Kate's side. As Nathan moved toward the door Kate put a restraining hand on his arm. "You aren't going to open it, are you?"

"How else will we know what's out there?" He went to the door then paused. "Do you know how to handle a gun?"

"I'll learn if I have to."

He handed Lawson the rifle. "I'll open the door enough to see what's out there. Sean and Kate, I want you to be ready in case I need your help to close it."

He put a hand on the door handle and braced himself, then pulled it open just a crack. He glanced at Kate with laughing eyes. A bad feeling settled in her stomach and she watched as he opened the door wider, then bent down. "Kate, here is your big scary monster."

He straightened and turned to her with a grin. She was distracted momentarily when she suddenly noticed his mussed hair and the twinkle in his eye. Shaking the thoughts from her head, she glanced down to the rather large bundle of fur cradled in Nathan's arms. It was anything but scary.

A brown short-haired puppy with all the fine qualities of a mutt took in the new surroundings and people intensely. His ears were alert, his eyes watchful. He looked about ten months old.

"It's a puppy!" Ellie squealed and carefully reached out to pet the dog causing its tail to rub happily against Nathan's stomach. "Oh, Kate, let me keep him. Oh, please."

"No."

"But we gave you Nathan, and Sean got Lawson and I don't have anybody."

"She has a point," Nathan commented.

Kate shook her head. "I'll just end up taking care of him."

Sean looked at her pleadingly. "He won't be any trouble. We can feed him table scraps and take him for a swim when he gets dirty. I'll help."

"Me, too," Lawson said.

"It might be someone else's dog," she reasoned.

"But if it isn't," Ellie pleaded.

Kate bit her lip. "I don't know."

"Please." The three children said, one by one.

She looked to Nathan to weigh his opinion but was confronted with his own version of puppy dog eyes that melted more inside of her than she wanted to admit. Finally, she looked at the dog that appeared to be smiling at her as he panted. "Well…"

She glanced at Ellie. The girl looked so hopeful that Kate couldn't disappoint her. "Oh, all right."

She waited until the whoops died down before saying, "Y'all better take care of this dog or I'll find someone else who will."

Nathan's chuckle reached her ear before he said, "There's just one thing left to say."

She refused to take the bait but Ellie eagerly asked, "What?"

He howled that eerie rendition causing the puppy to launch into his strange yowl. Ellie, Sean and then Lawson joined in to harmonize in some strange melody. Kate covered her ears then, glancing at Nathan, who grinned. She shook her head and laughingly let out a spontaneous howl.

It somehow felt good, not necessarily the howling because it hurt her throat a bit, but the freedom she felt to do it. As if, for a little while, she didn't need to carry the responsibility by herself. As if she could just be herself, Kate O'Brien. Her eyes caught Nathan's and her heart seemed to whisper—*Rutledge*.

Chapter Eight

Nathan carefully stretched his back and sent a silent prayer of thanks Heavenward. The pain was gone, his back was healing nicely and he was finally able to work again. He watched in anticipation as Kate uncovered the scythe. He stepped forward for a better view. The curved blade was impressive.

"May I see it?" Lawson asked, trying to peer around Kate.

Kate shifted, stepping back and to the side. Her heel landed right on the toe of Nathan's firm leather boots. He caught her around the waist to keep her from stumbling, then gently guided her heel off his boot onto the floor. She stilled then lifted her gaze to his apologetically. Their eyes held for a moment, then they both glanced away.

Nathan's gaze landed on Lawson who was looking back and forth between them with interest. Lawson turned back to the scythe and reached for it. "Do I get to use this?"

"Carefully," Nathan amended. "You get to use this carefully."

Kate leveled her serious blue eyes at him. "Nathan, have you ever used one of these?"

He frowned, then picked up the scythe to test its weight. It felt solid in his hand and the wooden handle fit nicely in his palm. "Absolutely not."

Under Kate's instruction, Nathan was soon wielding the scythe as though he'd been born a farmer instead of a rancher. He frowned as he thought about his family. He'd agreed to write a letter to them in a moment of weakness but he didn't regret sending it. They must have received it by now. He wondered if his pa would let the family read it, rather than burning it upon receipt.

He hadn't gone into detail about the events that had led him to answer Kate's advertisement. At the time, they'd been too fresh in his mind. Those nightmares had been more vivid than he'd had in a while. He had a vague memory of Kate soothing him during the worst of it but he hoped that was part of the dream. If not, that meant he'd been talking in his sleep. The images racing through his mind weren't meant to be shared.

He'd done his best to put them behind him but the image of one of his best friends dying right in front of him wasn't always easily shaken. The feeling of being cooped up in a jail cell and the accusations that sent him there weren't easily forgotten. Here with Kate and the children, that life felt an eternity away. He wouldn't ruin that by bringing it up or even thinking about it.

He knew that staying here would be difficult. He kept thinking if only. If only, things had worked out with Kate. If only, he had an entirely new life to make him forget his old one completely. If only, there was hope that something might change.

But there wasn't. He couldn't change the situation and dared not want to. If he did, he was destined to find a new kind of heartache spelled *K-A-T-E* with an apostrophe Sean, Ellie and now Lawson.

It was thinking about Lawson not Kate that caused him to look over his shoulder. Kate was helping Lawson pull the wheat into neat sheaves. Having already paused, Nathan wiped his forehead on his sleeve then pushed it farther up his arm. The sun had already taunted him into unbuttoning his shirt yet, in consideration for Kate, he'd refrained from removing it completely. He turned to survey how far he'd made it down the row in the past hour and had to remind himself not to become discouraged.

He lifted the scythe again but paused when he spotted Kate making her way toward him. Her cheeks were tinged by the sun and her hair was a bit mussed from removing her bonnet, but she looked beautiful. She shaded her eyes to meet his gaze. "I've left you two some water. I'll need to go inside for a while to do my own chores."

"That sounds fine," he agreed.

He watched as she turned and headed toward the house. Then, drumming his fingers on the scythe, he picked it up and prepared to swing.

"You like her, don't ya?"

Nathan stopped the motion quickly. "You shouldn't sneak up on me when I have this thing, Lawson. It's plain dangerous."

Lawson frowned back, "What do you mean sneak up? I was talking to you the whole way here."

Nathan didn't reply, waiting impatiently to get back to work.

"You like her, don't ya?" Lawson asked for the second time.

"You like her, don't *you*?" Nathan corrected.

Lawson grinned knowingly. "Sure, she's very nice. What I mean to say is, I like her but you like her in a different way."

"Lawson," he warned.

"Well, it's true. I may not be ancient but I'm old enough to recognize when sparks fly, and you two could start one of them prairie fires."

Nathan stared at the young man whose freckled face squinted to peer up at him. "Sparks and fires?"

Lawson nodded.

He pulled off his Stetson to let the slight breeze cool his face before setting it back on his head. He shrugged nonchalantly. "It makes no difference one way or the other."

"Of course it does. If you two got married—"

"We're already married. I assumed Sean or Ellie told you."

Lawson looked thoroughly confused. "Did you two have a fight?"

"Not exactly." He paused, looking at the boy's expectant face. "Sean, Ellie and Ms. Lettie got together and decided Kate needed a husband. I wanted a wife and happened to see the ad in the paper. I wrote a letter. The person I thought was Kate answered. We got married without seeing each other. Kate didn't know until I got here, so when the judge comes back we're going to get him to…unmarry us."

"Oh." Lawson seemed thoughtful then shrugged casually. "I'm sorry she doesn't like you back."

Nathan froze for a second, then opened his mouth to reply to the comment but Lawson had already turned and walked away. Nathan shook his head, muttering, "Yeah, well, so am I."

* * *

Kate placed her hands on Nathan's shoulders as his slid around her waist and he lifted her from the wagon. The warmth of his hold disappeared as soon as her feet touched the ground. She glanced over her shoulder and happened to catch sight of her sister. "Ellie, don't! You'll hurt yourself."

Ellie stopped just before attempting to hop out of the wagon. "The boys did it."

"Yes, but they weren't wearing a dress."

"I've got you," Nathan said as he lifted Ellie from the wagon.

Ellie thanked him then tugged at his hand. "Nathan, I want you to meet my friend. Come with me."

Nathan looked back at her to shrug his shoulders helplessly while Ellie led him away. Kate glanced around the crowded churchyard and a thin brunette caught her attention with a quick wave. The young woman hurried toward Kate, hesitating only a moment to eye Nathan as he passed. As she reached Kate's side she lifted her brows curiously. "Who was that?"

Kate rolled her eyes then gave her friend a wry smile. "Hello to you, too, Rachel."

"Sorry." Rachel laughed. "Hello, Kate. It feels as though I haven't seen you in two weeks."

"You haven't seen me in two weeks," she admitted.

"Part of that is my fault—my brothers and sisters started trading sickness so I had to stay home and help Ma last week," Rachel said as they slowly walked toward the church. "I came to church but you weren't here."

"Nathan was too sick for us to come," she said with a nonchalant shrug. This would be the first time they appeared together in public and she intended to make their relationship appear as innocent as it actually was. That way Nathan and Lawson could continue working at the farm while Kate's reputation stayed intact.

She wanted to keep the news of their marriage a secret from the town but she thought that her best friend deserved to know. "Rachel, I'm going to tell you something that you can't tell another soul. Do you promise?"

Rachel came to an abrupt stop then turned to Kate. "Of course I promise. What's going on?"

Kate quickly told her who Nathan really was. When Kate finished Rachel shook her head in astonishment. "At least something good came out of it. You have Nathan and Lawson to help with the farm for now. I've worried about you being out there all alone so much with your siblings in school. This is good."

"I don't think so."

"Why would it be bad?" Rachel stopped to look at her with new interest. "Does this have anything to do with the fact that he's married to you and happens to be one of the most attractive men in town?"

"No." Kate glanced past Rachel and smiled. "Besides, I thought you said Deputy Stone was the handsomest man in town."

Rachel's turned to watch the deputy walk toward the church. "He's all right, I guess."

Kate laughed. "Has he gotten the hint that you're in love with him yet?"

"Unfortunately, no." Rachel winked. "Here comes your hired hand."

Kate turned to find Nathan approaching. She introduced him to Rachel. It wasn't long before Rachel excused herself to join her family and Kate decided it was time to find hers. They started toward Ellie but only walked a few feet before Mrs. Greene suddenly appeared with her daughter in tow.

"It's wonderful to see you up and around, Mr. Rutledge," Mrs. Greene exclaimed while extending a hand to Nathan.

Nathan smiled charmingly. "Yes, well, it's good to be up and around."

Mrs. Greene twittered almost more than her daughter, and Kate could hardly keep from rolling her eyes. The golden-haired young woman smiled demurely. "Ma told me how you jumped in front of that runaway horse. It's quite thrilling. I meant your bravery and not your injury, of course."

Nathan nodded. "Thank you, Miss?"

"Greene. Emily Greene. Will you be in town long?"

Nathan glanced at Kate. "I don't think so. Probably only another month or so."

"Oh, I do wish you would stay longer," Emily protested with a smile. "Though this town is rather rustic, it can be very diverting if you give it half a chance."

Kate nearly choked at the blatant flirting but Nathan's smile grew and he looked as though he would say something else. Kate beat him to the punch with a gracious smile. "Emily is right. This is a very nice town, but speaking of leaving, I think it's time I rounded up Ellie and Sean. Mrs. Greene, Emily, it was nice talking to you."

Mrs. Greene stepped forward. "Mr. Rutledge, I don't suppose you've been able to see the gazebo the town is building. My husband donated a large portion of the funds. I think Emily could show you now. It's just around the corner of the church."

Nathan's eyes widened. "I don't think we'll have time. Perhaps after—"

"Nonsense. You have plenty of time." Mrs. Greene nudged Emily forward causing the girl to blush becomingly. "Go ahead, Emily."

Nathan met Kate's gaze for a long moment as though waiting for her reaction. She started to make up an excuse for him but suddenly realized he might not want one. She pressed her lips together then glanced away. Nathan offered his arm to Emily. "A quick trip wouldn't hurt."

Emily took his arm then pointed him in the right direction. Kate chewed her lip as she watched the woman's beribboned hat thread through the crowd. Mrs. Greene turned to give her a satisfied look. "I think they hit it off rather well, don't you?"

Kate turned, her blue eyes flashing as she whispered, "He's still a married man."

"Not for long," Mrs. Greene replied, then strolled away.

Kate took a steadying breath, inwardly warning herself to let the woman walk away and not say anything impulsive. She didn't see Ellie with the other children so she decided to check inside the church. Stepping inside, Kate almost ran into Lawson who proudly held the church bell, which was actually a cowbell, in his hands. He muttered an excuse before hurrying out the door. Sean and a host of little boys of a variety of ages followed him out.

As Kate sank into the pew beside Rachel, the bell clanged loudly. A moment later the sound of Ellie's voice drew her attention. She glanced back to see her sister walk inside with Mrs. Greene and her husband. She groaned. What was Ellie telling Mrs. Greene now?

It had to be a humdinger because the woman's face had grown even redder than it usually did when Ellie was around. Mr. Greene seemed to listen in amusement. Kate grimaced as Ellie waited in anticipation. Mrs. Greene loudly snapped, "No, I do not want to learn how to howl."

Kate covered her warm cheeks with her hands. What could she do with the girl?

Ellie patted Mrs. Greene's arm comfortingly, then headed up the aisle to Kate and sidled in next to her. Before she could scold Ellie, the girl looked up at her innocently. "I know you told me not to talk to Mrs. Greene, but I was sure her face would turn purple. Too bad that whenever I have a good one Mr. Greene always has to be around. He calms her down too much."

"You better be glad he does," Kate scolded in a hushed voice. "I really mean it, Ellie. I want this behavior to stop. What does the Bible say about how you should treat people?"

"'Do unto others as you would have them do unto you,'" Ellie supplied.

"How would you feel if someone was constantly trying to make you angry about something?"

"All right, Kate." Ellie sighed as if her world was coming to an end, then looked up at Kate. "After all, I don't think it's even possible for someone's face to turn purple. Is it?"

"I hardly know."

Ellie leaned toward Kate. "Wouldn't you like to?"

"No."

"Oh." Ellie sat back to stare sedately at the front of the church.

The first hymn started just as Sean and Lawson slipped into the pew. Ellie tugged at Kate's hand. She bent down and her sister's voice sounded just above the music. "Is he really going to sit with her?"

Confused for a moment, she followed Ellie's pointed gaze and found Nathan strolling down the aisle with Emily Greene still on his arm. A woman behind her spoke to someone in a low tone but one that Kate could hear over the singing. "It seems Emily has found a beau. Won't her mother be relieved?"

Kate, still watching Nathan, saw him glance toward the woman as he passed that row. His gaze then met Kate's. He sent her a panicked look as Emily made a big show of allowing him to precede her into the pew where her family sat.

Kate bit her lip. Short of reaching out and dragging him into the seat beside her there was really nothing she could do. She widened her eyes and lifted her shoulders in a minuscule shrug. She caught a glimpse of disappointment in his eyes before they dropped to the floor, then lifted to Emily. He guided her into the pew then settled on the end.

This might be a good thing, Kate realized. *By sitting with Emily, he's showing there is nothing between us, and Sean and Ellie see that he isn't really tied to our family.*

Ellie made a dissatisfied sound deep in her throat. It was loud enough to draw the attention of a few people nearby. Kate was sure others heard it but were too polite to acknowledge it.

Once everyone looked away, Kate sent her sister a reproving look, then gently poked her in the ribs which unfortunately caused the girl to gasp just as the music paused. Several more people turned to look at them but Ellie only seemed to notice Nathan. He looked back at them and winked. Ellie smiled in satisfaction, then leaned onto Kate's leg and stared up at her. "I think that means he still likes you better."

Warmth rose in her cheeks as the women from earlier began to murmur behind her. Ellie had just managed to undo all of Kate's efforts. She lifted a finger to her lips and whispered, "No more talking."

Ellie nodded, obviously satisfied that her work was done. Kate let out a frustrated breath. Lifting her voice with the rest of the congregation, she tried to shift her focus to God and ignore the tiny part of her that was relieved Ellie might be right.

Chapter Nine

Kate pulled the ties from her bonnet and glanced down the peaceful residential street as she waited for Ms. Lettie to respond to her knock. The door opened a moment later. Ms. Lettie stared at her in shock, then glanced past her. Realizing Kate was alone, Ms. Lettie's brow lowered in worry. "What's wrong? Is it the children? Did Nathan relapse?"

"Nothing is wrong. Everyone is fine. I just came to visit you." She lifted the small plate of tea cakes she'd baked for the occasion as proof.

Ms. Lettie watched her for a minute as though unconvinced. "I don't think you've ever just come for a visit, child. Are you sure nothing's wrong?"

Kate rolled her eyes. "Nathan and Lawson started harvesting last Friday. I tried to help them when I was done with my chores today, but they shooed me away like I was unnecessary. I believe Lawson's exact words were, 'Why don't you bake a cake and bring it to a friend or something. You do have friends, don't you?'"

"Oh," Ms. Lettie breathed, then a smile lit her face. "In that case, come right in. I was about to have tea. You can tell me all about it."

The woman ushered Kate into the breakfast room, then bustled into the kitchen for another place setting. Ms. Lettie returned just as Kate set her tea cakes on the table. Ms. Lettie smiled as she poured Kate a cup of tea. "I am so delighted that you came. I can't remember the last time we were able to just sit and visit. You said Nathan and Lawson took over most of the chores?"

"Yes, they've been doing all of the outside chores and the heavy labor. I've been doing more sewing, mending, washing, cooking and cleaning type of things." She frowned as she stared into her teacup. "Honestly, I don't like it."

"I'm sure you don't," Ms. Lettie said as she gingerly sprinkled a teaspoon of sugar into her tea. "I bet it's been simply awful having them take control over your farm. You've managed on your own for over two years. How dare they act as if you're unnecessary? Why, it's practically an insult."

"Thank you!" Kate exclaimed. "I'm so glad that I'm not the only one who sees it that way. I…" She narrowed her eyes at Ms. Lettie who was obviously struggling to keep a straight face. "You're laughing at me, aren't you?"

Ms. Lettie nodded as she pressed her lips together to keep in her laughter. "I'm so sorry, dear. I didn't think you'd take the bait. You really are upset, aren't you?"

"Yes, I am," she admitted as she shoveled two spoons of sugar into her tea. "I know it doesn't make sense to be angry that Nathan and Lawson are doing what I've hired them to do, but I am."

Ms. Lettie tilted her head and shrugged. "At least you know it doesn't make sense."

Kate set her teacup on the table and leaned forward. "I think what bothers me is that I'm not really paying them. In fact, it's the opposite. Nathan is practically paying me to let him work for me."

"I don't think that's really bothering you, Kate." Ms. Lettie took a sip of her tea then met Kate's gaze knowingly. "What bothers you is that you're sitting here enjoying tea with me while someone else takes care of the farm, and you're actually enjoying it. What's bothering you is that you like not having to work until you're exhausted, then go to bed to get up and do it all over again. Am I right?"

Kate took a nice long sip of her tea so she wouldn't have to admit the truth. "I was fine on my own."

"I'm not questioning that." Ms. Lettie took one of the tea cakes from the plate and placed it on her own. "In fact, I doubt anyone in town questions the fact that you can take care of yourself and your siblings. We all know you to be a strong, determined woman. My only concern is that you might become too strong."

"How could I be too strong?" Kate asked.

Ms. Lettie swallowed a bite of her cookie before continuing. "Before Nathan came along you shunned help from anyone. You were in danger of believing you could get through life on your own. You can't. No one can. God didn't create us that way. We need to give help and receive help. I don't mind telling you that you hadn't been doing either."

"What do you mean?"

"After your parents died you accepted help for a while until that episode with Andrew Stolvins. You say he didn't break your heart but I don't think you can deny he broke your trust. You shut almost everyone out. Rachel and I managed to maintain our relationships with you simply because we wouldn't take no for an answer. You were grieving, vulnerable and hurting then. What about now?"

"I've recovered somewhat."

Ms. Lettie nodded decisively. "You have and it shows. You're accepting help from others by allowing Nathan to work for you. You're helping others by opening your home to an orphan who has no real hope for a better life outside of the opportunity you're giving him." Ms. Lettie reached across the table to touch Kate's arm. "These are good things, Kate. You shouldn't fight them."

She glanced away from Ms. Lettie's sincere gaze. "I don't want to get used to it. I know Nathan is going to leave. When he does, the burden will fall back on my shoulders." She bit her lip. "Do you think God may have allowed this to give me a reprieve?"

"It's possible," Ms. Lettie said. "Or, God could have allowed this to happen because he wants you to fall in love with Nathan and stay married."

"No, that's why you allowed it to happen." Kate sent the woman a pointed gaze, then tried one of the cookies.

"Why don't you trust God to reveal it to you? Find out what He wants you to do in this situation."

"You make it sound so easy."

Ms. Lettie looked at her with new interest. "You mean it isn't?"

"I tried that with Andrew. Look how that turned out."

"He put on an act, dear. He was one person with you, and another person with the rest of the town." She smiled sympathetically. "You were so desperate for something good to happen after your parents' deaths that you ignored some of the more obvious signs. For instance, Sean and Ellie despised him. He talked about building that saloon whenever you weren't around." She shook her head. "Everyone in town knew he was wrong for you."

She set her cookie down and stared at Ms. Lettie. "So I really was just oblivious?"

"You were physically, emotionally and spiritually exhausted. It isn't surprising that you missed a few things." Ms. Lettie placed a comforting hand on her arm. "You made a mistake. That's all it was. It wasn't the end of the world."

"Why didn't God keep me from making it?"

"How would you ever learn?" Ms. Lettie laughed. "Besides, I think he kept you from making the greatest mistake of all."

Kate frowned. "What do you mean?"

"Your last name isn't Stolvins, is it?"

"No." She breathed a sigh of relief. "It's still O'Brien."

Ms. Lettie smiled as she raised her teacup toward her lips. "Actually, Kate, I believe it's Rutledge."

Nathan stopped outside the Post Office to stare at it, then removed his hat and fiddled with the brim. He nervously stepped inside the small building. A white-haired man peered up from the book he was reading. "Howdy. How can I help you?"

Nathan stepped up to the counter. "I wanted to see if you might have any mail for me. I'm Nathan Rutledge."

"I know they're here somewhere." The man grabbed a pack of letters and sorted through them. "Here you are."

Nathan stared at the letters the man offered to him. He checked the return addresses on the envelopes. The first was from Davis Reynolds in response to his job inquiry. He didn't need a job immediately, so he was free to focus on the other one for now. It was from Mariah Rutledge of Rutledge, Oklahoma. His youngest sister had written back. He swallowed the emotion rising in his throat, then choked out his thanks to the postmaster before he hurried out the door.

He glanced around the busy street for a private place to read the letter. With none in sight, he ducked into the alley next to the Post Office and opened the letter. Several other envelopes were inside but a sheet of paper enclosed them. It was a letter from Mariah. He decided to read that first.

Dear Nathan,
I can't tell you how happy I am to hear that you are alive and well. We are all fine but we've all missed you. Pa has, too, even if he won't admit it. I was only fifteen when you left but even I knew Pa was too harsh with you.

Oh, Nathan, I wish you had contacted us earlier. Even a few months would have made a difference. You see, Pa found out about what happened when you lived in Noches. Your business partner, Jeremiah Fulton, wrote him a letter about his brother's death, your trial and escape from justice.

I'm sure it can't all be true, although Pa believed every word. He had softened where you were concerned but now I fear all of that has been lost.

Mr. Fulton has written several times to Pa to check if we've received any information about your location. Pa usually tosses them in the waste basket after he's read them so I've enclosed them....

His sister went on to talk about what had changed since Nathan left, but he stopped reading to look at Jeremiah's letters. He glanced at the postmarks on the envelopes. If Jeremiah was trying to find him, he was looking in the wrong part of the state. He frowned as he scanned the contents of the letters. They presented an account of what happened skewed by Jeremiah's anger and grief and his stubborn certainty that Eli's accidental death was actually murder. No wonder his pa was upset.

He leaned against the wall of the Post Office and took a deep breath. Mariah had written back. That's what he needed to focus on. It was a big step in the right direction. Now if he could just get the misunderstanding that Jeremiah had caused under control, then perhaps he could improve his relationship with his pa. He walked back into the Post Office and wrote a response immediately.

Dear Mariah,
Thank you for writing me. I will send another letter soon. In the meantime, please write to the sheriff of Noches, Texas, and ask for a full explanation of what happened. I'm sure Pa will be pleased to find out the truth.
    Please refrain from giving Jeremiah my information. He doesn't seem to want reconciliation and I'd prefer to leave the past in the past.
Love,
Nathan

He mailed the letter, then tucked the others safely into his saddlebag. It wasn't long before he reached the edge of town. He pulled his Stetson lower with a jerky movement, then gave Delilah her head. The horse set out at a gallop. The ground flew beneath her feet but no matter how fast he went, he couldn't seem to outrun the memory of his past.

With the Fulton brothers in Noches, he had been so focused on his dreams that they'd blinded him to everything around him. If nothing else, he'd learned there were no "take backs" in life. There were no "do overs." There was only the present and it was to be lived, protected and cherished.

He reined Delilah in to a smooth canter. The stakes were higher now. He realized he could lose something much more important than any ranch. He'd tried to ignore the attraction he felt for his wife but he couldn't. Worse, he was starting to care for her as more than just part of an ideal future. If he couldn't rein in the emotions he was beginning to feel for Kate, then he could very well lose his heart. And not just to her. It would be too easy to love Sean, Ellie, Lawson—even the puppy they'd named Lasso. It felt like they were building a family, and he wanted to keep it more than he'd ever wanted anything before.

Nathan was stunned at the thought and even more at the truth of it. He'd just have to remind himself that this family wasn't his to keep. He would leave soon and he was determined to leave nothing behind but good wishes and fond memories. He had a feeling that was all Kate expected from him anyway.

He reined in Delilah and settled her in her stall of the O'Briens' barn, then grabbed his saddlebag and went in search of Kate.

He found her kneeling in the loose dirt of her vegetable garden. The sound of his footsteps on the softly packed earth made her glance up and give him what could pass as a welcoming smile. He met her gaze with a determined nod. She tilted her head questioningly. His gaze shot around the barnyard. "Are the children around?"

She shrugged, brushing her hair from her face with dirt-streaked fingers. "They've been running wild the past few hours so I haven't the slightest idea. Did you get everything taken care of in town?"

He realized he was still wearing his Stetson so he quickly removed it. "Yes. I just wanted to send off a letter."

"Good." She rubbed the dirt from her hands and glanced up at him curiously. "Is everything all right, Nathan?"

"Yes." He tapped his Stetson on his leg then decided to get on with it. "I just want to get a few things straight between us."

Suddenly incessant barking erupted from the house, followed closely by Ellie's scream. Nathan's heart skipped a beat. Kate scrambled to her feet and ran toward the house and he hurried after her. He reached the door a moment behind Kate and burst through it into the sitting room. His heart pounding in his chest, he surveyed the scene in confusion.

"What is going on?" Kate asked.

Sean whirled to face them and over the painfully loud barking managed to say, "There is something furry under the settee. Lasso chased it in."

"Is that all?" Kate met Nathan's gaze with shared relief. "I'll get the broom."

He set his saddlebag by the door then said, "We need to quiet that dog."

Sean jumped to orders, calling the dog's name over the frenzied barking. Ellie was standing on the settee and seemed to be trying to dance. "I think it's a rat. I think it's a rat. Oh! Get me down."

Lawson was hunkered on the ground trying to get a view of the animal. "Ouch, Ellie, that was my finger you stepped on!"

Kate reappeared holding the broom like a sword with one hand and covering her ear with the other. "Everyone calm down. We'll deal with this in an orderly way."

"What? I can't hear you," Sean yelled.

Nathan walked over to the settee, picked Ellie up and set her down beside Kate. Then he firmly commanded, "Lasso, sit."

The dog looked over his shoulder at Nathan and let out a moaning sound. Then it obediently lay down to stare under the settee. With the noise under control, Nathan turned to Lawson who was peering beneath the settee. "Now, do you have any idea what's under there?"

"I think it's either a cat or a skunk."

"A skunk!" Kate exclaimed. Ellie resumed her dance. Lasso took that as a cue to start barking again. Sean tried to shush him. Lawson hunkered down for a better look. Nathan took in a deep breath, commanding, "Sit, Lasso."

The dog growled deep in his throat.

"Sit."

Lasso moaned but lay down.

"With this racket, a skunk would have let us know it was here." His words seemed to have a calming effect on everyone.

"It's a cat," Lawson said confidently, then added, "I think."

"Nathan, we need to get Lasso out of here before we can do anything else," Kate said. "He needs to go to the barn."

"Right," he agreed. "Sean, do you think you can help me with that?"

"Yes, sir."

Nathan scooped up the gangly pup and headed out the door that Sean held open. He didn't stop until he'd set the dog in the barn. He quickly closed the barn door behind him then hurried back inside with Sean trailing after him.

As he walked inside, Lawson said, "It's a cat. Either that or a snake with fur."

Ellie gave a pronounced shiver.

Lawson grinned, watching the effect of his words on Ellie until she glared at him, then he turned to look under the settee again. "Listen."

Everyone was quiet a moment and they heard a soft hissing sound.

Sean shifted his weight. "If that's a cat it isn't happy."

"The poor thing it's probably scared to death," Kate sympathized.

"I have an idea," Nathan said.

Soon Lawson and Sean stood at one end of the settee while Nathan stood at the opposite end with a sack. He was ready to slip it over the cat upon its appearance. Kate stood beside Sean and Lawson just in case the cat went that way. Ellie had a sheet to throw over the poor animal in case it didn't go either way.

"On the count of three," Nathan commanded. "One. Two. Three."

The settee moved and Nathan saw the cat. He lunged for it but the cat was already moving his direction to get away from Sean and Lawson. It completely missed the sack and instead it ended up clinging to Nathan's shirt. He let out a startled yell then decided to catch it in the sack anyway. Just as he brought the sack up, the cat fell from its precarious position. It landed on its feet with a thump then took off running.

In a split second it was in Ellie's arms, its face hidden in the crook of her elbow. Everyone stared in astonished silence filled only by Lasso's faint bark from the barn. Ellie stared back at everyone for a moment before her large green eyes lifted to Kate. "May I keep it?"

Chapter Ten

Kate nearly groaned at the pleading look on Ellie's face. Instead, she shook her head. "No, Ellie. You have a dog. You do not need a cat, especially not that one. It can stay in the barn until we find another home for it, but that is it."

"But Nathan—"

"I'll not go against your sister, Ellie. We'll have to find another home for it."

Her little sister lifted her chin. "Fine, but at least I get to keep it until then. Come on, boys. Let's go play with it outside."

She flounced toward the door in her shirt and bloomers. Her pert little nose was in the air so high she tripped over Nathan's saddlebag. She would have fallen if Sean hadn't managed to catch her arm. Lawson knelt down to pick up the envelopes strewn across the floor. "Hey, what's this?"

Nathan hurried across the room to gather the letters. "It's a letter from my family."

Lawson stilled then glanced up at Nathan. "They wrote you back."

Nathan stacked the letters in his hands then nodded.

Silence sounded throughout the room for a heartbeat then the children erupted in cheers. Kate smiled at their exuberance. Ellie shifted the cat in her arms to get a better look at the letters. "Those are a lot of letters. They must have had a lot to say."

He placed the letters in his bag and set it upright. "Just one was from my sister. The others were letters she forwarded about some business I need to take care of."

Sean leaned against the door frame. "What did she say? Do they want you back?"

"I haven't read all of it yet. She said Pa is still upset but she's going to try to help me."

Kate smiled as she sank onto the end of the misplaced settee. "That's wonderful, Nathan."

He sat back on his haunches to glance up at her and shrugged. "It's a start."

She held his gaze, wondering why he didn't seem as excited about the letter as the children were. Perhaps he didn't want to get his hopes up. *Did* he hope to go back to his family? Would he head to Oklahoma after the annulment? He was working hard on their crop, but she knew he wasn't really a farmer at heart. The children began asking question after question but Kate admonished them, ignoring the fact that she had some questions of her own. "Nathan hasn't even had time to read the whole letter yet. If he wants to tell you about it later, then fine, but give him some time to think about it first."

Nathan sent her a grateful look as the children reluctantly went outside to play with the cat. He helped her set the room to right. Once they were finished, he slid the settee back into place then collapsed onto it. Kate settled beside him with a sigh. "I don't know what I'm going to do with Ellie. She knows just what to say to get her way."

He laughed. "She'll turn out all right."

"I certainly hope so. I'm all she has so if she doesn't we'll know who to blame."

"You're doing a good job with them, Kate."

She met his gaze. "You think so?"

He nodded. "I really do."

Kate smiled ruefully then, leaning her head back against the settee, she let out a sigh. "Well, at least that makes one of us."

He was quiet for a long moment before he cleared his throat. "Kate, I was trying to tell you something earlier."

She opened her eyes and shifted on the settee to face him. "Yes, I remember. You were behaving rather oddly and then you said something needed to be set straight."

He met her gaze seriously. "You remember when I spoke to Mr. Potters about the annulment and he said it would either be one or two months or more until the judge was back?"

Kate nodded and waited for him to continue.

"Well, this will be the fourth week since the judge left so he could be back at any time."

"Oh," she breathed. "I see."

Why did that leave her feeling strangely bereft? After all, she'd only know Nathan for little more than a month. She suddenly realized she would be sorry to see him go. Though she tried to convince herself there was nothing romantic between them, she couldn't deny the friendship they'd managed to eek out.

This is silly. I should be overjoyed. This is exactly what I wanted. He's leaving and that's the way it should be, she sternly reminded herself.

"Or," Nathan continued, "he might not be back for another month or more."

Kate's gaze flew to his. *Did he say another month or longer? I barely made it through this one without weakening my resolve.*

His warm brown gaze searched hers. "We'll just have to wait and see how everything works out."

She set her pride aside to smile. "Either way, I'm glad you came. You've been a great help to me and my siblings. I wish I could offer to let you stay on as my hired hand once this is over but I doubt I could pay you a fair wage."

His gaze seemed to shutter before he glanced away. "No, I couldn't do that."

Uncomfortable with the silence between them, she stood up. "I'd better start supper. I don't suppose Ellie will be any help." She paused to turn back to him. "If you aren't busy, I wouldn't mind," she hesitated, "I mean, if you just wanted to..."

"Help?" he asked, then smiled. "Sure, I'd like to."

After supper Kate set the dress she was mending down to glance around the empty room. She frowned, wondering where everyone had gone. She'd sent Ellie outside to help with the chores since the girl couldn't seem to sit still long enough to complete a stitch, but that had been nearly half an hour ago. She set her sewing basket aside, accidentally sending a spool of thread rolling across the floor. The cat shot from the hallway into the kitchen to chase it.

"Who let you in here?" Kate asked. As she stepped forward the spool rolled from the cat's grasp and she quickly covered it with her boot. Scooping up the cat, she set her aside. The cat rushed toward her boot again but Kate managed to pick up the spool before the cat reached it. "You're a feisty little thing, aren't you?"

The cat meowed pitifully.

"Oh, don't try that act with me. I know what you're really like." She set the spool back in the sewing basket. "I ought to put you outside. I don't like animals in my kitchen."

The kitchen door opened and the cat streaked outside a moment before Nathan stepped inside. "What are you doing?"

She'd been talking to the cat but she didn't want to tell him that. She settled back into her chair, then picked up her needle. "I'm just getting a head start on the mending for tomorrow."

He straddled the chair next to her. "You should come outside with me," he said. "Sean and Ellie say they're just dying to 'watch the stars,' whatever that means."

Her needle stilled. "It's something we used to do with Ma and Pa. Every so often after our nightly Bible reading, they would let us stay up really late to watch the stars come out."

"Maybe you should continue their traditions," he advised thoughtfully. "Since the children are already outside, you could start with this one."

She glanced down at the mending in her hands and saw it for what it really was. It was busywork to keep her mind off… Her gaze lifted to Nathan's. She wanted to groan. So what if she was beginning to like him? That didn't mean she had to pursue those feelings. She'd simply choose not to. There. She wouldn't like him anymore. She couldn't trust that feeling anyway. Every time she thought about liking him, she'd just remind herself of the mistake she'd made with Andrew Stolvins and eventually those feelings would dissipate.

Before she had the chance to try, Nathan stood and tucked his chair back into place. He held out his hand, then with a gentle smile of entreaty, he asked, "Are you coming?"

"I'm coming." But she certainly wasn't going to take his hand. She stepped outside and immediately spotted the children sitting along the pasture fence. She ducked beneath the top railing of the fence while stepping over the bottom. Sean smiled at her from his perch on the fence as she went to stand between him and Ellie.

She turned her back to the fence and was trying to figure out how to hoist herself up without landing in a heap on the ground when Nathan appeared in front of her. He caught her waist then set her carefully onto the fence.

"Thank you," she said as he claimed a spot on the other side of Ellie.

"We're watching for the first star," Ellie said.

Sean nodded. "Nathan said the person who spots the first star gets to make a wish."

"I spotted the moon but that doesn't count." Lawson pointed to the right spot.

"I see it," she said after following his gaze to where the half moon hung in the slightly clouded sky.

Several minutes later Ellie was sitting safely between Sean and Lawson. Kate had Sean on one side and on the other, entirely too close, sat Nathan. For safety sake, he'd said. Trying to ignore the man beside her without making it painfully obvious, Kate focused on her siblings' conversation.

She felt a presence behind her. Before she could react, Delilah's muzzle appeared over her shoulder. She gasped. The muzzle disappeared then pushed her forward. She would have fallen off the fence if Nathan hadn't caught her. She gasped then turned to stare at Delilah. The horse nudged Nathan's shoulder, only much more gently. Kate narrowed her eyes. "Do you think she did that on purpose?"

Nathan guided the horse's muzzle away from his shoulder then rubbed her nose. "No. I trained her better than that. She was just looking for attention. I'm sorry. Sometimes she doesn't know her own strength."

She wasn't convinced. "I don't think she likes me. She sneezed into my hand the first time I tried to pet her."

Nathan quirked an amused grin. "Maybe she's allergic to you."

"She seems fine now."

"I'll put her in her stall before she sneezes again." He jumped down from the fence and led Delilah away. When he returned he asked, "When did you say the combine and threshing machine would be coming through?"

"The day after tomorrow," she said then glanced around Sean to Lawson. "Did you hear that, Lawson? You won't have to work in the fields after that."

"I liked working in the fields."

Ellie leaned forward. "Don't you want to go to school, Lawson?"

He shrugged. "I've never had much use for it."

Ellie grinned. "Me, neither."

Once the sky was filled with stars the excitement was gone and the children jumped down from the fence. Sean and Ellie wanted to show Lawson how to catch fireflies in the fields. Kate glanced at the fields that were just beginning to sparkle. "Stay close enough that you'll hear when I call you in."

They waved in acknowledgment then scampered off.

Silence hovered in their wake. Nathan moved his arm from behind her to brace himself more fully. His hand landed close to hers on the rough wooden fence. She bit her lip. Glancing upward, she stared at the millions of stars twinkling in a dark sky. It looked so immense it was almost frightening.

"It's amazing, isn't it," Nathan asked upon observing the same view.

"Yes," she agreed, as she glanced out at the fields. The fireflies danced across the fields in what appeared to be a reflection of the sky on a still lake. She pulled in a deep relaxing breath. She couldn't remember the last time she'd allowed herself to appreciate the beauty of the land she was working so hard to save.

Nathan's deep voice should have jarred her out of her calm reverie, but its warm tones just enhanced the spell. "It's enough to make you feel weak and powerful at the same time."

"I know exactly what you mean," she breathed, then her entire being stilled when she suddenly wondered if he was still talking about the stars. His words perfectly described the feelings she'd been trying so hard to ignore.

Did he share those feelings? Did she want him to? No, she reminded herself. Because he wasn't staying—and she didn't want him to...did she?

"I guess I should call the children." She carefully lowered herself from the fence. Then she walked away from him and the question she was too afraid to answer.

As Nathan and Lawson returned to the cabin, Lawson spoke up. "You know, even if your pa doesn't accept you back, at least you've got a sister who loves you."

Nathan didn't point out that his sister seemed to have

some doubts about him, too. He hoped she followed his advice and wrote to the sheriff in Noches. If not, he doubted if he would ever have a chance to reconnect with his family. Lawson seemed to follow his line of thought, for he continued, "Even if you don't hear from them again, at least you, Kate, Ellie and Sean are all a family."

Nathan sent him a skeptical look. "If you consider me part of their family then you're family, too."

Lawson shook his head. "No, I'm not much like family to anyone."

"I disagree."

"Listen, I may be saying this all wrong but it all comes down to dreams."

"Dreams?" Nathan asked in low disbelief.

Lawson nodded. "Haven't you had dreams, Nathan? Things you hope for and keep close to you? Things you don't want to let go of?"

Nathan agreed slowly. "I've had a few of those."

Lawson took in a deep breath as he looked up at the stars. "Well, I've always wanted a ma and pa. Real ones."

Nathan silently waited for him to continue.

Lawson glanced at Nathan and the desperation he tried so often to hide would not be denied. "Nathan, I'm fourteen years old. I've never had a family. Not one that loved me enough to stick around. Being here, for the first time, I know what I missed out on and it makes the ache that much worse. Sometimes I just wish I was someone else. Someone good people might want to choose."

Nathan leaned toward him, resting a hand on the boy's shoulder. "Lawson, you are chosen. Not just by

Kate, Sean, Ellie and me but by God. Do you understand?"

Lawson shook his head. "I don't think so."

"He loves you. He never wants to be separated from you. He gave up everything He knew and came to this earth so that he could have a relationship with you." Nathan allowed those words to sink in for a moment before continuing, "If you accept that, you become His son and can trust that He wants the best for you. If that's a ma and pa then that's what He'll give you. If that's living with me then that's where you'll stay."

"You mean that?" Lawson asked quietly. "You'd let me go with you even if you have to leave?"

Nathan smiled, amusement lighting his eyes. "I reckon."

Lawson quirked a smile and gave him a short nod. "Thanks, Nathan."

He sat up. "Now wait just a minute. What happened to wanting a real ma and pa?"

"Nothing. It's just good to have a backup plan even if it is pretty shoddy."

"Shoddy, huh?"

Lawson grinned.

"I'll try not to be offended," Nathan said.

There was silence for a long moment, then Lawson asked, "Want to know what I think you should do about Kate?"

"Not particularly."

Lawson shrugged. "All I'm saying is it doesn't hurt to remind a girl she's pretty."

Nathan stared at him skeptically. "How would you know?"

"I have my ways."

Nathan snorted.

"I'm also saying it doesn't hurt to remind a girl you know she thinks you aren't too bad looking, either."

Nathan's opened his mouth to speak then closed it. He considered the idea for a moment then said, "Lawson, do me a favor. Stop thinking whatever you're thinking and go to bed."

Lawson smiled. "Yes, sir."

Chapter Eleven

A rough knock on the door prompted Kate to step away from the table where Nathan and Lawson sat eating lunch. Nathan moved to stand. She shook her head. "I'd better get it."

Today was the day the harvesters were coming. That meant it could only be one person at the door. She smoothed her stark white apron as she walked out of the kitchen, then paused in front of the door. Ready for the confrontation, she opened the door. Andrew Stolvins had wandered away from the door to stare at the field. She leaned into the door frame and placed one hand on her hip as he turned to frown at her.

"Kate, what happened to the field?" Andrew pulled his hat from his head to uncover his dark blond hair.

"I harvested part of it myself."

He looked mad enough to spit. "Why'd you go and do a fool thing like that? I told you we could negotiate some sort of payment."

She gave a dry laugh. "I don't even want to know what sort of payment you would have expected."

His innocent expression almost looked genuine. "I

was trying to help you just like I did after your parents died. I was here for you then, wasn't I?"

"Sure you were. Unfortunately it was the kind of help that pushes someone down when they're already falling." She lifted her chin as she gained control of her emotions. "We've gone over this before, Andrew. I don't want your help. I don't want to negotiate. I want you to treat me like you would any other farmer."

"Fine." He shifted in his fancy boots, then continued in a businesslike tone. "I insist you pay me the rate for the whole field since that was our agreement."

She narrowed her eyes. "Our agreement was that I would pay you eighteen percent of the wheat you harvest."

He smiled smugly. "No, it was eighteen percent of your total harvest. That includes what you've already done."

Kate gritted her teeth in frustration. It was his word against hers in their verbal agreement. He stepped closer. "I set up payment plans with a few farmers. If you'd like to do that, I'm sure we could come to some agreement."

Kate stepped aside as he tried to place a hand over on the door frame above her head. She watched him with suspicion. "What sort of payment plan?"

"That all depends on you. You could work three nights a week for a month and we could call it even or—"

"Is that the deal you set up with the other farmers?"

He looked her over appraisingly. "The other farmers weren't pretty enough to be a saloon girl."

Her fist clenched at her side.

He took note of her fist then raised an imperious brow. "I'd pay you eight dollars a week and you'd earn commission off the drinks you sold. Take the offer. It isn't as though your reputation could get much worse now anyway."

Kate froze. "My reputation? What are you talking about?"

"Half the county is talking about how you have that man living here."

"Nathan? He doesn't live here. He works here. He lives in the cabin about half a mile away."

"It makes no difference. I still can't take the chance. The only job I have to offer you is the one at the saloon." He lowered his head to stare at her. "There your reputation certainly wouldn't be a problem."

"I've heard enough."

Paying no heed to her objections, he continued. "In fact, it might even prove profitable."

Her breath caught in her throat. "Get off my land."

He ducked his head, finally realizing he'd gone too far. "Kate, won't you listen to me for a minute? The truth is—"

"You heard the lady." Nathan's voice cut him off. Relief filled Kate as he stepped from the house to stand beside her.

Andrew stared at Nathan for a moment then sent him a mocking smile. "Ah, this must be the man all of Texas envies."

Nathan's jaw clenched with anger. "Leave now."

Andrew laughed. "I don't take orders from no-account drifters like you. You have a lot of gall standing there like you aren't after the same—"

Kate gasped as suddenly Andrew flew through the air and landed on his backside in the dirt.

"Lord," Nathan muttered as he rubbed his aching fist and watched the man struggling to sit up. "I believe you'd agree there is such a thing as righteous anger."

He heard a laugh escape from Kate's direction but he didn't look her way. He was too busy trying to see if the man was going to throw a punch of his own. That was the only trouble with defending a woman's honor. In doing so you might find yourself in an all-out brawl. Not that the pain wasn't worth it, of course. He waited while the man regained his equilibrium and tried to get to his feet.

"I'm sorry I had to do that, Stolvins," Nathan said. "You see, my pa didn't raise me to sit back and do nothing while a lady's honor was being wrongfully challenged. I think we both know you deserved it."

The man eyed Nathan as he stood to his feet. He drew his arm back as though ready to throw his own punch but then his hand relaxed and covered his stomach. "You sucker punched me."

"I did. Now, I'd appreciate it if you would be so kind as to remove yourself from the lady's presence. For your own good, you understand? I'd surely hate to have to do that again."

Stolvins stared at him in defiance then reached down to pick up his hat. Setting it on his head he said, "You remember what I said, Kate."

"I believe I've already forgotten."

"Then you can forget my help with your crop. Do it yourself. I'll be glad to see little Miss High and Mighty fail." Stolvins gave them both a dirty look which Nathan returned with a polite nod. Nathan didn't relax until the man galloped away.

Lawson tumbled from the doorway with a grin. "That was amazing. I saw the whole thing through the window."

Kate shook her head with a soft smile. "Thank you, Nathan."

He shrugged. "I only did what any decent man would."

"Do you suppose what he said about my reputation was true?" she asked. "Is that what people think of me?"

"I truly hope not, Kate. If so, it's my fault. I should have realized there would be talk. However, you have to realize the worst thing the townspeople could do is force us to get married."

Lawson's eyes widened. "You already are."

"Exactly," he agreed, then frowned. "Listen, Kate. Why don't I go into town and see how things stand?"

"What about the wheat?"

"We can start tomorrow. We'll need to buy a few more scythes and Sean may have to stay home to help."

She sighed. "I hoped it wouldn't come to that but I suppose there is no other choice. If you're going to town then I'm coming with you. What better way to find out what people think of me?"

Nathan didn't like the idea but knew he wouldn't be able to convince her otherwise. "I'll get the horses."

Kate frowned at the glass of lemonade in her hands as she sat in Ms. Lettie's parlor. "So there has been talk?"

The woman smiled kindly. "Barely snatches of it, Kate, and those people were quickly put to right."

"I see."

"As far as I know, it's only that horrible Mr. Stolvins and his saloon people who speak of such nonsense. Everyone else respects what you've done with the farm and is happy that you have help. I wouldn't worry about it. Now, tell me. Have you any idea how you'll bring in the harvest?"

"Nathan suggested we keep Sean at home. Other than that, I suppose we'll be working dawn to dusk."

"And you'll be keeping more of your hard-earned money." The widow paused in thought. "Kate, I have an idea that will bring you more workers than you can manage."

Kate smiled but watched her in suspicion. "What are you thinking?"

"Just leave it to me." Ms. Lettie leaned forward. "Oh, Kate. I'm so glad you came to town. I have news of my own. Luke has finally proposed!"

"I'm not surprised," Kate teased. "I wondered when Doc Williams would get around to it. I'm so happy for you!"

"Yes, well, it seems I've found myself in desperate need of a maid of honor and seeing as you're like a daughter to me I was hoping…"

"Oh, I'd love to!" She squeezed Ms. Lettie's hand. "You were my mother's best friend, after all. You took me under your wing when she died. This is the least I could do."

Ms. Lettie smiled. "Wonderful. We'll need to pick out some fabric then. I was thinking blue for you but I'm not at all sure of what color I should wear. Nothing white, of course. You'll have to help me choose."

Kate followed Ms. Lettie into the kitchen to place her cup in the sink. "You don't have to buy a dress for me."

Ms. Lettie smiled. "My dear, you are getting a new dress. I want you to have one so fancy and becoming you'll be half ashamed to wear it."

"Wait a minute—"

"It will be perfect," Ms. Lettie soothed. "There's no

better time than the present. We'll go pick out the fabric then visit the seamstress."

The two were soon talking over the fabric and possible embellishments at the mercantile. Glancing up, Kate caught sight of a familiar set of shoulders. Nathan stood at the counter talking with Mr. Johansen. The two scythes that lay across the counter spoke of the nature of their business together.

"Should we ask Nathan's opinion about the dress?"

Kate's eyes widened. "No. Why should we? Men hardly know of such things."

"I've found that doesn't stop them from having an opinion," the woman quipped as she waved at Nathan.

"Ms. Lettie, I hate to say this, but you're embarrassing me."

"I'm sorry, dear. This has to happen every once in a while. It's hardly fair for you to miss out on this type of thing because your dear mother is gone." When Nathan arrived Ms. Lettie held up sample of the two cloths. "Nathan, we need your help to decide which shade of blue suits Kate best."

Kate sent him an apologetic look. "No, we don't."

"Do you think the lighter or the darker shade would be better?"

Nathan seemed all too amused as he considered the two fabrics. Finally, he pointed to the bolt of medium blue fabric. "I'd have to say this one matches her eyes almost exactly."

Kate looked at him in surprise. Her eyes? He hadn't looked at her to compare, which meant he didn't need the reference. She tried not to let that thought flatter her but when her gaze met his she couldn't seem to look away. Mrs. Lenworth's voice broke the moment, allowing Kate to glance away though she still felt his eyes on her. "It's a beautiful color isn't it, Nathan?"

"Very beautiful," he replied then took a step back. "Was that all you needed?"

"Yes, thank you."

As soon as he was out of earshot Kate turned to Ms. Lettie with a tired sigh. "I wish you wouldn't waste your matchmaking on me."

"We must pick out my fabric. I'll take this dark blue one and I think this pretty cream ribbon would complement it nicely. We need buttons, of course. For you." She looked at the lighter blue fabric. "Let's go with white ribbons. I suppose you should purchase some white fabric now to be prepared," she muttered, then hurried toward the buttons.

It took a moment for the meaning of her parting comment to dawn. When it did Kate gave a sharp laugh that caused a nearby customer to look up. Grimacing, Kate followed Ms. Lettie.

Kate and Lawson waited in the wagon with the few supplies they'd gotten from the mercantile while Nathan stepped into the Post Office. He pulled the letter he was sending from his pocket and set it on the counter. The older gentleman with the white hair searched under the desk for the appropriate stamp. "Did that fellow find you?"

Nathan stilled. "Was someone looking for me?"

"Sure was." The man smoothed the stamp onto the envelope carefully. "It was a man about your age. He wanted to know if you were around. I told him I'd seen you a while back. He wanted to know where you were living but I couldn't remember and didn't care to speculate."

"Do you know if he stuck around?"

"He said he'd be back." The man handed Nathan his change back. "He was a tall fellow but skinnier than you. He had real dark hair and light blue eyes. That caught me as strange or I never would have remembered him. Do you think he might have been a friend a yours?"

"Probably not," Nathan said before he could catch himself. He didn't like the idea of Jeremiah Fulton coming to Peppin. Eli's death had changed a lot of things including Jeremiah's friendship with Nathan. The man's bitterness and anger didn't belong in this place where Nathan had tried to make a fresh start. But judging from all those letters Jeremiah had sent his folks, Jeremiah wouldn't stop tracking him.

Perhaps it was time for them to finally talk about what had happened. If he showed up, Nathan would try to reason with him. Maybe they could part as friends. Doubt pulled his mouth into a frown. Trying to talk rationally to his friend hadn't worked at the time. He could almost hear Jeremiah's screams after Eli fell dead.

"You're going to pay."

Nathan's gaze flew to the postmaster. The man stared back at him. Surely, he'd misheard. "What did you say?"

"I said I can only mail the letter if you're going to pay." The man lowered his bushy white brows. "You were expecting to pay, weren't you?"

Nathan ignored the chill that brushed over his skin, and paid the man. "Do you have any mail for me or the O'Briens?"

The man shuffled through his stack of mail but came up empty. "There's nothing today."

Nathan thanked him then couldn't get outside fast

enough. Kate glanced at him in concern when he climbed into the wagon. "Are you all right? You look so pale."

"I'm fine," he said brusquely then set the wagon in motion. "Everything will be fine."

Kate placed her hands on her lower back and leaned into them. It felt wonderful to stretch her aching muscles. She leaned farther back and felt a satisfying pop. She had just turned back to her work when Sean called. "Kate, look."

She followed her little brother's gaze to find her friend Rachel riding toward them on a small black horse. The young woman grinned and waved.

"Rachel!" Kate exclaimed in surprise before hurrying toward her. The petite brunette slipped off the horse to give Kate a hug.

"What are you doing here?"

"I'm with them."

"With who?" Kate asked but turned in distraction when Sean let out a whoop and hurried past her. It was then Kate noticed a group of ten or so men walking toward the field, scythes in hand.

"Ms. Lettie said you could use some help."

Kate frowned. "But I can't take you all away from your farms. You have your own harvests to worry about. We'll be fine."

"Of course you'll be fine—because you'll have our help. There should be a few more men coming this afternoon. Ashley Walker, Cynthia Pikes and Erika Pikes should be waiting near the house. We all brought food, of course. Lena and John Talbot said they would come tomorrow since Mr. Stolvins is harvesting their fields today. This will be so much fun, Kate!"

"But I can't just accept your work for free," Kate protested.

"Naturally not," Rachel agreed. "There are two things we want as payment. First, you all have to come to the Harvest Dance. It's been two years since we've had O'Briens there, and we miss you." Rachel grinned. "It's just not the same without Ellie's antics."

"And second?" Kate pressed.

Her friend smirked. "One punch to Andrew Stolvins. That was paid in advance."

Kate couldn't help but smile at the recollection as the men approached. Jeffery Peters slapped Nathan on the back. "Sure wish I could have seen it."

Deputy Stone laughed. "Sure wish I could have done it."

"I've been aching to for years," said old Mr. Murphy. The kind eyes that always seemed to twinkle landed on her. "Miss Kate, we come offering our services. Do you accept?"

Her pride urged her to say no, but for once, she pushed it back. These were her friends and neighbors, come to help out of the kindness of their hearts. Just this once, she was going to let them. "How could I not? Thank you all for coming."

Her gratitude was waved off. Billy Joe said, "I don't see how we'll do you much good standing around here talking."

"Truer words were never spoken," Mr. Ives agreed.

As the group of men moved toward the field, she walked arm in arm with Rachel as they made the short trip to the house. Giving her friend a sly look, Kate said, "So tell me how things fare with the deputy."

Rachel laughed. "Only if you tell me how things fare with Nathan."

Kate rolled her eyes. "The two are hardly comparable."

"You're right. The absolute nothing happening between Deputy Stone and I hardly compares to what's happening with you and Nathan." She sent Kate an expectant look. "What *is* happening between you two, anyway?"

"What makes you think something has happened?"

Rachel shrugged. "He's been here for a while now. Your feelings have had time to change. Have they?"

"I don't think so," she said quietly as her gaze trailed back to the field.

"That isn't a firm no, so maybe there is hope after all."

"There's more hope for you than there is for me." Kate smiled teasingly. "Perhaps I'll be attending another wedding soon."

"Perhaps you will," Rachel agreed. "It may not be mine, but perhaps you will."

Nathan crept silently through the early morning darkness. He'd hoped the full day of harvesting would be enough to ensure a good night's sleep. Unfortunately, memories of Eli had been stirred up by the postmaster's mention of Jeremiah and kept rest at bay. He hoped a hard ride might do the trick. An owl hooted over his head, rivaling the low creaking of the barn door as it opened and closed. He made a note to himself that it was time to oil the hinges. The sound was loud enough to wake the dead. Walking toward Delilah's stall, his hand trailed to the reassuring weight of the holster belted low on his hips.

Delilah welcomed him with a soft neigh as he neared her. Nathan smiled. "That's right, girl. We're going for a ride before we both get stir crazy. It will be just the two of us like old times."

He opened the stall then moved to get the bridle. Draping it across his neck, he placed the saddle blanket on the saddle in order to carry them both. At the plodding sound of horse's hooves he spun just in time to see Delilah heading for the barn door.

"Delilah," he scolded but the sound of his voice sent the horse bolting through the door by widening the crack he'd unknowingly left there. He rolled his eyes. Maybe he'd made a mistake naming the horse. She should have been named something like "Sugar." Then maybe she'd act that way. Nathan snorted, knowing he would never allow a horse the disgrace of being named something like that.

He walked through the door, lugging the saddle with him. He was all prepared to whistle to Delilah, a sound she instinctively came to, when his gaze landed on a dark figure walking across the barnyard. He froze as apprehension shot through him.

His gaze flew to the dark house where Kate, Ellie and Sean lay sleeping. He had to protect them. Yet, as he watched, it became apparent that the figure seemed more interested in Delilah than anything else. *Yes, that's right, take the fool horse,* he thought, then immediately felt guilty.

A voice reached his ears, sounding clearly in the early morning stillness. "How did you get out here?"

He relaxed. *It's Kate. What is she doing out here alone at night?* he wondered.

Delilah moved toward Kate, blocking her from his view. He almost called out to her but before he could she said, "Well, no need to pretend. I don't like you, either."

Nathan smiled.

"Why don't you like me? Is it because of Nathan?"

Surely he had nothing to do with this.

"I understand that you might feel angry since you were taken from your life as a cowpony to get stuck on this farm. Technically, it was Nathan who made the decision so you and I were just innocent bystanders."

I wonder if Delilah really doesn't like Kate. She does seem a mite edgy the way her hooves are dancing around like that. Nathan swallowed a laugh knowing he should make his presence known but things were just getting interesting.

"Unless, of course, you're only jealous," Kate continued. "It's hardly my fault that he likes me better than you though I can see why. I am a sight prettier since my nose isn't half as big as yours. But then, you can run much faster than me, so I suppose we both have our good points. Perhaps you would temporarily agree to share him with me until the judge comes back."

He decided it was time to stop Kate before she said anything else she might not want him to hear. He heard Delilah snort loudly which probably covered the sound of his approach.

"What am I talking about?"

This time he answered. "I haven't the slightest idea."

There silence was penetrated only by the sound of his footsteps and Delilah's soft breathing.

"Nathan, is that you?" Kate asked. He walked around the horse and came face-to-face with Kate. Instead of trying to discern her expression, he shifted the saddle so that he could place the blanket on Delilah. He smoothed it down then placed the saddle over it. That bulky hindrance removed, he turned to Kate.

She stepped closer. "What are you doing out here?"

"I'm going for a ride." He tilted his Stetson up for a better view of her.

"In the middle of the night?"

"It's nearly morning now. The sun will be rising in a little less than an hour." He shrugged his broad shoulders. "I couldn't sleep, anyway."

"Why not?"

"Bad dreams," he admitted.

"Bad dreams about Eli?" she asked hesitantly.

He caught her arms. "How do you know that name?"

"You mentioned him when you were sick." She placed a hand over his. "I guess he's the business partner you said died. If you ever want to talk about it…"

He shook his head. "It only makes the dreams worse not better."

Besides, he'd been forced to tell his story so many times he'd resolved to never tell it again. He suddenly became aware of the cold metal touching his arm. He glanced down then lifted her hand in his. "Were you coming to do me in?"

She seemed flustered as she tugged her hand from his grasp and slipped the gun into her pocket. "No."

"Delilah, then?"

"Of course not."

"That's good," he said before turning to tighten the saddle's cinches and slip on the bit and halter. "It's hard to find a good cowpony."

She stiffened beside him.

Placing his hat on the saddle horn, he stepped closer. "Though I must admit your nose is twice as pretty as hers."

Chapter Twelve

Kate turned away from him to face the house. He'd heard every word she'd said. She was sure of it. Oh, what had made her go spouting off to a horse? Better yet, why had she deemed it necessary to get out of her safe bed to investigate the opening and closing groans of the barn door? Who would have guessed she would find Delilah standing in the middle of the barnyard unsaddled, unbridled and looking downright ornery?

She was pulled from her thoughts when Nathan's rich low voice reached her ear and skittered down her backbone. "I do like you better than Delilah."

She turned to face him. "You could have told me you were there."

"Well, I didn't know it was you at first."

She narrowed her eyes and took a step closer to challenge him. "Didn't you?"

"No, I didn't," he said with what sounded like a smile. "Besides, I'm glad I overheard you. How else would I know I was being shared?"

"Maybe I should let her have you."

"Maybe I don't want to be had."

"Good. Maybe she doesn't want you."

Nathan's eyes narrowed as he stepped so close she had to look up to meet his gaze. "Maybe she does and she won't admit it."

She scowled. "Maybe she doesn't and freely admits it."

His gaze trailed over her features in such a searching way she wanted to turn her face away. She didn't. She had nothing to hide, nothing at all.

"It could be," he said and she felt his warm fingers on her waist just inches above where her own were perched on her hips. "Or it could be she's too afraid to look past her pretty little nose to see what's right in front of her."

"What is in front of her?" she asked slowly.

"She has to find out for herself."

"How?" The question was out before she could stop it. "How does she find out?"

He reached down, cradled her cheek. His thumb brushed lightly across her cheekbone. He lowered his head to say lowly, "I reckon that would be up to her."

Kate searched his dark brown gaze. It seemed to hint at feelings mysterious to her yet amazingly familiar. A strange ache filled her heart, moving throughout her chest. Something inside her begged for the freedom to dare to throw caution to the wind and...do what? Trust that she was right this time? That Nathan was someone she could or perhaps even should love?

The thought startled her so much that she caught her breath. "I think I should go inside."

He gave a slow nod then released her just as slowly. She didn't move. She just watched him for a moment intrigued by the emotions that played across his features in the nearly nonexistent light. Finally, she took a step backward then turned to walk into the house.

Once inside, she closed the door behind her, leaned

against it and closed her eyes. Was she right this time? Was God leading her down this path? More importantly, could she trust Him enough to believe it would end well?

She slowly shook her head. "I don't think I can, Lord. I'm sorry."

She pushed away from the door then locked it behind her before carefully making her way back to bed.

Nathan watched her until she closed the door to the house. He stepped into the saddle and immediately pulled his Stetson over his eyes as though he needed to block out the moonlight. With a soft nudge to Delilah's sides, he set off at a moderate pace to allow her muscles to warm up. Once they moved past the field, he let her run like she begged to. He needed the speed, too—needed to feel like he could outrun his problems and his doubts. If only it was that easy.

They raced across the open meadow before turning toward the woods. He reined her in as they entered the forest then allowed her to pick her way through the trees. When he could no longer bear the load on his shoulders, he dismounted and led the horse to ease her heaving sides. Eventually he released the reins and continued walking forward allowing Delilah to follow if she wished. He stopped to stare up at the sky as the stars did what little they could to fight the darkness.

He was in love with Kate. The knowledge came with enough power to pull the wind from his body, leaving him to take in a sharp breath.

He'd done his best to keep this from happening but it had been a lost cause from the start. He was in love with his wife, God help him, and there was nothing he could do to change that. He might as well stop trying. Nathan stilled. *Stop trying.*

None of this made sense. He'd been so sure God had given him this dream. He'd been equally sure God was taking it away. What if He wasn't?

Nathan had given up at the first sign of trouble. Yet it did not matter how many times he tried to do as Kate had asked and walk away, circumstances outside of his control always brought him back. It couldn't all be a coincidence. Perhaps God still had a plan in all of this. Perhaps this had been His plan all along.

"God, I don't want to do anything outside Your will so if I try, please warn me." He swallowed. "If, however, You have me here for a reason beyond what I have allowed myself to imagine…if You have me here for Kate and her family, then I'd like to follow You in that."

He shook his head then smiled wryly. "Since her father is no longer here, I guess what I'm really asking is for permission to court your daughter, Kate, my almost-wife."

He waited in the stillness of the morning just before dawn as the rest of nature seemed to hold its breath in wait of answer. He heard no audible voice, not even a small internal one. All he felt was a sudden and acute blossoming of hope in his chest.

Hope. It was something he'd been missing of late but it settled within his chest with nearly tangible warmth. It called him to believe and even to love. He put his hand over his chest then pulled in a long breath.

It wouldn't be easy, he realized. Achieving a dream never was. He knew, because he'd tried before and failed. But this time things were different. This time hoping was worth the risk of disappointment and refusing to hope was not an option. He gave a short nod of appreciation toward the Heavens. "Thank You."

Kate took in a shallow breath since it was all that the formfitting bodice allowed. "It's a beautiful dress, Ms. Lettie, but are you sure it isn't too small?"

The bride eyed her laughingly. "No, Kate. It looks perfect. You look perfect. Stop worrying!"

Kate shook her head incredulously. "I hardly think this is worrying."

"Then what do you call it?"

"Fretting."

Ms. Lettie laughed.

"Oh, that's fine." Kate lifted her chin playfully. "Laugh at my expense. I don't mind. Just make sure someone is behind me should I faint dead away."

"Women have gotten by without breathing for centuries."

"That doesn't encourage me."

Ms. Lettie smiled mischievously as she handed Kate a bouquet. "Then be encouraged that if I even see you so much as sway I will alert Nathan in plenty of time for him to catch you in his arms."

Kate lifted her gaze from the flowers suspiciously. "How convenient."

Ms. Lettie's picked up her own bouquet of flowers, then glanced at Kate with dancing brown eyes. "Yes, it seems we've stumbled upon the reason women have gone without breathing for centuries."

Kate laughed as they moved to wait outside the double doors of the small chapel's inner sanctuary. She could hear the piano warming up as she took her place in front of Ms. Lettie. She glanced down at the bouquet in her hand as she tried to concentrate on pulling in short, frequent breaths and willing away the light-headedness she felt.

Suddenly she was aware of being watched. She looked up to see pews full of people all staring at her expectantly. Quickly turning her grimace into a smile she hoped would take the focus from her burning cheeks, she took her first step down the aisle. The second was easier than the first. By the third she managed to look at something besides the plank floor. On the fourth her gaze lingered on Doc who looked very distinguished. The fifth step she looked behind him to Nathan.

She lost count. Her breath caught in her throat but didn't go very far into her lungs for lack of space. She managed to avoid his gaze as she continued down the aisle. Once she reached the spot where she'd been told to stand, she turned toward the entrance to watch Ms. Lettie walk down the aisle.

A moment later the couple held hands before the preacher and everyone waited while the two exchanged vows. Doc's voice sounded strong and clear and she found herself wondering what it must be like to have the man you loved pledging those words to you. She found herself watching Nathan as he pulled out the rings.

Their eyes met and he gave her a grin. Kate was suddenly reminded that Nathan had taken these very same vows toward her with every intention of keeping them. Of course he hadn't known her then—except for what the letters had told him—and certainly hadn't loved her. No. The words couldn't have been spoken with the same tenderness that Doc said them.

Kate pulled her attention back to the woman who spoke softly but firmly. "With this ring, I thee wed."

"Then by the power vested in me through God and this church, I now pronounce you husband and wife." The preacher nodded. "You may kiss your bride."

Nathan watched Kate as she laughed at something Ms. Lettie said, then forced himself to stop staring at the woman.

Hearing Doc's voice speak his vows had reminded him of when he'd said his own. He'd had no idea what he was getting into with that proxy wedding. If he had known, would he have gone through with it? He gave a short nod. Without a doubt.

Even if he never changed Kate's mind, at least he'd met her, Sean, Ellie and Lawson. At least he'd been able to help them. At least being a part of their family for a short time had inspired him to reach out to his own. But he wanted more. He wanted so much more.

He turned to search for the children. He'd only gone a step toward the door of the chapel when a man paused in front of him to buckle his shoe. Stopping short, Nathan glanced down. The man was wearing cowboy boots. His gut clenched in wary surprise as the man straightened. Hate-filled eyes met his and instead of saying "excuse me" the man muttered one word, "Graveyard."

Nathan gave a nod and kept moving in his original direction but he couldn't help glancing back to make sure what he'd just seen was real. Yes, the man was still there and he was also looking back, but not at Nathan. The man had his eye so locked on Kate that he nearly ran into the person in front of him. In a move similar to what had just happened, the man muttered something then moved around the person.

Nathan detoured to exit out the back of the church.

When he stepped outside he found the man waiting for him.

"Good to see you again, Jeremiah." Nathan extended his hand in a gesture of hopeful reconciliation. The man eyed his extended hand with something so akin to contempt that it made Nathan's skin crawl. Even so, he managed to retain a polite air. "It's been quite a while since we've seen each other, hasn't it? How have you been?"

"This isn't a social call, Rutledge," the man warned tersely. Nathan was saddened at the change in his friend. A man who had once lived with enthusiasm, ever ready for a joke, now stared back with cold blue eyes.

"Well, then," Nathan drawled. "What brings you to this part of Texas?"

"I want justice for what you did to my brother." Jeremiah stepped closer. "You and I both know what happened in that barn and I don't care what any two-bit jury has to say about it."

Nathan gave a weary sigh. So much for his hopes that the passage of time would help Jeremiah see things more clearly. "Jeremiah, why do you still believe I'm guilty after the jury found me innocent?"

"You'll always be guilty in my book. I can't get back my brother but I aim to take back the money you stole from us."

"I can't give you what I don't have."

"You're lying," Fulton growled. "You think you have a great setup here, don't you? The people in this town don't even know who you are. Does your wife know you're living a lie?"

Nathan felt the blood drain from his face. "My wife?"

He smiled coldly. "Yes, I know all about her. The

record of your marriage is what finally helped me track you down."

Anger rose in Nathan's gut causing him to step forward and grip the man's collar. "You listen to me and you listen good. If I even see you so much as look in her direction, I'll bring the law down on you quicker than you can blink."

The man tried to pull away. "I'm not afraid of the law."

"Then you'd better fear me on this one thing, Fulton." Nathan released him with a jerk. "I'll say it only once more. I don't have the money you're looking for. I never did. The sooner you realize that, the sooner you can get on with your life. I have nothing more to say to you." As he walked away, Nathan hoped that would be the last of it. Jeremiah was angry, but surely no amount of anger could turn his one-time friend into a violent man. Yet he couldn't shake the creeping sense of dread that told him his troubles were just beginning.

In seconds flat, Nathan pulled, cocked and shot the gun at one of the metal cans nailed loosely to the corral fence. Metal punctured metal with a satisfying bang. He was slow on the draw, slower than he'd been for a while. He couldn't allow himself to be lazy anymore. He hadn't seen nor heard from Jeremiah Fulton since the wedding nearly a week ago and he hoped more than anything that the man had moved on for good. But if Nathan was going to try to stay and become a permanent part of this family, he had to be sure he could protect it.

He frowned as he slipped the gun back into his holster, then tried again. The shot came off much quicker that time. *Better,* he acknowledged to himself, then continued shooting at the cans one after the other in a familiar rhythm until he ran out of bullets. He lowered the gun.

They'd finished with the harvest yesterday. Today he'd taken the children to school early to talk to the teacher about Lawson. As far as he could tell, the boy was seriously behind on his schooling. The teacher had promised to do his best to help him catch up. Once Nathan had returned to the farm, he'd decided to carve out a few minutes of target practice.

"Very impressive," Kate's voice lilted.

"Thanks." He turned to offer her a distracted grin as he reloaded the gun.

"Where did you learn to shoot like that?"

"I picked it up here and there," he said, slipping his Colt in the holster and walking toward her. Adjusting his Stetson, he propped his leg on the fence between them. He figured this was just as good at time as any to continue the courting he'd begun over the last few days. "How about I give you a shooting lesson?"

"I don't need a shooting lesson."

"You've already learned?"

"No," she said slowly.

"Don't tell me you're afraid of this little thing." Nathan pulled the gun from its holster and watched her blue eyes drift over it.

She lifted her chin. "I'm not."

"Prove it."

She bit her lip then met his challenging gaze with one of her own. "Fine. I will."

He waited while she slipped through the fence. Then reaching up, she knocked the Stetson from his head only to catch it and place it on her own. She paused to tug the gun from his hand and moved to where he'd been standing earlier.

She glanced over her shoulder impatiently. "Are you going to tell me how to do this or what?"

"No need to get testy." He took the gun from her and dropped it in his holster. "We're going through it without the gun. First, you have to find your stance." She was soon standing in the correct position. "Now, keep your wrist strong so the barrel stays level."

"What barrel?"

"Not the one that points at my feet. Focus up." He stepped in front of her, guiding her chin upward. Suddenly her liquid blue eyes focused on him and he knew he'd made a mistake. She stilled. His gaze trailed down to her lips.

"Pow." Kate jerked as if she'd shot something and Nathan realized that something was him.

He stared at her. "Of all the nerve—"

Kate's blue eyes filled with the laughter she barely kept from showing on her lips.

He chuckled then pushed her arms to the side and away from his chest. He kept a hand on her arm then slipped behind her. She froze. "What are you doing?"

"I'm teaching you to shoot," he said as he pulled the gun from his holster. He cocked the gun then showed her how to hold it. "Remember to keep your arms taut but not perfectly straight. Your wrists need to stay strong. Keep that right foot slightly back."

"Nathan, I can't remember all of this."

"Sure you can. Keep your finger off the trigger but go ahead and aim." He watched her adjust the gun while she gazed intently at the can. "You want the piece on the end to line up with your target. I'm going to stay where I am and all I want you to do is pull the trigger."

A bang followed as she fired. Unfortunately, a second tinnier sound did not. She stumbled back. He was there to steady her. She glanced up from under his Stetson and he smiled. "That was good. Try it a few more times."

Each time he had to remind her less about her form and keeping the target in her sights. "Try it by yourself. Mind the kickback."

Nathan crossed his arms as she shuffled back into place, aimed and fired. Nothing happened. He paused then said, "You didn't cock it."

A click announced the cock. Another bang sounded and the kickback caused them both to fall backward, which unfortunately for Nathan meant being sandwiched between the dusty corral and Kate. Somehow he managed to rise up on his elbows then brace himself with his hands. He took in a Kate-scented breath which surprisingly was like a mixture of cinnamon and gunpowder. "Kate, are you all right?"

She turned her face to the side giving him a very close-up look at her profile. "Yes. Are you?"

"Yes, I suppose that means we should get up."

"Right." She quickly leveraged herself to sit beside him, then scrambled to her feet. He slowly followed suit. Kate's pretty mouth grimaced. "I'm sorry."

"That's quite all right. I shouldn't have assumed I would be safe that close to you," he said, wondering if she would realize how true those words were.

If she did she didn't acknowledge it because, though she huffed, she glanced at him with concern. "I didn't hurt you, did I?"

"Not too much." He picked his hat off the ground and shook his head to clear it. "Maybe we should stop for today."

She rubbed her elbow with her free hand. "I didn't hit the can."

He extended his hand for his gun. "You don't need to hit the can. I doubt you'd ever shoot at anything that small. Besides, you didn't even want to come anywhere near the gun when I first asked."

"You convinced me and now I want to hit the can."

Nathan shrugged. "Then hit the can for all I care."

Her blue eyes narrowed. "You needn't be rude."

"Who was being rude?"

"You were getting close."

He looked down at the Stetson in his hands. "I was about as close to being rude as you were to hitting that can."

They eyed each other. Challenges were issued and accepted. His arm gave a sweeping motion toward the target as he stepped back. Kate turned. She aimed then shot dead through the middle of the can. It actually came off the nail and tumbled from the fence to land in the dirt.

Kate smiled and turned to him triumphantly. "Well?"

He tilted his head. "Well, what?"

"I hit it, didn't I?" She narrowed her eyes at him. "Don't you have anything to say about that?"

He shrugged. "Congratulations?"

She pointed the gun at him. Nathan's fingers twitched near his gun belt before he stilled them and stepped out of the way. He stared at the gun until she presented him with the handle and not the smoking barrel. He reached for the gun but Kate didn't release it. He looked up questioningly.

"Thanks for the lesson, Nathan." A smile danced across her lips before she continued, "It was fun."

"Whoa. Let's not get carried away." He grinned

slowly. "I'm just glad shooting me gave you so much pleasure."

"Oh, it did." Her eyes sparkled as she pressed the gun into his hand, forcing him to take it as she stepped past him. She suddenly spun toward him. "I almost forgot why I was looking for you in the first place. Since Andrew Stolvins didn't harvest our wheat, we'll have to take it to market ourselves. I need you to bring it to Colston. There are two mills close to the town."

He thought of his lingering concerns about Jeremiah and frowned. "Kate, now might not be the best time. I'm not entirely comfortable leaving you and the children here alone. You see—"

Kate narrowed her eyes at him. "Don't be silly. I ran this farm just fine on my own for two years. I think I know how to take care of myself and my siblings. Lawson will help out while you're gone."

He placed the gun in his holster. "Kate, really—"

"We have no choice, Nathan. We have to sell the wheat. Without selling, I won't be able to pay the mortgage and the farm will not survive." She blew out a heavy breath and glanced at the sky. "Nathan, I need you to go."

"To Colston, right? I actually have a friend who lives there. Mr. Reynolds may help us out." He slowly nodded. "I'll go, but I'll ask Deputy Stone to keep his eye on the place."

"That is hardly necessary, but thank you," she said. "You can leave right after the Harvest Dance. That should leave you plenty of time to prepare."

He tipped his hat up as he watched her begin to walk away. He hesitated for half a second before he called after her. "Kate, wait! When we were in town for the wedding, I saw a man who…" Nathan didn't know what to say.

"Who what?" Kate asked.

He shook his head. There was no way to warn her without explaining the whole situation, and that dark part of his life wasn't exactly something he wanted to show to the woman he was trying to impress. Besides, he still couldn't bring himself to believe that Jeremiah was serious in his threats. "You'll be careful while I'm gone, won't you?"

She promised she would, and Nathan prayed that that would be enough.

Chapter Thirteen

Kate sat reading the large family Bible in the living room as she and her siblings waited for their parents to come home. It had been raining since early that afternoon but the strength of the early winter storm had only increased since nightfall. It raged outside, spewing sleet and sometimes even hail. The thunder bellowed like a madman and sent tremors through her little sister's body while putting a grimace on her little brother's face.

She placed the Bible in her lap and closed the covers. Obviously her attempts to cover the storm's ferocity had failed. Instead, silence filled the small room as they each sat lost in their own thoughts. Kate tried to speak over the storm. "I think we should go to bed."

Sean frowned. "But Ma and Pa aren't home yet."

"They probably decided to stay in town once they saw how bad the storm was getting," Kate reasoned. "I'm sure they'll leave first thing in the morning."

Quiet descended once more as they all sat still waiting for their parents to return. Finally, Kate stood and ushered everyone to bed. The dark loft she shared with Ellie flashed bright in cadence with the storm. A small hand searched for hers on top of the covers. Suddenly she awakened to the sound of someone banging on the front door. She grabbed her housecoat and hurried down the stairs in time to see Sean stumble from his room. She opened the door, only to stare blankly at the man before her.

"Sheriff Hawkins," she said in surprise. "Is something wrong?"

The man glanced over her shoulder then stepped backward. "Perhaps it'd be better if we spoke outside, Ms. O'Brien."

She glanced behind her at Ellie and Sean then stepped out the door. The sheriff opened his mouth to speak but his lips moved silently. She struggled to hear. Finally his words whispered past her ear in small phrases filled with words like accident, dead, joint buri-als.

She couldn't breathe. She couldn't move. Then his voice grew strident, demanding her attention. He was asking if she wanted help with the children. She said she didn't know. There had been no time to think. Her breath caught as she'd spun toward the door. What would she say? How would she tell them?

Suddenly there was nothing around her but that wooden door. She tried to back away from it but her hand was already on the knob, turning it. She would have to tell them. She would have to tell them just as the sheriff had told her, quietly and calmly but with a firmness that left no room for doubt.

She lifted her chin and stepped through the door, closing it firmly behind her. She avoided looking into the eyes of her brother and sister, knowing she would have to tell them the unthinkable. She swallowed, then lifted her eyes as courage won out...

Kate gasped and forced her eyes open as she sat up in bed. Dim morning light spilled from the windows and painted the room in soft purples and blues. Ellie's slow steady breathing countered her accelerated gasps. She pushed her loose hair away from her face and turned to sit on her side of the bed. She forced herself to pull in deep, even breaths. It had been nearly a year since she'd relived that moment in her sleep. Perhaps it was the end of the harvesting that brought it on. The wagon was loaded, and Nathan would leave for Colston the next morning, after the dance that night. It had been a good harvest, and Kate no longer worried about the mortgage. But the knowledge that she'd saved her parents' farm was cold comfort when she thought of how much she still missed having them in her life.

Why can't I relive the good moments we had together? Why must it always be that night? She longed for her father. At a time like this, he would have pulled her into his arms and told her not to be afraid. He would have reminded her, in his subtle Irish brogue, to trust in the Lord so He could direct her paths.

Had God been directing her parents' path the day of the wagon accident that took their lives? If so, why hadn't He directed them to wait out the storm in town? She buried her face in her hands as she whispered, "I do love You, God. You know I do. It's just so hard for me to trust."

Ellie shifted in the bed. Kate froze then slowly opened her eyes. The girl continued sleeping so Kate pulled in a deep breath, then continued with one last request. "Lord, help me. I don't know how You can or will but I need You to do something. Prove Yourself. Let me know You're real. Let me know You care about my future. Right now, it's just a little too hard to believe."

* * *

That evening Kate stared at herself in the reflection of the only looking glass they owned. Her hair was piled high on her head. A frown painted her face and it was caused by more than just the new freckles that had appeared on her nose from spending so much time in the sun. The first month of her marriage had been over for two weeks and the judge had not made his appearance. She had given up all hope that he would return soon. It looked like she would be stuck with Nathan Rutledge for the long haul. She was frowning because right now that didn't seem like such a horrible thing.

Ellie peered over Kate's shoulder into the looking glass. "Your hair is a mess."

"I know." Kate released her hair from the fancy hairstyle she'd attempted. She met Ellie's gaze in the mirror as she fished the hairpins out of her curls. "Why aren't you dressed?"

"I can't reach the buttons."

"Turn around then." Kate turned from her task to help her sister.

"I don't understand why the buttons are in the back."

"I sew them that way to make things difficult. Didn't you know?" she asked.

"I would be perfectly happy wearing my day dress rather than this scratchy old thing."

Kate buttoned the last hole then turned around to survey her sister. "You look lovely."

Ellie couldn't seem to figure out whether to take that as a compliment or an insult. The girl smiled mischievously. "No one there will care a fig about what I wear except Mrs. Greene, but everyone will be watching you and you haven't done a thing to get ready."

"Yes, I have."

Ellie sent her a disbelieving look and plopped on the bed with her skirt inching up past her knees. She frowned and managed to pull her skirt down to the proper length.

Kate lifted her chin. "I'm nearly ready."

"You plan to go with your hair undone and your petticoats showing in the back?"

She glanced behind her and sure enough Ellie was right. "No."

"Then I suggest you hurry up."

Kate looked at her sister sitting so properly on the bed strewn with clothes. Before her eyes her ten-year-old sister was ever so slowly shedding her tomboyish ways and turning into a young lady. She still preferred her old bloomers to her new skirts but there was a beginning to be a perceivable softening to her sister's demeanor. Kate decided Ellie would turn into a proper young lady yet. She sensed it would probably happen gradually over time. She wouldn't rush the girl but vowed to enjoy the process.

Ellie frowned. "What?"

"Nothing," Kate responded with a smile. "Fix my dress back there, will you?"

Downstairs, Nathan leaned back onto the wall near the front door as he waited with two very impatient gentlemen.

"Aren't they ready yet?" Sean asked from his seat near the fireplace.

Nathan glanced toward the stairs and shook his head. "I don't think so."

Lawson frowned. "What takes them so long anyway?"

He shrugged. "They have more to put on, I suppose."

"What do you mean?" Sean asked.

Nathan glanced toward the two boys with the answer on his lips, then paused to take in their freshly scrubbed faces and pressed shirts. He shook his head. "Never mind."

Lawson shifted on the settee. "At this rate, the dance will be over before we get there."

"I don't think they'll let that happen." Nathan laughed. "Besides, if I know anything about women it's that the longer they take the more it's worth the wait."

Sean looked at him. "What is that suppose to—"

Lawson's low whistle cut him off.

Nathan followed Lawson's gaze then straightened from the wall. Kate moved toward the bottom of the stairs and paused to say something to Ellie as she pulled on her gloves. She looked so beautiful in her pale green dress with its rounded neckline and fitted waist.

Kate turned to find them all watching and met their stares with a curious look. "Shall we go?"

"Yes, please," Sean moaned and walked out the door.

Lawson turned to follow Sean but paused to hold the door open for Kate, then glanced back at Nathan with a laughing gaze. The boy's smirk plainly said, *you are in so much trouble.*

Ignoring him, Nathan caught the door to allow Lawson to precede him. Ellie hung back to frown at her shoes. Seeing the problem, Nathan knelt down to fix the button on her shoe. He paused to look up at her. Tapping her nose gently, he grinned. "You look very pretty, Ellie."

She looked at him seriously for a moment before chancing a small smile. "It's not too fussy, is it?"

He shook his head. "Not at all."

"Good."

He stood and waited for her to exit the house before closing the door firmly behind them.

Kate pulled her skirts toward her as she slipped through the doorway of the crowded hallway leading to the hotel's small ballroom. Glancing to the right, her gaze faltered as it landed on Nathan. Ever since that night with Delilah he seemed to be behaving differently toward her.

He'd always been kind in the past but lately there seemed to be a bit more motivating his actions. She would catch it every now and then in the tone of his voice or the way he looked at her. Something seemed to have subtly shifted in their relationship and she wasn't entirely sure what to do about it. She had decided the safest thing was to avoid him whenever possible.

Their eyes held for a moment longer as she stepped past him. Moving away, her lashes drifted down and up, then biting her lip she glanced back in time to see Nathan shake hands with the sheriff. He met her gaze again and he pushed from the wall. Her eyes widened and she stepped into the main room that was crowded with dancers. She moved toward the punch bowl then felt Nathan's hand on her back. Steeling herself against his warm gaze, she turned to face him with a smile.

"Are you enjoying yourself?" he asked.

"Yes, thank you. Actually, I was looking for Rachel. Have you seen her?"

He turned to scan the room. She reached for a cup of punch and took a cooling drink as he faced her. "She's dancing with Deputy Stone."

She nodded and took another sip.

"Would you like to dance?"

"What?" she asked, using the excuse of the noise of the hoots and hollers coming from the dance floor to stall for time to think. Dancing with Nathan would be a very foolish thing to do. It would, however, be rude not to dance with him at least once, she reasoned.

Nathan leaned closer to say, "Would you like to dance?"

"Well," she began, then set her cup back on the table. "Yes, I would. Thank you."

He guided her through the crowded room to the dance floor. She felt as though everyone was watching to determine the familiarity of their relationship. She allowed him to take her hand. She placed her other hand lightly on his shoulder, then followed him as he led her into a fast waltz. She glanced up to find him frowning. "Relax."

"I am relaxed," she said, though she knew she was lying through her teeth. Rather than focus on her partner, she allowed her mind to wander. Although the waltz was still considered a controversial dance in other towns, Peppin had accepted it long ago. Town protocol demanded that the dance was never done slow enough for a person to do much more than move his or her feet, thereby avoiding any complications.

She grimaced as she stepped on Nathan's toe. When she glanced up apologetically his smile was so painfully polite that Kate vowed to redeem herself. She forced herself to relax and allowed Nathan to lead her carefully across the floor but a moment later the song came to an end. He stepped toward the punch bowl but she stayed where she was. "Let's dance another set."

The music began again. This time it was a quick two-step and she missed the first step. She tilted her head up to frown at him. "I do know how to dance, I promise."

He grinned. "Prove it."

She allowed herself a smile and placed her hand in his once more. This time they moved easily into the dance. Kate pushed all the doubts from her mind and allowed herself to truly relax in his arms. He led her through the steps simply and naturally obviously feeling at home on the dance floor. The longer they danced the easier it was to move in sync with each other. When she could no longer contain her curiosity she asked, "Where did you learn to dance like this?"

He laughed. "I have three sisters. Who do you think they practiced with?"

She would have responded but the music stopped for a split-second then began at a faster pace. They were caught off guard for an instant but quickly caught up. Suddenly Nathan angled his steps, causing her to step sharply to the left then right. Kate's eyes flew to his as she smiled in delight. He grinned then slowly turned her under his arm while they two-stepped. Once she faced him again she didn't falter but instead moved right back into the dance.

"Do you believe me now?" she asked with a triumphant smile.

"Maybe." He smiled and her heart skipped a beat. Wait, no. The music skipped a beat then continued even faster. This time they were ready for it and easily moved into the faster step. She twirled under his arm without missing a step. The music picked up its pace again.

Her eyes widened as she glanced over her shoulder at the ragtag group of musicians. She barely had time to place her feet before it was time to pick them up. She heard someone let out a whoop and looked over to find the deputy grinning ear to ear as he and Rachel danced. Kate's laughter blended with Nathan's low chuckle. Finally, the music made by a lone fiddle, harmonica, banjo, washboard and other makeshift instruments swirled to a halt.

"Enough?" Nathan asked.

She looked at him innocently. "Why? Are you tired?"

He began to speak but the caller's words sounded over his. "Fellers, grab your gals. It's time for the 'Courting Game.'"

Chapter Fourteen

Nathan looked at the man in surprise then transferred his gaze to Kate. "The 'Courting Game'?"

"Oh, that." She waved her hand as if dismissing the game completely. "It's a square dance. We don't have to play." She was already moving off the floor.

Nathan frowned. "Wait—"

He was cut off when the caller said, "Kate O'Brien, where are you going?"

Nathan's gaze flew to Kate, who was waving the man off.

"You send that young man up here so I can talk to him."

Her eyes widened and flew to his. Nathan made no attempt to hide his amusement as he shrugged. He walked over to the man who said, "Now, you just position yourself across from that gal and I'll make sure one of you gets a hat, you hear?"

"Yes, sir," Nathan said then did exactly that. Kate looked at him from across the circle and shook her head. He ignored that, hoping she wouldn't leave the two circles of dancers that were being formed with the men on the outside and the women on the inside.

They were suppose to thread through each other, he was told. Between the hats and the name the 'Courting Game,' Nathan was sure mischief was afoot. To clench it, the caller said, "Now in years past the parson demanded that the kiss be given on the cheek…"

Kiss? Nathan glanced across the circle at Kate who pointed to herself then away from the circle. He shook his head and pointed to the ground motioning that she should stay. However, the action was poorly timed for it was done just as the caller robustly exclaimed, "But he ain't here tonight!"

Kate frowned at him then turned to talk to the brunette beside her. He watched suspiciously as the lady responded to Kate then glanced around the circle to look at him. The woman laughed and whispered something to Kate. As the two giggled, the caller continued, "Seein' as we got ourselves a room full of gentlemen, I think tonight we'll allow the ladies their preference."

There was much laughter around the circle and not all of it came from the men. Nathan caught Kate's gaze. She gave him a satisfied smile. One of the men near Nathan called, "Start the music, already!"

The caller grinned and gave a nod to the rusty band of musicians who managed a pretty good semblance of "Turkey in the Straw." Nathan soon caught on, extending a hand to one woman. Passing her, he took the hand of the next lady. He knew from glancing across his shoulder that Kate stayed opposite him as the distance between them diminished.

The music stopped and so did the dancers. Everyone searched for the bearer of the hats and Nathan saw a man a few spaces in front of him collect a kiss on the cheek. The caller told everyone to pass the hats back three people. He wasn't surprised when a hat tied with a green handkerchief landed in his hands. He glanced at Kate, but she was looking at the hat that landed one person ahead of her.

The music started again and many women eyed the hat whether he extended that hand to them or not. He could no longer look across and see Kate. Then suddenly the music stopped and Kate was nowhere to be seen.

Kate laughingly watched as Nathan smiled wryly at Mrs. Redding. With infinite care to propriety, he leaned forward and placed a smacking kiss on the woman's cheek before glancing around in search of an irate husband. The music started up again and Nathan threaded through the line once more.

As he passed by she lifted her cup of punch in a silent salute and grinned at the feigned reproachful look he sent her. Draining the rest of her punch, she turned to look for Ms. Lettie but suddenly stopped short. "Mrs. Greene."

The woman glared at her, obviously annoyed about something.

Kate searched for any sign of Ellie but found her innocently talking to a few girls her age. "Is something wrong?"

"I should say so. Why, the way you're throwing yourself at that man is disgraceful. It's all over town."

"Ah, yes. The rumor industriously circulated by Andrew Stolvins," Kate acknowledged. "I wasn't under the impression that you frequented the Red Canteen, Mrs. Greene."

The woman bristled. "Sinful, that's what it is. All the while knowing the man is going to leave you. To think, I once imagined him suitable for my Emily!"

"Mrs. Greene—"

"Well, you've done your parents proud, haven't you? Your poor mother would roll over in her grave if she heard the words I did."

Kate lifted her chin. "My mother wasn't poor in any respect. She lived fully and completely with a compassion for others I doubt I'll see again on this earth. Unlike you, my mother would never have entertained malicious gossip much less spread it."

Silence stretched for a moment. Mrs. Greene seemed to tremble in silent anger. When she did speak it was in a very cool, almost icy tone. "Young lady, if I had any doubts about the truth of what I have heard about your reputation, they have just been destroyed. I have never met such a disrespectful young woman in all my life. Why, if I hadn't kept my mouth shut about this business in the first place—"

"You may say what you like but I'm long past the point of caring what you think about me, Mrs. Greene. Good evening," Kate said. Setting her cup down with a decisive thud, she turned and rushed quickly away.

Nathan looked past the colorful swirl of dancers in search of Kate and moved to where he'd last seen her at the punch bowl. He paused in his search when he nearly ran into Doc Williams.

"Nathan," Doc said reaching out a hand.

Nathan shook it firmly. "Hello, Doc. How's married life treating you?"

"Very well," he said, then grinned. "A better question is how's it treating you?"

Nathan smiled wryly. "It isn't."

"Kate is still adamant about you leaving then?"

"As near as I can tell."

"The children will be disappointed to see you go."

"Yes, so will I." Nathan's gaze tripped nonchalantly over the doctor's shoulder to survey the room.

Doc frowned. "What will happen to Lawson if you leave? Do you think Kate will take him in?"

"I'm not sure. When I spoke with the sheriff he said he was still looking for a home for the boy. I figured if he hasn't found one by the time I head out, I'll take him with me."

"I should think Lawson would be easy to place," Doc mused. "He's a good age to help around a farm."

Nathan glanced to the left and spotted Kate talking with Mrs. Greene. "Yes, but everyone knows he tried to steal from us and no one is willing to take the chance that he'll run off with their possessions."

"Even now that the boy has proven himself trustworthy?"

Nathan nodded. "The more I talk to him, the more I realize that he's really just a victim of poor circumstances. He's done the best that he can by himself. Unfortunately, that wasn't enough to keep his belly full. He resorted to stealing in order to survive."

"I'm sorry to hear that," Doc Williams said. "I'd like to see what he could make of himself given the right opportunity."

"Maybe you should give him a chance then," Nathan challenged.

"The thought has passed my mind." Doc Williams nodded thoughtfully. "I'll talk to Lettie about it. I won't keep you."

"Wonderful." Nathan grinned as he took the doctor's offered hand. "It's always a privilege, sir."

Doc moved away, giving Nathan a clear view of where Kate had been standing, only to find her missing. Frowning, he searched the crowd then glanced back at Mrs. Greene in time to see the woman glare at something to his left before she turned on her heel. Following a hunch, he glanced to his left then moved that direction.

Kate sat on the second step of the stairs spilling from the hotel's small yet well-constructed wooden porch onto the lawn of an overgrown garden. The winsome call of the fiddle carried through the air, melting into the sounds of cicadas and crickets calling to each other. A puddle of light slowly spilled from the doorway onto her dress, alerting her that she was not alone. She glanced behind her and smiled seeing it was Nathan. "You found me."

He left the door open behind him but stepped onto the porch. "You disappeared. I wanted to make sure you were all right."

"I'm fine." She paused then admitted, "I just had a horrible fight with Mrs. Greene."

"Who hasn't?"

She laughed. "You haven't. She wanted you to be her future son-in-law for a while."

"I assume I have since been disowned."

She gave an amused nod. "Quite viciously at that."

"Lucky me." He gestured toward the stairs and with her nod of approval he sat on the bottom step. He was quiet for a while before he asked, "What did you fight with Mrs. Greene about this time?"

She rolled her eyes. "My poor reputation. What else?"

He met her gaze sincerely. "I'm sorry, Kate."

"Don't be." She sat up proudly with a glimmer of

laughter in her eyes. "I think I did very well for myself. Her face nearly turned purple. Ellie would be proud."

He laughed just as the fiddle wound down, leaving near silence. They were quiet for a moment, each content in their own thoughts. He looked toward the door. "I should go back inside. We don't want to fuel more gossip."

He began to rise but she quickly caught his hand. "Stay."

He glanced at her in surprise.

"The gossip ignited without any fuel so it hardly matters now." She shrugged. "Besides, you left the door open."

His gaze trailed to where her hand rested upon his. He stilled. She followed his gaze and quickly released her grasp just as he turned his hand over to tighten his. She knew if she tugged her hand once more he would have to release it. He knew it, too. They both waited in the breadth of the moment for her to make her decision.

She bit her lip then slowly relaxed her hand in his hold. The music started again as if it had been waiting for that cue. Nathan sat facing her then gently intertwined his fingers with hers. "I've been waiting for a month and a half to hear that word. It sure sounds good."

Her breath stilled in her throat. "Nathan…"

His gaze was gentle, undemanding yet seeking. She didn't know how to respond. For the first time in a long time she wanted to believe that she had correctly discerned God's will and it was this. It was him. She wanted it to be him so badly.

What if it was? Slowly, trepidation rose in the pit of her stomach, then turned into pure fear. She turned away and tugged her hand from his grasp. He immediately leaned back. His hand lifted toward her cheek then dropped once, twice, back to his side. "Kate."

She turned toward him.

His eyes spoke to her gently. "It's all right."

Tears suddenly pooled in her eyes, blurring her vision. She turned to face the garden and placing her elbow on her knee she buried her face in her hands.

"I might think it's something I did, but it's more than that, isn't it?"

She nodded.

He moved to sit on the same step as her with his shoulder touching hers, but kept his hands clasped and propped on his knees. He didn't try to talk about it. He was just there, waiting if she needed his shoulder to cry on.

How could she possibly explain that she was crying because she thought God might actually want them to be together? He wouldn't understand. He would be happy but all she felt was fear of what that might mean to her heart and the plans she'd made for her future. She leaned against the stair railing so she could look at him. "Nathan, you said God led you here, didn't you?"

He looked perplexed at the sudden change of subject but nodded. "Yes."

"Do you still believe that, after everything that has happened and hasn't happened?"

He smiled. "Yes, I still believe that."

She shook her head in confusion. "But, why? I mean, aren't you the least bit angry that God allowed you to believe he was leading you in one direction when you ended up arriving somewhere else entirely? Doesn't it feel like..." She bit her lip, almost afraid to go on.

He straightened with new interest. "Like what?"

She swallowed then met his gaze more fully.

"Doesn't it feel like God lied? In Jeremiah, He says something about having thought of peace toward us and not evil. He says He wants us to have 'a future and a hope.' It doesn't seem like that's true. It seems like every time I let Him direct my path I just end up going through heartache. The same goes for my parents. They always prayed God would direct their paths but look what happened to them."

"You're right," he said quietly.

"I am?" she asked in surprise.

"God never promised that if we followed His will life would be easy or even make sense. He just promised that in the end it would all work together for our good. He promised that if we'd follow Him He'd take us to the best possible future, but He never said the journey would be easy. We're supposed to go through hardships knowing that we'll end up better for them in the end."

"You think I should stop focusing on the painful paths God has led me through and focus on where I'm going instead," she said thoughtfully. "What if I'm not sure that He's leading me to a good destination?"

"I guess that's where trust comes in. You have to trust that His word is true. You have to believe that despite how it seems now, He hasn't lied. At the very least, ask Him to prove His word is true."

She nodded thoughtfully.

"I think the same goes for love," he said quietly. "You have to be willing to trust the other person. You have to be willing to depend on them. You have to let yourself be weak enough to find strength in others."

Her gaze slowly lifted to his. "I'm not good at any of that."

"Maybe not yet, but I think you could be." His gaze seemed to say that he was counting on it. "We should go inside, but first—" He reached out and gently lifted her chin to its familiar defiant tilt, then winked. "That's much better."

The next morning, Kate bit her lip as she watched Nathan say goodbye to her siblings and Lawson. *Goodness, the way everyone was acting you'd think he was leaving permanently.* He'd be back in a week with the money that was supposed to keep her from needing him. Of course, by then the judge might be back and Nathan *would* be leaving permanently.

An awful feeling settled in her stomach at the thought. Perhaps it would be best to treat his departure now as a practice for the real thing. Maybe it would make things easier for her siblings when that day came. Perhaps, her heart seemed to whisper. But, would it make it easier for her?

She watched as Nathan gave a kind word and an affectionate gesture to each of the children. Ellie wouldn't settle for anything less than a hug, but was also rewarded with a grin and a tap on her pert nose. "Try to stay out of trouble, Ellie."

"Yes, sir," Ellie said as she slipped her hands behind her back and rocked from her heels to her toes and back again. "It probably won't do any good but I'll try."

Nathan clasped Sean on the shoulder. "You just keep taking care of your sisters. You're doing a fine job at it."

Sean nodded solemnly but Kate didn't miss the way his chest swelled at the praise. Nathan moved on to Lawson, who stood with his arms crossed in front of him. Nathan didn't try to penetrate that barrier. Instead, he surveyed his young friend carefully. "Remember what I said about keeping up with the chores and school. Don't run off before I get back."

Lawson shrugged. "I'll be here. It's not like I've got anywhere else to go."

Kate braced herself with a casual smile as Nathan stepped in front of her. He didn't say anything at first. The silence made her nervous. She spoke first. "I left a satchel with a few more provisions under the seat of the wagon. If you think you're going to stay more than a week, write a letter and let me know."

He tilted his head slightly as though to question her businesslike demeanor after what had passed between them last night. Her gaze strayed to where the children watched them with eyes that missed nothing. She didn't want to do or say anything that might get their hopes up about her relationship with Nathan. It wouldn't be fair to them.

"You'll be careful, won't you?" Nathan asked. "Be wary of strangers. Keep the pistol with you at all times."

She glared at him. "Really, Nathan, if you tell me to be careful one more time, I'll—"

"You'll what?"

She began to respond out of her bristled pride but stopped herself before the words did anything more than form on her lips. He was only trying to keep them safe. She gave up with a minuscule shrug. "I'll be careful."

A disbelieving smile tilted his lips as he caught her arms and gently tugged her closer for a better look at her face. "Are you feeling all right?"

She lifted her chin threateningly but smiled reluctantly. In her peripheral vision, she saw Ellie hit Sean on the arm to make him pay attention to what was happening. Nathan's gaze slid from hers to the children then he casually released her. "It's probably best that I didn't hear the rest of that sentence, anyway."

"I'll be back." He squeezed her hand then stepped into the wagon. He placed his Stetson on his head and tipped it at them all before urging the horses onward. She crossed her arms as she watched him disappear around the curve in the road. For one week, life was going to go back to the way it had been before Nathan Rutledge had ever shown up. That was a good thing. Wasn't it?

Chapter Fifteen

Nathan squinted against the afternoon sun then finally pulled the brim of his Stetson down to block it. He pushed open the heavy wooden door in front of him and stepped into the lobby of the hotel. He glanced at the clock realizing he would make it to his appointment at the agreed-upon time. He hurried across the lobby to the restaurant and paused inside the door.

"Are you looking for someone, sir?" asked a young man dressed in the uniform of the hotel.

Nathan glanced up from searching the tables to meet the youth's gaze. "Yes. I was supposed to meet a gentleman here named Mr. Reynolds."

"Yes, sir. Right this way." The young man led the way through the tables, stopping at one near the large-paned windows.

"Nathan, my boy, it's good to see you," the older man exclaimed.

"Davis, it's been a long time." Nathan grinned, extending his hand for a hardy shake.

The large Nordic-looking man motioned to a chair. "Sit down. Tell me how you're doing. I don't suppose you've had any contact with your family?"

"Actually, I have." He grinned at Davis's shocked look. "Mariah wrote to me. She says they're doing well."

"That's wonderful, Nathan. I always knew that girl had gumption."

"She sure does. It's nice to know that at least one member of my family is willing to risk Pa's wrath to contact me," he agreed. "How is your family, Davis?"

"Oh, we're just fine. Faith is just approaching her sixteenth birthday and of course Tyler is spending his days out on the range. He's a wanderer for sure. Just like you were, the last time I saw you."

Nathan smiled then shook his head. "Not anymore. I've been looking to settle down."

"That's good. I hope one of these days Tyler will do the same. The missus is doing as well as can be expected with both of her children nearly grown. I'm sure she hardly knows what to do with herself these days except to plan one function or another." He paused to take a drink of water then pointed to the lemonade in front of him to indicate it was for Nathan. "But you didn't come all the way over here just to hear an old man blather. We have business to discuss."

By the end of the conversation, Davis promised to personally introduce Nathan to a wheat buyer who was a good friend of his. "I'm sure he'd be willing to buy what you have. Since you're a friend of mine he'll definitely offer you a good price for it."

Nathan let out a smile in relief. "Thanks for your help, Davis. I appreciate it."

"You're welcome, Nathan." He pushed his plate away to show he was finished. "Farming is a hard market."

"I don't mind farming." He especially wouldn't mind if he was doing it for Kate.

"You're at the mercy of nature day in and day out. That's a hard way to live. It certainly wasn't what you came to Texas to do," he said as a waiter came to take the plate away. "Personally, I think you should go back to raising horses. You've always had an interest in it."

"It developed into more than an interest. When I was a partner at my old ranch it became my passion." Nathan smiled wryly. "Not that I'd do it again."

"Why not?"

"I already failed at it once."

"No. You were failed at it. Someday you might be ready to try again. When you are, let me know." The waiter extended the check. Davis grabbed it, then smiled. "I hope you know you're staying with us tonight. My wife would have my head if I didn't bring you home."

He smiled. "Yes, sir."

So this was what life was like without Nathan Rutledge, Kate thought to herself as she sat grimacing at the cow's udder. Funny she hadn't remembered it being so empty.

How pathetic. He's only been gone three days but I'm already waiting for his return, she thought.

Flick meowed loudly. The sound pulled Kate's gaze from the milk streaming into the bucket. She caught sight of Flick, then with an unpracticed twist, Kate shot a stream of milk toward the cat as she'd seen Nathan do. She missed. The small stream landed few feet from Flick rather than in her mouth.

She closed her eyes, tried to picture what she'd seen Nathan do. She tried again. This time it flew over her own shoulder, barely grazing her hair. Giving up, she lifted her shoulder to wipe away the few droplets that clung to her cheek. Looking toward Flick she shrugged. "Sorry, pretty kitty, none today."

The cat let out a plaintive meow and slunk toward Kate to rub against the milking stool. Kate stood to stretch her arms. Flick jumped toward the bucket almost as if to submerge her entire body in the warm liquid. Kate gasped but managed to block the cat from reaching its goal.

"Flick!"

The cat continued to struggle toward the bucket.

"That is quite enough, young lady. I fed you this morning so you needn't act as though you're starved. Have some dignity." She moved her legs to guard around the bucket. It took only a few more minutes to get the rest of the milk. Standing, Kate gave the cow an appreciative pat and reached for the pail. "Thank you, ma'am."

She slowly yet carefully made her way toward the barn door then glanced up as Delilah gave a loud neigh. Kate smiled sympathetically. "I know you miss Nathan, but he really did have to take the wagon. He'll be back soon. Don't worry. You aren't stuck with me forever."

Delilah snorted.

Kate hurried across the barnyard lugging the heavy bucket. She paused to stare as she noticed a rider coming toward the house, then continued walking to keep the milk from sloshing onto her skirt. She looked in the direction of town with concern. Why would anyone be riding out this way? Hopefully nothing was wrong.

Her straining arm forced her to hurry to the kitchen and leave the milk on the table before rushing back out the door. She stepped outside just as the man was dismounting. Remembering her promise to Nathan, she wondered for a moment if she should have grabbed a gun before hurrying out to meet a stranger while she was alone, but the friendly smile the man gave her quickly put her at ease.

"I'm looking for—" he glanced down at a paper "—Nathan Rutledge."

Nathan? This man knew Nathan? She bit her lip. "He's not here. Is there something I can help you with?"

He frowned. "That depends on who you are. You wouldn't happen to be his wife, would you?"

She tilted her head and met the man's gaze suspiciously. How could this stranger know she was Nathan's wife? Only a few people outside her family knew she was married. "How do you know him?"

The man laughed. "We're old friends. He's probably told you about me."

Her suspicion grew. If they were old friends he shouldn't have needed to check the paper for Nathan's name. Kate swallowed and stepped back toward the house. "Well, you should come back later. I'm sure he'd be glad to see you."

The man looked at her oddly but what did it matter? She stepped back inside and closed the door. She heard him moving toward it and hurriedly tried to lock it but her hands fumbled nervously. The door flew open making her stumble back. She grasped for something to hold on to but her hand knocked painfully against the rocker and she found herself on the ground.

She stared at the floor in disbelief while a shadow fell over her. Her head jerked up at the sound of a gun cocking. She stared at the barrel of a gun before her gaze followed the strong arm up to cold blue eyes. The man's voice was like steel. "Get up."

Kate swallowed the dread settling in her stomach.

She stood, wincing when she placed weight on her injured wrist, to survey the man before her. His hair was a remarkable shade of raven black at odds with his threateningly cold blue eyes. His features were just far enough from plain that he might be considered attractive if not for the anger that radiated from him. His gaze found hers with the look in his eyes bordering on hostile.

She met his gaze evenly then lifted her chin as she tried to speak. He cut her off by sharply asking, "Where's the nearest table?"

"Table?" she asked in confusion. "It's in the kitchen."

The gun flicked in his hand. "Go."

She slowly turned and led the way into the kitchen.

"Sit down," he commanded and she had little choice but to obey.

Kate sank into the nearest chair. She tensed, feeling the tip of the gun barrel press between her shoulder blades as a piece of paper and a pencil were set in front of her. "You'll write exactly what I say, do you understand?"

She nodded then wrote mechanically as the man dictated that he was taking Kate hostage. He requested that a large sum of money be deposited at a bank in a larger town that she remembered was about fifteen miles to the east. When his diatribe came to an end, she stared at the paper for a long moment, slowly realizing what she'd written. He snatched the paper from beneath her fingers and stepped up beside her to read it.

How did I get caught up in all of this? She set her lips in a grim line. She wasn't sure but one thing was certain. She was ready to get out of it.

She eyed the gun he'd extended too close to her nose for comfort. Pulling in a deep breath, she slowly leaned back. Once she was in position, she slammed the man's hand on the table as hard as she could. He cried out at the same time the gun discharged, sending a bullet into the wall.

She spun out of her seat and took off running. Her first fumbling steps sent her through the living room and out the door. She saw the man's mount waiting patiently and ran toward it.

Her foot connected with the stirrup as she swung into the saddle. She heard the man shout and knew he must be coming toward her. She turned the horse and urged it toward town. A shrill whistle rent the air and the horse turned sharply; moving back toward the house.

"No," she whispered, trying to control the horse. Her efforts almost worked until the man whistled again. The horse tossed its head in protest to her leading and trotted back to its owner. The man jumped on the horse behind her, grasped the reins from her hand and spurred the horse on.

Chapter Sixteen

She couldn't bear to ride another moment. Any minute now the children would walk into the house and find her missing. What would they do? What could she? Every step the horse took carried her farther away from them. "Can't we stop now? I'm so tired I can hardly see straight."

"We have a half a mile before another camping spot. We'll stop there."

Minutes later, he lifted her off the horse. Her legs were stiff from hours in the saddle so she carefully walked to a nearby tree and collapsed near its base. He glanced her way and threw her a strip of jerky. "Rest up, we need to travel a few more miles today."

She stared up at him. "I want to go back to my family. They need me."

His gaze traced her features before he nodded. "I plan to let you go, but not until Rutledge pays his due. He owes me that much—and more—after what he did."

She couldn't fathom what he was talking about. "There must be some mistake."

He laughed. "You think he's a good man, don't you?

He certainly has you fooled. He's nothing but a liar, a thief and a murderer."

"Impossible."

He knelt in front of her to grab her arm while his blue eyes sought hers in anguish. "You don't know. You don't know what he's done."

She winced. "You're hurting me."

He released his grip. "What did he tell you about his past? Did he tell you about his arrest? His jail time?"

She shook her head. "You're delusional."

"Delusional?" He stared at her for a long moment then strode to his saddlebag. He pulled out a rolled-up piece of paper and handed it to her. "I guess the wanted posters didn't make it this far upstate."

She pulled her gaze from his to unroll the poster. She stared in shock at the rendering of Nathan's face with the word *Wanted* above it and a reward offered under it.

"The courts may say he's served his time, but he owes me more than that—and I mean to see to it that he pays."

Shock and betrayal made her shake her head. "I don't understand."

He grabbed her arm more gently but with a decided urgency. "He killed my little brother, Kate. He shot him down like a dog. Eli was my best friend. When he died a part of me died with him. I haven't been the same since."

He released her and began to pace. "I can't stop thinking about him lying on the ground lifeless in the hands of the man who killed him." He lifted his tortured gaze to hers. "Rutledge's hands were covered in blood—my brother's blood. All to cover up his own dirty, rotten thieving. Since the money meant so much to him that he'd kill Eli to keep it, that same money is what I'm going to take in return. It won't bring Eli back, but maybe it will help his soul rest in peace."

Her thoughts flew back to Nathan's feverish mumblings about Eli. He'd mentioned blood, hadn't he? He'd also said he didn't do it, but he'd never said what "it" was. She should have asked him. Now all she could see was the anguish in Jeremiah's eyes. She'd felt that anguish before. It was awful.

"You haven't fully grieved for him," Kate recognized softly.

"I haven't had the chance. I've been too busy trying to bring him justice." He wiped a hand over his face to forestall tears. "If you knew what I'd been through, you'd want to help me."

Kate swallowed. "I do want to help you find some peace. My parents died two years ago. I know what it's like to lose a loved one."

"Then you won't fight me?"

Perhaps she could lull him into a false sense of security. "I don't want to fight you, Jeremiah, but why did you have to bring me into this? Why not just confront Nathan yourself?"

"I tried. He wouldn't listen. And the lawmen…" He shook his head. "They shouldn't have let him go. That's not justice. This is the only way I can make him pay for what he did." He took the wanted poster from her and stuffed it in his saddlebag. "We have to keep moving."

Kate opened her eyes slowly to find the sun streaming through the green canopy of trees. She'd watched her captor wander from camp through her lashes, then immediately began pulling at the knots that bound her feet. It had taken the whole night to free her hands.

She'd succeeded at daybreak just as her captor began to stir. The knots binding her legs came free. She cautiously rose to her feet.

"Where are you going?" a voice demanded and she whirled to find her captor only feet from her.

"I have to use the necessary."

He surveyed her carefully. She tried to look tired even though her exhaustion was being replaced by adrenaline. She had to get away. Despite his promise not to hurt her, he was obviously unstable. She couldn't trust him. He frowned at her.

"You have three minutes then I'm coming after you."

"I'm afraid it's going to take more than three minutes," she warned.

He looked annoyed. "Five then."

Kate turned on her heel and moved toward the thickest part of the woods and just kept marching. When she was a good distance from the camp, she picked up her skirt and ran like she'd never run before. After all, she had a five-minute head start, maybe more. He would probably stew over whether she was really trying to escape or just taking a long time. Well, let him stew. She wouldn't go down without fighting every inch of the way.

Ten minutes passed and her legs screamed for mercy but she pushed even harder. She knew she would only have a few more minutes before unwelcome company would arrive. She needed a place to hide. Suddenly the trees stopped and so did the land. She skittered to a halt on an outcropping rock and looked down. There was water, a lot of it. And mist—a lot of that, too.

She glanced back the way she'd come, looking for any sign that she was being pursued. Finding none, she stared down into the murky depths of the water. She took a deep breath, then jumped into the lake. Her skirts billowed out around her as she landed in water up to her chest. Her breath caught in her throat as the cold water soaked mercilessly through the layers of her dress and petticoats to her skin. Lying on her stomach, she pushed off from the dirt outcropping and swam beneath the water, only coming up for air when absolutely necessary.

The water grew deeper as she swam toward the center of the lake. She paused a few moments later to stare back toward the outcropping. Through the mist she thought she saw a horse and rider. Her heart sped in her chest. Had she been seen?

She slipped under the water and swam farther toward the center of the lake. A few minutes later she again looked toward shore and this time she was sure she heard a horse's neigh echo across the water. The rider turned his horse away from the outcropping and disappeared back the way she'd come.

She let out a relieved breath and allowed herself to float for a moment in the water to gain her bearings. She found herself in the middle of a lake covered with mist and dawning sunlight with a looming tree line surrounding it. It would have been beautiful had not she been running from danger.

She closed her eyes. *Lord, I know I haven't been the best at trusting You in the past but, please, I need Your help.*

Something scaly brushed across her right leg. She flinched to the left. That was sign enough for her. It wasn't long before she stumbled onto shore. She sat for a few moments to catch her breath before she finally began walking.

Suddenly a sense of foreboding gripped her. She

stopped walking and looked into the woods around her. She took a step back. She sensed movement to her left. She impulsively dashed back into the water. She swam beneath the surface and came up on the other side of the lake. She staggered to shore dripping wet and gasping for breath but instantly felt peace.

She set out at a quick but steady pace. Glancing at the sky, she was thankful she had many hours to walk in the daylight. She wouldn't even think about the night. Not yet. She had to trust that the Lord would provide.

Nathan reluctantly slowed the wagon as he entered the outskirts of Peppin. He wanted to rush to the farm so he could show Kate the envelope in his saddlebag. He was sure the check was enough to cover her mortgage payment. In fact it was probably more than she'd ever yielded off a crop before since she'd planted more wheat and hadn't paid the harvesters.

"Nathan." He turned to see the deputy wave at him as he passed the sheriff's office. Nathan nodded in return but didn't stop to talk. The closer he got to the center of town the busier the streets became and the more often people began to wave at him. He returned their waves at first but soon became thoroughly confused. Why was everyone so happy to see him?

He slowed the wagon and stared more carefully at the next person who waved. He realized they weren't waving. They were trying to get his attention. He reined in the horses just as Ellie's voice cried out, "Nathan, stop!"

He turned to see her running after the wagon on the raised wooden sidewalk. He set the brake and jumped down. He rounded the side of the wagon just as she nearly stumbled off the sidewalk. He caught her before she could fall, then guided her into a hug. Wrapping her arms around his waist, she immediately dissolved into tears. "Ellie, what's wrong?"

Sean and Lawson came to a panting stop in front of him. He glanced past them to search the gathering crowd. "Where's Kate?"

Sean straightened. "A man took her yesterday while we were at school. He left a note saying we can't get her back unless you pay him a lot of money."

Nathan felt the blood drain from his face. Thoughts and feelings rushed through him so quickly that he could hardly grasp any of them. Shock, fear and anger battled for dominance. They were superseded by guilt. He should have known. He should have protected her.

He'd known that Jeremiah was desperate yet the man he knew would never have stooped so low as to harm an innocent woman. That Jeremiah didn't exist anymore. A stranger had Kate. That stranger might try to hurt her or may have already have done so just to get even with him.

He felt like he was going to be sick. Sean, Ellie and Lawson were waiting for him to say something. He pulled himself together. Kneeling in the dirt in front of them, he set a firm hand on Sean's shoulder and looked him in the eye. "I'm going to find her, do you hear me?"

Sean nodded while his face turned red as he struggled to contain his emotions. Nathan met Lawson's worried gaze. "I'm going to bring her back." He turned to capture Ellie's tear-filled gaze. "I promise." She nodded causing a large tear to drip from her chin.

He stood to his feet. "I need to talk to Sheriff Hawkins. Do you guys want to ride with me?"

They immediately nodded. The crowd began to disperse. He turned the wagon around in the direction of the sheriff's office. Minutes later, children sat on top of the deputy's desk while Nathan sat in the chair across from the sheriff's. He barely held back a frustrated growl. "Sheriff, I understand you're just trying to do your job, but it sounds to me like you want me to sit here and twiddle my thumbs while Kate is in danger."

Sheriff Hawkins's calm demeanor leaned a little too close to disinterest for his taste. "Nathan, we all want to find Kate, but you must be reasonable." Nathan watched the sheriff point to the map stretched out on the desk between them. "Here is Peppin. Here is Colston."

He drew a large circle with his finger. "This is the area where they could be. Notice I said 'could be' because they might have taken an alternate route. Even assuming they stayed on one of the main trails, it would still be a guessing game. I can't authorize a search. There is just too much space to cover. It would be a waste of manpower and supplies. The ransom letter shows me the man won't harm Kate as long as she remains his bargaining tool."

The sheriff sat back as if his point had been made. "He gave us four days and that's plenty enough time to get an operation in the works. We'll catch him when he comes to town."

"I don't care about your operation. Kate needs help *now.*"

"I understand but—"

"Pardon me, but no, you don't understand. Your wife is safe at home."

"Well, yes—"

Nathan placed his Stetson on his head and stood. "I'm going after her."

"You're searching for a needle in a haystack."

"At least I'll be searching." Nathan glanced at the

children's satisfied faces and tipped his head toward the door. "Let's go. I'll need to get a few thing squared away with Ms. Lettie before I head out."

"Sheriff, I'd like to apply for a leave of absence." Deputy Stone's voice made Nathan pause and turn. He met the deputy's eyes as the man said, "It seems a friend of mine could use some help."

The sheriff eyed both of them. "Very well, Deputy. Go if you must. I just don't think it'll do any good."

Nathan shrugged. "Then we'll make it our mission to prove you wrong, sir."

Sheriff Hawkins looked at him for a moment then gave a nod. "You do that, son. You do that."

Kate cupped her berry-stained fingers and brought them to her lips, allowing the cool water to caress her dry throat as she swallowed it. She lay back allowing the sun to beat down on her. Its heat continually stole her energy the way hungry children pilfered bread. She closed her eyes against its glare only to feel a slight burning sensation beneath her lids. She knew it must be from lack of sleep. Perhaps it would be best to rest during the heat of the day and travel when the heat tapered off in the afternoon.

"Lord, were You proving Yourself by letting me escape from Jeremiah?" she whispered though no one was around to hear her. "Or, did you allow me to be abducted to show me I shouldn't trust Nathan?"

She didn't want to believe that Jeremiah's accusations were accurate. Yet she had recognized within his words a disconcerting ring of truth.

Who was Nathan Rutledge? She had felt such an immediate connection with him. She had invited him into her home. She had shared so much of herself. Yet what did she truly know about him? What if the little she knew was really a lie? What if it was an act, covering up the fact that he really was a thief and a murderer?

She covered her face from the glare of the sun but she couldn't hide from her fears. She'd made mistakes before. What if this time wasn't any different? Questions roiled through her mind but other memories rose against them. The sound of his voice as he read their family Bible every evening. Nathan kneeling in the dirt to comfort Sean and Ellie. Nathan's hand on Lawson's shoulder, praising him for his hard work while the boy smiled bashfully in response. The laughter in his eyes when he twirled her during the Harvest Dance. She didn't know what he'd done in the past, but he wasn't the heartless killer Jeremiah had described. She was sure of that. As sure as she was that it was past time for her to get home.

She'd barely rested since she'd escaped. Yet even then, the hungry gnawing of her stomach refused to let her truly rest. Her feet ached, her legs were tired, and her mind was nearly numb from fatigue. Her every thought was directed toward home—to where her boots were hopefully carrying her.

She closed her eyes tightly and imagined herself there, surrounded by her family. She would make it home soon. She had to.

"The prints stop here." Nathan tipped his hat back as he frowned at the ground.

"She must have jumped into the lake," the deputy concluded.

Nathan's eyes scanned the lake. "She tried to escape and by the looks of the other prints she was chased."

"So did she escape only to be recaptured?" The

deputy searched the woods around them with his gaze. "We'll follow the horse prints and see if we pick up Kate's."

Both men remounted and followed the trail running counterclockwise around the lake. A little more than a quarter of the way Nathan pulled Delilah up short and let out a whoop, then dismounted. He was almost too busy to notice the deputy's sharp halt and questioning look. Nathan pointed to the tracks heading away from the lake. "She's free. Look how the horse's tracks continue that way and hers head off in that direction."

Joshua dismounted before squatting for a closer look. "She stepped right on this print." Looking up, he grinned. "You're right. She is free, or was at this point."

Nathan nodded soberly but could not deny a relieved smile. "We'll need to follow the other tracks to be sure."

After following the tracks around the lake, Nathan found they headed back off into the woods.

Deputy Stone reined in his horse. "Sorry I have to leave like this, Rutledge, but if I go now I might have a chance at finding this man."

"Are you sure you want to take him without backup?"

Joshua shrugged nonchalantly. "I figure I can handle him about as well as you can handle Kate."

"I reckon I'll ignore that," he said to the laughing man. Turning Delilah around, Nathan said, "You just worry about catching that outlaw and let me worry about Kate."

Joshua snorted causing Nathan to roll his eyes before tipping his Stetson toward the man. "Nice riding with you, Deputy. Do me a favor and don't get shot."

"Same to you, Rutledge." He tipped his Stetson. "On both counts."

* * *

Kate stepped quietly from the cover of trees into the moonlit clearing before her. The loud song of a katydid drowned out the sound of her footsteps and covered her approach. With each step she took, she prayed the Lord would forgive her for what she was going to do.

Her steps slowed cautiously as she neared the campsite. In the dim light Kate could see the still form of the man who would unwittingly provide her first real meal in days. Her gaze scanned the campsite. There must be food somewhere.

Perhaps it was in his saddlebag? Her gaze faltered. He was sleeping on it. She continued her search from the shadows. There. On the other side of him, partially hidden by the shadows, was a small jar.

She moved out of the fire's light and circled around toward the man. Kneeling in the dirt dangerously close to her sleeping benefactor she reached for the jar. Her fingers felt only the maddening brush of its cool glass. She scooted herself forward a little more then reached for it again.

Just as her fingers touched the jar a strong hand caught her wrist. She gasped, jerking her arm back and away. The hold on her wrist slipped for a split second allowing her to wrench free. Before she could pull away entirely a second hand clamped around it. Her free hand pushed at the ones that held her captive.

"Let go of me," she demanded.

She heard the dark figure's sharp intake of breath and immediately realized she'd made a mistake by speaking. Now he knew she was a woman. She braced her free hand behind her to pull with all her might. The grip on her wrist slackened enough for her to break free. The man called out but she scrambled to her feet.

Her worn boots crashed through the knee-high weeds as she ran toward the woods. Her heart galloped ahead of her as she realized the man was chasing her. Fear tangled her thoughts as the torn hem of her skirt tangled about her legs. Finally reaching the woods, Kate wound through the trees in a ragged fashion until she could no longer hear the running tread behind her.

She lifted a hand to brace herself against a nearby tree trunk. Her breath resounded heavily in the stillness of the woods around her. Her hand went to the stitch in her side and remained there as she turned to rest her back against the tree. Leaning her head back, she closed her eyes against the swaying branches above her and focused on pulling air into her lungs.

Tears burned her eyes as she murmured a scattered prayer so soft that she couldn't hear it over the sound of the gentle breeze. A twig snapped to her left. Her eyes flew open. She froze for a moment then whirled toward the sound.

Powerful arms came around her, catching her hands and pinning them behind her. She struggled to free herself but was forced backward until the tree's rough bark scraped against her knuckles. She couldn't move.

She opened her mouth to scream but the man covered it with his hand. "Hush, Kate. It's me. It's Nathan. I came to take you home."

Chapter Seventeen

She froze. Slowly her eyes lifted to survey his shadowed features. Her breath caught in her throat. How could it possibly be him?

"Nathan?" she questioned in a whisper only realizing after she said it that he'd released her completely. It must be him. No one else would let her go so easily. A sob of relief hitched in her throat. Before she even thought to question the wisdom of it, she stepped into his embrace and let her cheek rest against his chest.

He placed a kiss in her hair then tilted her head back so that he could look at her in the dim light. "Did he hurt you?"

It took her a moment to realize who he was talking about. When she did, Jeremiah's accusations flit clumsily through her mind like an annoying light bug hitting the lantern glass. She searched his face. Pure regard, concern and compassion stared back at her and her heart warmed under his gaze.

Jeremiah's words faded away along with any lingering doubts as she faced the reality she'd been running from since the night she'd found Nathan outside with Delilah. She loved him. Her hand reached up to trace the angle of his jawline. He caught her hand and pressed a kiss into it. "Answer me, Kate. Did he hurt you?"

"What?" she breathed, then forced herself to focus on his question. "No, he didn't hurt me."

He paused. "You're sure?"

"Of course, I'm sure. I think I'd know if—" Her words stumbled to a halt when he leaned down to kiss her. Their lips barely brushed before his muscles tensed beneath her fingers. He pulled away to stare into the forest around them.

Then she heard it. A rustling just above the breeze announced the presence of yet another stranger. The slow nearly muffled sound of hoofbeats confirmed it. Her fists clenched against the tension.

"Kate," Nathan whispered tersely. "Promise me you'll run if I tell you to."

"But—"

"Promise me."

She nodded. His hand crept down to his holster. A steely voice spoke from the surrounding forest. "Pardon me, but I couldn't help but wonder if that woman you've captured is Kate O'Brien."

Nathan spun to face the man with his guns at the ready just as the man stepped into the clearing ready to do battle. Everyone seemed to freeze for a moment then Kate stepped out from behind Nathan. "Deputy Stone."

"So it is you, Kate." The man grinned then waved his Stetson. "I was just making sure."

Nathan holstered his gun. "I suppose this means you couldn't find Jeremiah Fulton."

"I tracked him as long as I could but he took the main road toward Bensen. I figured I'd have better luck getting their local law enforcement on the case than if I went off alone. What do you think?"

"It makes sense to me." Nathan glanced back to her. "I'm sure Kate is tired. Why don't we go back to camp and we can start home first thing in the morning."

She nodded. "I admit I'm a little shaky and sleep sounds good but food sounds even better. I've lived on berries for the past few days."

Nathan grinned. "That's something we can fix."

"Then what are you two standing there for?" she asked. "Lead me to it!"

Nathan lifted Kate from the saddle and carried her sleeping body to the bedroll. She moaned as he set her down and lifted her tired blue eyes to his. "Food."

He lifted the blanket toward her chin. "In the morning."

"Promise," she murmured, her lashes drifting down.

"I promise."

She turned on her side and went to sleep. Nathan let out a deep breath in relief. She was safe. He rubbed a hand across an unshaven chin then squaring his shoulders he moved back toward the camp.

"Is she all right?" Deputy Stone asked as he moved toward the fire with his bedroll in hand.

"As far as I can tell," he said then glanced over to her sleeping form. He hated the fact that Jeremiah was still out there somewhere but the important thing was that Kate was safe. He planned to keep her that way for as long as she allowed him.

Nathan felt himself being watched. He glanced over to meet the deputy's gaze. During the time they'd spent searching for Kate, they'd created the beginnings of a friendship. Nathan hadn't had a friendship with a man his age in a while and the last ones obviously hadn't turned out well.

The man grinned knowingly. "You've got it bad, Rutledge."

"You think I don't know that?" he asked with a wry smile. "Keep it down, will you? I haven't told her yet."

"Sure you have." He smirked. "She just hasn't noticed."

The smell of coffee tantalized Kate's senses. It pulled her slowly from her scattered dreams and made her aware of the insistent beams of sunlight that spilled across her eyelids. She sat up abruptly to stare through her knotted hair at the scene before her.

Nathan knelt near the outskirts of the campfire as he added wood to maintain the hungry flames. The deputy stood across the fire from him and stirred something in a small round bowl. A pan sat in wait on a log that had been rolled close to the fire. She didn't know what was in that bowl but her stomach growled at the mere implication of food being made.

She pushed her hair away from her face, drawing the attention of the two men. They both wished her a good morning but it was Nathan's smile that made her gaze linger upon his. He pulled the tin coffee kettle from the fire and poured her a cup. He knelt beside her to hand her the mug. "How do you feel this morning?"

"Better than I felt last night." She took a small sip of the coffee and winced. "It's rather strong."

He smiled. "Good. You'll need the energy."

She turned to meet his gaze. "The children, are they—"

"They're fine. They've been staying with Doc and Ms. Lettie."

"Good," she said then glanced away from him to where Deputy Stone poured a circle of batter into the frying pan. "Are you making pancakes?" she asked hopefully.

The deputy looked up with a grin. "I sure am. Are you telling me you might want one?"

"I'm telling you I might want a few."

He nodded. "It will only be a few minutes."

"I can hardly wait," she said. In fact, she wasn't sure she could wait at all. A hole seemed to be developing in the middle of her stomach and she wasn't at all sure that she'd ever be able to fill it. She pulled in another sip of Nathan's wicked brew. Lowering her hand, she noticed a streak of dirt on her wrist. She rubbed it but it wouldn't come off.

"There's a small stream not far from here if you'd like to freshen up," Nathan said.

She met his gaze for a long moment, barely daring to hope. "Do you have soap?"

Nathan produced a bar of the precious substance and showed her the way to the stream. He left her alone for a few minutes promising that he wouldn't be far should she call for help. She scrubbed the dirt from her face and hands, then, since she'd lost her hairpins long ago, she combed through her hair the best she could before pulling it back into a long braid.

When she realized nothing more could be done at the present, she returned to the camp with Nathan and was delighted to find a large plate of pancakes waiting for her. She didn't care that they boasted no preserves to sweeten their taste but took the plate and sat down on the log near the fire. She picked up a nearby fork. It was making its descent toward the pancakes when the deputy turned from the skillet. "Wait, Kate. That was for all of us."

"Oh," she breathed. Her fork wavered then came to

rest beside the pancakes rather than on top of them. "Where are the other plates?"

He nodded toward them then turned back to the fire. Nathan picked up the plates then held them out toward her. She frowned in concentration as she carefully transferred pancakes onto the other plates so that each held the same amount. She quickly cut into the golden cakes on her plate, then placed a large triangle of it into her mouth.

She closed her eyes. Ecstasy. She swallowed. Unsatisfying ecstasy. She continued to eat but the more she ate the hungrier she became. The fork moved the pancakes to her mouth in what seemed to be increasingly unbearable slowness. She was only halfway through when Nathan noticed her desperation. "Kate, slow down. You're going to choke yourself."

She glanced up in questioning innocence.

He narrowed his gaze. "You heard me. Slow down."

Kate gave him an unappreciative look. Yes, she'd heard him but she could not imagine obeying him.

"Nathan is right, Kate. If you eat too much too soon you won't be able to keep anything down," Deputy Stone chimed in.

"Is that right?" she asked after another swallow.

He nodded.

She smiled then cut a particularly big chunk off her pancake and crammed it into her mouth. *Let's see them try to make me slow down. Don't they know I've been starving for days? I had nothing to eat but berries. Berries. Berries. I don't think I'll eat another berry again in my life.*

She closed her eyes to concentrate on chewing and suddenly her plate was snatched from her hand. Her eyes flew open to connect with Nathan's determined gaze. She narrowed her eyes. "What are you doing? Give me back my plate."

"You're going to make yourself sick."

"I don't care."

"Well, I do."

"Nathan Rutledge," she warned as she watched him scrape the rest of her pancakes onto his plate. "What are you going to do with them?"

She gasped as he cut into them and began to eat them along with his own. "You're eating my pancakes."

"I'm keeping you from getting sick."

"I'd rather you didn't."

He leaned forward. "Kate, listen to me. This is very important. Your body has existed on barely anything for days on end. You can't shock it by putting in so much food at once. I am not saying that you can't eat. You must eat. However, you should eat small meals throughout the day. You've had enough for now but I promise there will be more food later."

She looked at him for a long moment then glanced to the deputy. At his supporting nod, she sighed. "Fine. Not that you've given me any choice."

Nathan held his plate out toward her. "It's yours if that's what you want. I only wanted you to know the truth."

She shook her head. "No. You are right. I'll do as you say."

He almost choked. "What did you say?"

She lifted her chin and met his gaze with an attempt at a threatening smile. "You heard me. Just don't get used to it."

The deputy laughed. "Well, I'm finished. Let's get things packed up and take this young woman back home."

It only took a few minutes to put out the fire and destroy the evidence of their campsite. She soon found herself staring up at Nathan as he waited for her to mount Delilah ahead of him. He looked completely disreputable with the shadowy three-day beard of his. He could almost pass for an outlaw if not for the warmth and caring in his eyes.

She glanced away. *I can't believe I've fallen in love with a man who has tangled with the law. Maybe he didn't kill someone but he definitely hasn't told me the whole story of what happened before he answered that advertisement.*

She couldn't allow herself to envision a future with a man with a questionable past. She owed it to herself and to her siblings to find out the truth. As soon as she got home she'd cull through the letters he'd sent to see if he'd offered some explanation that she'd missed. If not, she'd demand he explain himself. In the meantime, she didn't even want to think about his problems until after she laid eyes on her brother and sister.

As she debated the wisdom of riding with him for several hours, with the weight of her unanswered questions and unresolved feelings bearing down on her, Delilah turned her head toward Kate and bared her teeth. Repeatedly. Kate caught her breath. "Did you see that?"

Nathan glanced at her questioningly.

Of course, not. Kate narrowed her eyes at Delilah. The horse would probably bolt the moment Kate put her weight in the stirrup. That clinched it. Kate shook her head and took a step back. "I think I'd rather ride with the deputy."

He tilted his head to survey her carefully. "You think so? Well, Deputy Stone has plans of his own so it appears you're stuck with me."

She glanced to where the deputy was tying his bed-roll to his saddle. "What does he have to do?"

"He's going to scout around to make sure we don't get any unwelcome visitors on the way back."

"Oh," she breathed in frustration. Praying Delilah wouldn't bolt, she placed her muddy boot in the stirrup and swung onto the saddle. The horse must have remembered their truce, for though Kate braced herself, Delilah stood perfectly still. Nathan quickly settled into the saddle behind her.

She let out a breath of relief. The saddle was bigger than it appeared. There was plenty of room between her and Nathan. Then his arms came around to hold the reigns and she stilled as his chest brushed her back.

"There, that's not so bad, is it?" he asked.

No, it's worse, she thought but instead let out an affirming mumble. She didn't want to be distracted by him or the emotions he so easily raised in her until she had time to sort out the past few days of her life.

They soon parted ways with the deputy. A few hours passed and the early morning sun inched its way across the sky until it shone directly overhead.

"Aren't we going to stop for lunch?" she asked.

"We don't need to." Nathan presented her with a long stand of beef jerky. "Here. You can eat this as quickly as you like."

Ignoring the sardonic grin in his voice, she took it from him and broke a piece off with her teeth. Chewing it, she glanced around at the landscape. It was pretty enough but still unfamiliar to her. "How far away are we now?"

"Probably a good four hours," Nathan replied from behind her in the saddle.

"Better than a bad four hours, wouldn't you say?"

"I would."

She felt her spirits rising. They were getting closer. She glanced around but the deputy's horse was nowhere in sight.

"Why don't you try to rest, Kate?" Nathan asked, pulling her from her thoughts. "Just lean back and close your eyes."

She narrowed her eyes. "Lean back and close my eyes, is that all?"

"I'll have you know my intentions are nothing but honorable, Mrs. Rutledge, so you needn't worry yourself." He paused thoughtfully. "Unless, of course, it isn't me you're worried about."

"Don't be ridiculous," she breathed, although his comment hit a little to close to the truth.

His drawl was nothing if not casual. "Well, you were the one to send for a husband."

She tensed. "You know very well that I did not send for a husband."

He shrugged a broad shoulder. "No, but you didn't exactly send me packing, did you? I reckon that must count for something."

She was not in the mood for his games. She turned in the saddle so he could see that fact for himself. She lifted her chin and pinned him with her gaze. "Don't tempt me."

Their eyes caught and held. He read the fire in her eyes just fine but instead of backing down, he inclined his head questioningly. His brown eyes flashed with gold then trailed down to her mouth before meeting hers. His voice was low and serious. "I'd say that's a fair warning."

She caught her breath. Her gaze clung to his for a long moment before she turned to stare at the road before them. "Are you sure I can't ride with the deputy?"

"I'm sure," he said calmly. "Why don't you eat your lunch?"

An hour and a half later, the horse's gait had long since become a lulling rhythm. Her eyes were slowly but surely closing on her. Perhaps Nathan wouldn't mind if she dozed for a bit. She grimaced. The man had obviously reverted back to his cowboy days. For the past hour he'd done nothing but hum, whistle or even occasionally sing. Strangely enough, all of the songs were slow or lullabies.

She knew he was trying to get her to relax. It was working. Her eyes closed and she felt her head nod forward. She snapped it back up. She decided she didn't want to break her neck by falling from the horse.

Staring at the piece of road framed by Delilah's dark ears, she slowly began to lean back. Small bursts of yellow against the green indicated the spattering of flowers growing beside the road. She blinked sleepily then looked back at the road.

She waited one last moment, then steeled herself by taking in a breath. Finally, her back met the warm solid strength of his chest. She waited a moment and was not disappointed. Nathan's whistling came to a halt with one last down-spiraling note.

She bit her lip then waited for his whistling to start again. It took another moment but it started up again slowly. Kate firmly decided that she was wrong. Exasperating couldn't fully describe Nathan Rutledge. A reluctant smile tilted her lips as she drifted to sleep.

Chapter Eighteen

Nathan leaned against the wagon as he waited outside the schoolhouse for the children. He hadn't liked leaving Kate at the farm all by herself but she'd been desperate for some time alone to rid herself of the dirt she'd accumulated during her days in the wilderness. She and Deputy Stone both seemed convinced that Fulton would move on. Nathan wasn't entirely sure. He had fooled himself into a false sense of security by believing that same thing before, and each time he'd been wrong. It wasn't over. That much he knew.

He'd already been to see Doc and Ms. Lettie, both of whom had promised to drop by the farm as soon as Kate had a chance to rest. He'd also stopped by the Post Office and was surprised to find a letter from his family. He slipped it out of his pocket, wondering if he should give in to the temptation to read it or wait until he got back to the cabin.

He glanced at the schoolhouse door. Realizing the children would probably be another few minutes, he turned the letter over to break the seal. He began to read it and smiled in relief. Mariah had done as he'd asked and written to the sheriff in Noches for a full account of the incident Jeremiah had mentioned to them. She wrote that their parents were satisfied that he'd been found innocent of all charges.

Her letter was short so he moved to the next sheaf of paper included in the envelope. He glanced down at the signature and his heart began beating harder in his chest. This letter was from his pa.

Dear Nathan,

I've wanted to write you for a while now but I didn't know how to contact you. I guess that was my own doing. It looks like you've gotten yourself into a heap of trouble since you left but you've also gotten yourself out of it. I'm proud of you for that.

I just wanted to let you know that I regret the way things have been between us. I know you must think I've been too hard on you and the truth is, I probably have been. The reason might surprise you. You may not have realized it but I'd been grooming you to take over the ranch those past few years before you left. I know it was supposed to go to your brother but you have a head for business that would have made the Rutledge holdings grow into an empire.

I never told you that. I didn't think I needed to until you decided to leave. Everything I'd envisioned for the future came crashing down around me. Perhaps it was selfish of me but I didn't want to share you with anyone else. I wanted you to stay and work with me. When you rejected my offer it felt like you were rejecting everything I'd worked to provide for you. Your last letter showed me that wasn't the case.

Mariah tells me that you got yourself hitched to a girl who may not let you stay around. If she doesn't, I want you to know that you're welcome here. The position of foreman is available for your taking. Just send word ahead to let me know you're coming.
Pa

Nathan stared at the sheaf of paper, his thoughts in an uproar. His pa not only wanted to reconcile but was also offering him a way out. *Is this from You, God?*

He'd wanted so much to believe that he could leave his broken dreams behind him to embark on a new future here in Peppin with Kate and her siblings. Now he was beginning to wonder if that was even possible. His past continued to haunt him through the specter of Fulton's anger and need for revenge. As for his relationship with Kate, he wasn't at all sure where he stood with her.

He could hardly hold her to the emotions that had almost led her to accept his kiss. She'd been out in the wilderness for days without adequate food, water or rest. Before he'd left with the wheat, he'd thought he was making progress. Her attempts to avoid him on the ride home had left him second-guessing that assumption.

The schoolhouse door flew open and he slipped the letter into his pocket. Children began to scurry out the door, with some hovering in the schoolyard while others immediately went their separate ways. It wasn't long before Nathan spotted Sean in the bustle of children.

The boy's eyes lit on his, then grew wide with cautious hope. He skirted the other children to hurry

toward their wagon. Staring up with world-weary eye
too old for his age, Sean asked, "Did you find her?"

Nathan smiled. "She's waiting for you at home."

A smile grew across the boy's face until it explode
into a grin. "I'll get the others."

Kate was tucking the last hairpin into her damp ch
gnon when the creak of wheels drew her gaze to th
window. She dashed down the stairs, then opened th
door just as the wagon came to a stop in front of th
house. Ellie jumped down. The little girl's eyes four
hers and began to fill with tears. Kate sank to her kne
as Ellie traveled the few last steps into her arms.

"Ellie," Kate consoled as the girl wept in her arms

"I was so scared. We couldn't find you." Ellie
shoulders gave a small shudder.

"I know, but God protected me and He was with yo
even when I wasn't. You know that, don't you?"

She nodded, which set free a few large tears tha
spilled over her cheek and off her chin. Kate wipe
the tears from her sister's cheeks then smiled. "It's a
right."

She waited until Ellie gave her a trembling smil
in return before she released her and looked for he
brother. Sean was just hopping down from the wago
He smiled as his gaze caught hers, then he quickl
walked toward her and pulled her into a strong hug. H
stepped back to look at her in concern. "Are you su
you're all right?"

She nodded.

He shook his head seriously. "If he hurt you—"

"He didn't. I promise you."

His eyes filled with desperation. "I should have bee
here. I should have protected you. Since Pa died, I'

the man of this family. It's my responsibility to keep us safe."

"No, Sean," she said. "If you had been here he would have tried to hurt you. What happened wasn't your fault. Don't ever believe that."

Kate glanced behind Sean to Lawson. He stood beside the wagon looking unsure of what to do. She realized he probably wasn't used to such open familial displays of emotion but she didn't let it stop her. She stepped forward and pulled him into a hug. It took him a stunned second to return it.

"I'm glad you're back," he said in her ear before he released her.

She smiled. "Thank you."

Nathan cleared his throat from where he stood near the wagon bed. "Now that everyone is finally home, we have a lot of things to get inside the house. Everyone is responsible for their own things. This looks like Sean's."

He began tossing the children their belongings, making a game out of it, and easing the moment for all of them. When all of the children had disappeared into the house Kate shaded her eyes to look up at Nathan. "Is there anything I can carry?"

Nathan grinned then jumped down from the back of the wagon. "As a matter of fact, there is. Ms. Lettie sent an entire meal with us. She didn't want you to have to cook on your first day back."

"Bless her for thinking of that," she said as she joined him.

"Doc is planning to visit you in the next few days."

She nearly rolled her eyes but instead turned to look at him. "I'll be fine. All I need is a little rest."

"I know that but people are concerned." He shrugged

then began gathering as much food as he could. He met her gaze. "They can't help it. They love you."

The door to the house flew open and as the children hurried out Nathan gave her a parting smile before carrying the load of food inside.

Sean and Lawson took what remained into the house, leaving Kate alone with her sister. When the girl moved to follow them inside Kate called her back. "Ellie, do you remember where you put the letters?"

Ellie stared at her in confusion. "What letters?"

"The ones from Nathan, silly."

"Oh." The girl tilted her head to stare up with a curious look in her eye. "Why do you want them?"

"I just want to read them."

"I see," Ellie said while staring at Kate as though trying to discern all of her secrets.

She glanced surreptitiously at the door of the house then back at Ellie. "Where are they?"

Kate slipped toward the back of the empty barn where several small wooden crates stored some of their father's old tools. She lifted the cover off one of the crates and there, partially buried by broken halters and old tools, rested their father's tackle box. Kate pulled it out and placed it on her lap. The lid opened easily to display a small stack of letters.

She shook her head. The lengths that her family had gone to, to secure her a husband never ceased to amaze her. She reluctantly had to give them credit for their cleverness. She never would have stumbled upon the proof of their guilt unless she had been told where to look.

It had been hard to ignore Ellie's curious glances throughout the evening. It had been equally difficult to disregard her own unanswered questions until the children had gone off to school and Nathan was distracted by his chores on another part of the farm. She pushed down the guilt she felt for leading Nathan to believe that she was content to spend the day resting when she was really planning to discover the truth about his past.

She pulled the letters from the tackle box, then settled beside the crates to open the first letter. She was surprised to find the missive wasn't from Nathan at all but rather a letter of inquiry from another suitor. She smiled as she read the letter written by an older gentleman looking more for a companion than a wife. She set it aside then continued to read through the others in the stack. It seemed the advertisement had elicited quite a response.

The stack of letters began to dwindle and Kate had yet to come across one of Nathan's letters. She leaned back against the barn wall with a reluctant smile. Based on the letters she'd read from other potential suitors, she had been fortunate to end up with Nathan. She realized she probably would have made the same choice that her family and Ms. Lettie had made.

She let out a sigh and let one more letter float to the haphazard pile around her on the floor. Nathan's letters had to be in the stack somewhere. She opened the next letter, then glanced down to the signature. She hesitated at the sight of his name scrawled across the bottom of the missive. He'd signed it, *faithfully yours*.

Suddenly a wave of guilt swept over her. She stared unseeingly at the letter, then realized she couldn't do it. She gently folded the letter closed. It might be the most foolish thing she would ever do but she decided that she was going to trust Nathan Rutledge to be the man he'd presented himself to be. At least until she asked him about Fulton's accusations face-to-face.

As far as she could tell, Nathan had not had an easy life before he'd married her. She might never be sure of all the details of that life but she did know he was not the person Fulton had portrayed him to be. Her experiences with him were proof of that. She would have discovered such outrageous flaws in his character, especially since she had been looking so desperately for some reason, any reason, not to love him.

They had been living and interacting so closely that she had been given the opportunity to observe his character in many different situations. As it was, she had discovered that though Nathan was far from perfect he still strove toward and displayed the characteristics of his Father.

She realized her legs were aching from her sitting on them and slid them out in front of her. She wondered just how long she had been here in the shadows of the barn between the feed sacks and the crates, trying to peruse the pages of Nathan's past. Sighing, she began to gather all of the letters around her and fold them neatly back into stacks.

She had just lifted the pile of letters back into the tackle box when the sound of the barn door opening caused her to freeze. Glancing up in dread, she watched Nathan walk in. She bit her lip. What would he think if he found her here with all of these letters? Maybe he'd just get what he needed and leave. She carefully put the letters down and attempted to back farther into the shadows of the barn.

Nathan grabbed the muckrake from its post near the back of the barn. He heard the door creak open behind him.

"I thought you were going to rest," he called over his shoulder as he reached for the broom. He heard a quiet gasp from his right and glanced that way only to see the flash of a familiar blue skirt disappear behind the feed bags. *Kate,* he noted in confusion. *If that's Kate, then who...?*

"Fulton," Nathan growled and spun to face his adversary just as the man stepped another pace toward him with his guns at the ready.

"Drop your weapons," the man commanded. "All of them."

He considered his options then set the tools aside and slowly unbelted his holster. He dropped it to the ground so that it would slide closer to where Kate hid. Fulton tilted his head to Nathan's left. "Move away from them. You and me, Rutledge, we're going to settle this once and for all."

Kate blew the floating dust from where it tickled her nose and shifted on her knees for a better view. Peering around the sacks of feed near the ladder to the loft, she watched as Nathan's brown gaze slid over Jeremiah Fulton's shoulder and met hers. His face gave away nothing, not even a flicker of recognition. He looked down and away from her. She followed his gaze to where his gun rested on the ground. She had to get it.

"Why are you here, Fulton?" Nathan's voice drew her attention even as it drew the interest of the gunman. "I don't understand. You could be free from the law some place farther west or across the border."

"You would still be here walking around free. As if you deserve that. As if you didn't kill my brother," Fulton said.

Kate swallowed and glanced at the gun then slowly

made her way toward it. Her heart thumped in her chest. All he had to do was turn around and she would be spotted. She carefully reached for the gun. She wasn't close enough.

"I didn't kill your brother, Fulton."

"Liar."

She glanced up. If she went any farther she'd be in Fulton's line of sight but she knew she had to take the chance. She placed a stabilizing hand on the ground in front of her, then reached her right hand to grasp the barrel.

"Listen," Nathan said sharply, barely stopping Jeremiah from turning to pace and inevitably spotting Kate. "You need to face the fact that your brother took your land right from under you. He did the same to me. We were both dense enough to sit by and let it happen."

In the corner of his eye, he watched Kate begin her slow and careful trek back to her original spot.

"I don't believe you." The man combed his fingers through his hair.

Nathan spoke in calming tones. "I didn't want to believe it, either, but there comes a time when we have to face facts no matter how painful they are. Eli was my best friend. I never thought anything was wrong when he made such a fuss about handling the financial end of things. It freed me up to work with the horses. That was where I wanted to be and Eli wanted to be in the office so that worked out real nice.

"I went over the records after everything fell apart. It looks as if the ranch hit some rough times because of poor management. Not his fault, at first—the job was too big for one person. Instead of asking for help, Eli borrowed from other areas to balance the books. You and I were those areas but mainly you."

Fulton looked down, shaking his head and Nathan used that opportunity to look at Kate. *Leave now. Slip out the back.*

She sent back a message loud and clear though she didn't say a single word. *You have to be kidding. I'm not leaving you with this crazy person.*

Nathan nearly growled in frustration but managed to withhold the urge in order to protect her. Instead he pulled his gaze back to his former friend and business partner just as the man looked up. He continued speaking as he tried to think of some way to get them out of this. The truth was the only weapon he had.

"He was probably more comfortable borrowing from you, thinking he'd pay it back. When that didn't work he started gambling. He lost more than he won. He realized everything was going to crumble so he got desperate. He pinned what he could on me and was going to hightail it out of town."

Fulton began to appear more agitated. He turned to pace. Nathan had no choice but to continue, hoping that for once the man would listen to what the courts had already proclaimed. "I stumbled upon him leaving and confronted him. He didn't come after me. He turned the gun on himself and said he was going to kill himself. I tried to talk him out of it but he wouldn't listen. That's when I tried to wrestle the gun from him. Somehow in the scuffle he managed to get a shot off. He killed himself, Fulton."

"Lies!" Fulton shouted.

"No. It's true. As to the money you think I have, it doesn't exist." Nathan tilted his head toward the door hoping Kate would read the message he'd carefully disguised. It was time for her to go. Things weren't going to get any better. She needed to make a break for it.

Either Kate didn't catch his signal or she ignored it. He was leaning toward the latter. Her inaction forced Nathan to continue his efforts to make Fulton see the truth. "Check the receipts. I barely broke even on what I paid for my share of the land and what I sold it for. I even offered you the land at more than a fair price. You wouldn't consider the deal. In fact, you threatened me."

The man snorted. "Of course I did. You tried to sell me what was rightfully mine."

"Fulton—"

"I'm tired of listening to this," he said then stepped forward with his gun at the ready.

"Stop. It doesn't have to be this way."

A chill went down Nathan's back as Jeremiah cocked his gun. This was it. It was best to take it bravely. *Lord, if only Kate didn't have to witness this.*

Kate. As a last effort Nathan shot a glance toward her with only one word echoing in his gaze. *Shoot.*

Chapter Nineteen

Kate's eyes widened. She raised the gun and pulled the trigger. Instead of the loud bang she was expecting all she heard was a click. Her mind stopped working for a moment. Then she glanced down at the gun and pulled again. *Click.* She caught her breath. The hammer was still down. She pushed it up then pulled the trigger again. *Bam!*

She glanced up to find both men shying away from the blast only now they were both facing her. Jeremiah's expression was filled with rage while Nathan's showed a mix of impatience, exasperation and relief.

Minutes later Kate's wrist chafed at the rough rope as she found herself in an all-too-familiar situation. She tried to wriggle her wrist yet found she was unable to do so. She tried wiggling her arms then her feet. Nothing below her shoulders or ankles moved.

It looked as if Fulton had learned his lesson. Escape for her seemed impossible. She glanced at Nathan. A thought hit her and a laugh bubbled up in her throat.

She managed to turn her upper body so that she could lean her head against the wall. "I never really thought about it but when one must die tragically, dying next to a handsome man is definitely the best option."

Nathan looked at her as if she was insane. "Kate, aren't you the least bit concerned about this situation?"

"Not really," she confessed. "Somehow I can't see your friend killing us. He's had so many opportunities. Yet, the most he's ever done is tie us up and push us around. He could have killed you after my gun went off but he didn't do it then, either."

Nathan shook his head and looked away. "I don't find that comforting."

Delilah edged toward Kate, nickering softly. She watched the horse warily. "Nathan, if you let that horse step on me—"

"She's not going to step on you."

"You keep saying that but I'm not sure it's true."

"It's true. Besides, when have you ever been afraid of horses?"

Kate looked at him impatiently. "I'm not afraid of horses. It's just a well-established fact that Delilah has a grudge against me and I don't like my head being in kicking range!"

"Would you calm down?"

"I'm not excited!"

"Then stop arguing!"

"Who's arguing?"

Nathan growled and turned away.

Kate scooped up a handful of hay. She turned her back to Nathan, which took considerable effort, and weakly threw it at him.

"You missed." His tone was a maddening mix of amusement and indulgence.

She didn't bother to turn around but instead leaned

sideways into the wood of the stall. "I don't care. According to you, we're going to die anyway."

Nathan snorted. "It's not my fault you forgot to cock the gun."

She bristled. "I wouldn't have had to cock the gun if you'd done what you were supposed to do."

"Which was?"

"How would I know? Whatever it is you failed to do."

There was silence a moment, then Nathan asked, "Why don't we pray?"

"What?" she asked, caught off guard. Throwing her weight, she rolled to face him.

"Let's pray," he repeated, his eyes dark and serious. His head bowed. "God, You know where we are and how to bring us out of this. We know it isn't Your will for us to be murdered so we ask for Your protection, for Your mercy. We ask that You send Your angels to guard us lest we dash our foot against a stone. Be our shield from persecution. In Jesus's name, amen."

"Amen," Kate echoed. She sat in thoughtful silence. "What's that smell?"

Nathan comfortingly clucked his tongue at Delilah when the horse moved toward him. "Fire."

Kate froze. "Fire?"

He glanced her way. "Yes, fire, as in burning wood, scorching flames and unbearable heat."

"Then why are we still sitting here?"

Nathan's voice was irritatingly patient. "Where would we go?"

She responded in kind. "Somewhere besides here."

"How do we get there?"

"We move? I don't know. How long have you known the barn was burning?"

"Why do you think we prayed?"

"Oh." It came out as a laugh yet nothing was actually funny.

Nathan used the wall to push himself toward her. "Scoot over here and try to untie me."

With a new sense of urgency, she turned and backed toward him.

"I just wish I had my knife. Why, today of all days, did I lend it to Sean?"

Kate paused. "You lent it to Sean? I can't believe that. Not after I made him give me his pocketknife just this morning. He convinced Ellie her dress was on backward again."

Nathan turned to look at her and licked his lips. "Kate, there is something I've been meaning to say."

His voice droned on but her mind stumbled to a halt. *Pocketknife.* Her gaze snapped up to look at Nathan. "Pocket."

"What?" he asked distractedly.

"His knife is still in my pocket."

She watched Nathan freeze then hope flared like gold in his brown eyes. "Scoot over and I'll get it."

"Scoot over," she said more to herself then anyone. She half rolled and half scooted toward him.

Finally, Nathan had the knife in his hand and had managed to flip it open. A moment later his hands were free and he was bending to cut his feet lose. He turned his attention to her and she was free in a matter of seconds. In that short span of time, the fire had spread so that most of the north wall of the barn had flames licking at its wooden walls.

"Go open the doors," Nathan commanded. "Then come back and help me get the animals out."

She broke into a run toward the door and tried to push it open. "Nathan, the lock is jammed!"

He barely paused in his flight toward the milking cows to pick up a gun lying on the floor. She stepped aside. He shot the lock. She pushed at it again. It barely budged. "It's stuck!"

Nathan rushed for the door. "Get the cows."

She hurried toward the north end of the barn and went to the cows closest to the fire first. Their pens opened without difficulty. She herded them in the direction of the door just in time for Nathan to exchange glances with her as he ran for the hatchet. She went back for the last two cows and found the fire was spreading even faster. The heat of the flames caused her hair to feel wet with sweat.

"God, please let those doors be open when I get there," she mumbled to herself. She reached the entrance of the barn just as the doors flew open letting in a rush of cooler air. She breathed a *thank You* as she and Nathan shooed the cows out, then ran toward the south side to get the horses. They opened the gates to the stalls as they went, then turned to shoo the horses out the door.

They were headed outside when Kate heard a pitiful meow. She gasped and stumbled to a halt. She coughed out the smoke she'd drawn into her lungs.

"Kate," Nathan's voice yelled over the confusion. "Let's go. This place is burning up."

She shook her head and moved deeper into the barn in the direction the sound had come from. "Flick is in here."

The meowing was louder and almost incessant as Kate moved closer to the south side of the barn. The fire was already making its way toward her yet Kate couldn't ignore the cat's desperate call for help. She came to the last stall yet saw nothing.

She glanced up. The cat was sitting on the ledge of the wall. The ledge was no more than a few inches wide but somehow Flick had managed to climb up there and get stuck. Kate looked around for some way to reach the cat. Dragging over the ladder, she managed to pull the reluctant cat into her arms. Kate was carefully climbing down the ladder when Flick let out a loud meow. With that battle cry, Flick sprung from her arms and shot out of the stall in the direction of the barn doors.

Kate stood in disbelief for a moment, then hopped from the ladder onto the floor. The smoke and fire were now making their way toward her. She had to get out. Now.

She hurried into the smoke making sure to keep her wits about her. There were four stalls before the door. One. Two. Three. Four. She turned to her right and walked through the open space to the barn door. But where was the air? Where was the sunlight? She froze. She'd miscounted the stalls. She glanced around and saw through the smoke barely enough to find that the stall around her was on fire.

Eyes wide, she turned and stumbled back the way she'd come. This time she went too far. She found herself at the stairs to the barn loft. She held on to the stairs and closed her eyes. Think. If she was at the stairs near the loft, it meant the door was directly behind her. She opened her eyes even as the smoke stung them. The heat was becoming unbearable.

Nathan couldn't believe Delilah had thrown him. He barely had time to notice that the roof was on fire before he was on his feet following the horse through the dense smoke. When he spotted Kate struggling to get on the horse Nathan felt a smile touch his lips. So Delilah had had a reason for knocking him flat on his back. He'd been leading her in the wrong direction. *Good girl,* he thought. Then slipping behind Kate, he lifted her onto Delilah's back and quickly swung up behind her.

The steel band of Nathan's arms was all that kept Kate from tumbling off the horse as it bolted into a strong canter toward the exit. With one hand on Nathan's arm and the other tangled in the horse's mane she searched for the rays of sunlight that pierced through the intoxicating smoke. Then she heard it, the moaning and groaning of a roof begging to cave in. Her breath caught in her throat and echoed in her ears as desperation clawed at her chest.

Nathan's weight was heavy against her back as Delilah moved into a gallop. They were almost there. Nathan muttered something unintelligible, then placed a heel into the horse's side. Delilah picked up speed. The barn was nothing more than a blur of smoke and fire. Kate felt her eyes close. The muscles under her tensed as Delilah leaped. Kate bit her lip. With a whoosh, hot air rushed by her ears and was replaced with cooler air.

Her eyes flew open. Her gaze took in the house, the chicken coop and the barn animals that were milling about where they shouldn't be. Clean air met her lungs and surprisingly caused her to choke. A stiff breeze fanned the flames behind them. The horse hardly came to a stop before Nathan slipped off. He lifted Kate from Delilah's back, then glanced toward the barn.

"We'll have to round up the animals and put them in the pasture for now," he said over the roar of the flames. "First, I have to find Fulton."

"What about the barn?"

He shook his head. "There's no time."

She pulled her gaze from his to turn toward the flame-ridden building. She'd worked so hard to maintain everything. She'd spent two years trying to prove to the town that she was able to take care of her siblings and the farms alone. There was no way she would have the money to replace the barn.

What would they do come planting and harvest time? What would they do when winter set in and they had no place to keep the animals? How would she take care of her family? Visions of her working at the Red Canteen for Andrew Stolvins danced through her mind.

She shook her head. "No, we have to save it. Help me!"

"Kate," Nathan warned but she paid him no heed.

She ran toward the house and grasped the bucket she kept close to the door. She needed water. She hurried around the back of the house then stumbled into the kitchen. She pushed the lever for the sink up and down as quickly as she could. Precious water gushed into the bucket. She lifted it from the sink then turned toward the door—

—and came to an abrupt stop as she saw Jeremiah Fulton leaning in the doorway, blocking her way out. He looked ready to collapse. Blood dripped from his shoulder to the floor. He seemed to consider lifting the gun in his hand then dropped it to his side as he met her gaze.

She stiffened. "Why are you doing this?"

He shook his head. "The fire was an accident."

"I suppose bolting the door was an accident, too."

"My brother—"

She set the heavy bucket on the counter. "He has

nothing to do with this anymore, does he? This is about revenge. Killing won't get rid of that anger you feel."

He stared at her for a long moment then dropped his head. "How do I stop?"

"Pray," she suggested.

He glanced up in surprise.

She smiled. "And give me your guns."

He stared at the gun, then turned it over in his hand to grasp the barrel. He lifted his arm to hand her the gun but it slipped from his grasp to the floor. Kate watched a world of pain flash across his face as he groaned from the strain the movement caused on his arm. The man would have collapsed onto the floor had not Nathan appeared in the doorway to keep him from going down. Surprise and agony painted Fulton's features in a grimace.

Kate watched him glance at Nathan. Fulton's other arm began to move. She erased the distance between them with one quick lunge. Her hand made it to the gun still in his holster a second before his did. She wrestled it from its spot at Fulton's hip then stepped back to point it at him.

His dazed blue eyes met hers and for the first time since she'd met the man, he smiled. It was a weak smile but a smile nonetheless. "I guess you figured out who to trust after all."

She nodded. "I guess I have, at that."

Nathan sent her a questioning glance.

Kate lifted the other gun from where it had fallen and pointed the pair toward Fulton. Both men flinched. Nathan shook his head slightly as if to warn her that she couldn't shoot two-handed no matter how hard she tried. Her eyes narrowed then she set the hammers of the guns in place. "There. Now, they're both cocked. Why don't you tie him up while I hold these on him?"

Nathan stared at her for a moment then seemed to curb a smile. He nodded toward her. "Hold those guns steady. This shouldn't take long."

Chapter Twenty

Nathan lifted his hands from the pail of water and splashed the cooling liquid on his face hoping it would rid his eyes of the burning caused by smoke. Wiping his face on the inside of his shirt, he glanced around the barnyard lit by the golden sunset. Everywhere he looked, people gathered in small groups watching the fading embers consume what was left of the barn's standing structure. Five men circled the fire, throwing buckets of water onto the debris to control what was left of the flames.

The rocking chair had been pulled onto the lawn of the house. Sean sat there with his arm around his little sister as the chair rocked slowly back and forth. Lawson sat on the ground on the other side of the chair. Doc and Ms. Lettie stood near them. Nathan glanced around for Kate and found her standing nearer to the barn. One arm was wrapped around her waist while the other hand supported her chin as she stared at the fire.

He was drawn to the sight of her solitary figure standing alone in the midst of all that movement. She glanced over her shoulder at his approach and her lips lifted into a small smile. He returned the smile with one of his own. "I'm glad to see you can still smile after a day like this."

Her gaze traveled back to the fire and she shrugged. "I've realized that no matter how hard you try, there are just some things you can't control. This fire was one of those things. You were right. I couldn't have saved the barn. I probably would have gotten hurt trying."

He shook his head. "I'm really sorry about that, Kate."

A glint of determination lit her eyes. "We'll just have to rebuild, that's all. I'm not sure how or when we'll be able to, but by God's grace we'll rebuild."

"At least the fire did one good thing by drawing the sheriff over here to check out the smoke. He showed up just in time to take Fulton into custody."

"He'll be going to jail for a long time."

"That's what I'd guess. We'll know for sure when the judge gets back," he said. "I still can't believe you were able to get Fulton to hand over his guns."

She met his gaze with a smile. "Neither can I. I'm glad you arrived when you did. I wouldn't have known what to do with them." Her smile turned rueful. "Obviously."

He tilted his head, considering. "You kept him from killing me. That counts for something."

She lifted her chin. "I suppose I did."

"I was wondering about that earlier. Why were you hiding in the barn? I thought you were inside resting. Had you already seen him?" He was surprised to watch her eyes widen and her cheeks turn an alluring shade of pink before she turned to stare at the fire again. He stepped closer. "Kate?"

She frowned at him and glanced around. "You shouldn't be so close. People will talk."

"Will they?" She was trying to distract him but he could play that game as well. He lifted his hand to brush away the black streaks that painted her face. She stilled beneath his touch. "You're covered in soot."

"Nathan," she said warningly, though it came out a bit too breathless to carry a real threat.

"Kate."

Kate rolled her eyes and stepped away from Nathan's touch. Of course it would be too convenient for him to have forgotten the small fact that she had been hiding in the barn. She glanced up at his curious gaze. "You really want to know?"

He smiled. "I really do."

"You'll think it's silly."

"So what if I do?"

"I was looking for your letters."

"My letters?" he asked in confusion.

"Yes, the ones you sent me before you came here."

He took a moment to digest that, then nodded slowly. "Why?"

"I'd never read them before." She shrugged innocently.

The man seemed to have developed an uncanny ability to read her mind, for he inclined his head toward her and searched her features carefully. "Was that the only reason?"

She couldn't maintain her flippant attitude another moment. The tension dropped from her shoulders. "When I was with Fulton he made a few accusations about your past. I didn't want to believe him. At the same time I discovered I hardly knew anything about you in that sense. I wanted to see if you had offered any information about what happened."

"So you read the letters to find out about my past," he said, his gaze intent on hers. "What did you discover?"

Kate allowed herself a smile. "Nothing. I didn't read them."

"Why not?"

"I didn't need to. It was probably very foolish of me not to read them but I decided that I trust you." She laughed. "Don't look so shocked. I still wanted to know. I just planned to ask you in person instead."

He grinned wryly. "I wouldn't have blamed you for asking. I should have known Fulton would have tried to make you believe his version of things. I'm sure he said some pretty awful things."

"Don't worry. He did."

He tilted his head. "Well, if you have any other questions about my past you just let me know."

"Actually, I still have a few and, since your letters are most likely gone forever, it seems you are my only source."

He grinned. "Ask away."

She bit her lip. "He showed me a wanted poster with your face on it and a pretty hefty award."

"That is an interesting story within itself. After everything happened with Eli, I went to the sheriff's office for questioning. Once he finished, I thought he was done with me. I had a lot of my mind so I wandered here and there for a few days until I ended up at the next town and saw the wanted posters. Apparently, the sheriff had called on me for more questioning. When I wasn't around, Fulton convinced him I'd run off to Mexico. It kind of shattered his story when I turned myself in."

He shook his head. "Things were a mess for a while.

I was charged with murder, and there was a trial. But I was found not guilty. I wasn't sure that I'd ever be free again. When I was let go, I did the best I could to find a new life. It seemed like God was smiling on me again when I saw that advertisement in the paper for a husband."

She watched as he seemed to gather his thoughts then he faced her again, obviously in search of more questions. She pursed her lips. "How old are you?"

He smiled again. "Three years older than you."

She did the math. "Twenty-three."

He nodded. "You've been wondering that the whole time?"

"No. I just wondered off and on." She paused, debating whether she should continue. Seeing that he was waiting expectantly, she gathered her courage. "Have you ever been married?"

He grinned slowly. "Well, now. That depends on what you consider married."

She felt her cheeks warm. "Before me."

"Never."

"Betrothed?"

"Once."

"What happened?"

"We got married."

Her eyes narrowed. "Then what?"

"I don't know yet."

She sighed.

He leaned closer. "Mrs. Rutledge, don't look so exasperated."

"Don't call me Mrs. Rutledge."

He tilted his head. "Well, isn't that like the pot calling the kettle black?"

"What? How?"

"You just finished making sure I was as single and unattached as any slightly married man can be."

"I assure you, that isn't at all what I was doing."

"Than what were you doing?"

"I was only making sure that you are the man you've presented yourself to be." She realized how close they were and stepped back. "You are exactly who I thought you were."

"Yeah, and who is that?"

"A good, honest, Christian man and a very trustworthy friend," she said seriously then smiled at Nathan. Her smile faltered when she met his gaze. He looked completely flummoxed. She frowned. "That was a compliment."

He bit off a tight smile. "I understood that. Thank you."

She watched in confusion as he gave a brief nod and stalked off to speak to the men controlling the dying embers of the fire.

Nathan banged his Stetson against his leg in agitation as he strode down the wooden sidewalk of Peppin. He couldn't get Kate's words out of his head. Didn't that beat all? After courting the woman for weeks she still only saw him as a friend. He pulled in a calming breath. Being friends was definitely better than nothing but it was so far from what he wanted to be for her and her family.

He set his Stetson on his head and tugged it low. His hand immediately strayed to the letter in his pocket— the one he'd reread a thousand times. His pa wanted him to come home. Kate seemed to want nothing but friendship. The children obviously wanted him to stay. What did he want?

He paused in front of the sheriff's office and stared at the building. One thing he wanted was to leave the anguish of the past behind him once and for all. To do that, he had to talk to the one man who probably never wanted to see him again. Maybe some sort of reconciliation would lead to a complete end to the nightmares that now visited his dreams less frequently. That's what he was hoping for, but these days he'd take whatever he could get. He removed his hat and stepped inside. Soon he met Jeremiah Fulton's glare through the harsh metal bars of the jail cell. The man frowned and stepped closer to the barrier between them. "Look, I don't know why you're here. I have nothing to say to you."

"I'm here because I have something to say to you."

"What then?"

Nathan took a moment to swallow then said, "I'm sorry."

Fulton froze. "You're sorry?"

He nodded. "I didn't kill your brother and I think you know that. All the same, I'm sorry for the way things turned out. I'm sorry if I said or did anything that caused you more pain than you were already feeling."

"Just leave me alone," he said, distrust apparent in his gaze.

Nathan lifted the book in his hands. "I brought this in case you get bored."

Fulton backed away from the bars. "Why are you doing this? I am not your friend and you are certainly not mine."

"We were friends once."

"That was a long time ago." Fulton sat down on the bunk and wouldn't look at Nathan. "You should go."

"You're right." He slid the Bible he'd cleared with the

sheriff through the slats between the bars. "I'll leave this."

Jeremiah frowned but otherwise didn't respond. Nathan left him to his solitude and turned toward the sheriff. The man stood from his desk. "I guess Kate probably hasn't had a chance to think about a barn raising, but you let me know when you're ready to put that new barn up. I'll be glad to hammer a few nails."

Nathan agreed and was ready to bid the sheriff farewell when a knowing expression shifted across the man's features. "By the way, Rutledge, I heard tell Judge Hendricks was looking for you."

He curbed his surprise. "Judge Hendricks? You don't say?"

"Sure enough." Sheriff Hawkins gave a twist of a smile. "He didn't seem all too happy, if you ask me, so if I was you I'd get over there real quick. He's like a rattlesnake—the longer you wait the madder he gets."

Nathan smiled though he didn't find the analogy amusing. Thanking the sheriff, he waved at Deputy Stone and stepped from the dim jail into the brightness of the early afternoon sun. Pulling the brim of his Stetson low over his face, he allowed his eyes to adjust then paused beside the dark form of his horse. Nathan felt his fondness grow for the dark beauty. She'd done exactly what he'd needed her to do during the fire, practically without his help. Delilah gave out a huff as if to express her annoyance.

He grinned at her and gave her nose a pat before he moved past her. "Just give me a minute more, girl."

The sound of horses' hooves near the front of the house piqued Kate's curiosity enough to set the soapy dishes into the sink. She dried her hands on her apron as she walked to the front door. Opening it, she was surprised to see a fancy black buggy and two beautiful matched horses waiting in front of the house.

She stepped cautiously around the buggy to find a tall older gentleman surveying the barn's destruction incredulously. It took her a moment to believe what she was seeing. When she did, her heart filled with dread even as her lungs let out a happy gasp. "Judge Hendricks!"

The dark-haired man who had been her father's closest friend stepped forward with a concerned smile and pulled her into a warm embrace. "Kathleen Grace O'Brien. I just arrived in town and heard what happened. I had to see for myself that you were all right."

She shook her head in amusement. "My, news travels fast in Peppin."

"You just have to have the right sources," he said then stepped back to survey her. "I heard no news of the children. Were they injured?"

"No, they were still at school when it happened."

"You must be exhausted. Perhaps we should sit down."

"Come inside. I have a lot to tell you." Kate led the way inside and sat in the rocking chair while the judge settled near her on the settee.

He removed his hat and met her gaze. "First of all, I want to assure you that I will see this matter through to the full extent of the law."

"Without partiality, of course," she teased as she removed her apron.

"Of course," he agreed then shook his head. "I admit I've learned about the fire and your abduction from the sheriff but I'm still unclear on the details. I heard your abductor was the friend of a new man you hired."

She folded the apron and sat it in her lap. "I doubt the two men involved would call each other friend and Nathan isn't really a hired hand at all."

"Who is he then?"

She bit her lip. "I'm afraid he's my husband."

"Your husband!" Judge Hendricks stared at her until he surmised she was serious then asked, "Since when?"

"We met a few days after you left."

"Mr. Potters couldn't approve a marriage license."

"He didn't." She laughed. "Actually, neither did I."

He shook his head in confusion. "Perhaps you'd better explain."

I'd rather not, she thought. Then she looked into the judge's brown eyes and suddenly couldn't hold the story in. "I hardly understand it myself. It seems Ellie, Sean and Ms. Lettie decided I needed a husband so they found one for me. I didn't find out they had married me to him until the poor man showed up at my door with our marriage license in hand."

"That does not make sense. How did he get a marriage license if you didn't know about it?"

"Well, I knew a little about it," she admitted. "They told me they wanted to marry me off by proxy. I signed the silly affidavit in a moment of weakness but I never intended to send it."

He sat back and stared at her with a thoughtful look on his face. "So he's been living here since then?"

"Yes. Well, not exactly. He's lives out at the Mac-Gregor cabin with a runaway boy we took in," she said.

"Runaway?"

She sent him a warning glance. "That's a whole other story."

He nodded.

She set the apron in the chair beside her, then stood

to pace. "We've been waiting for you this entire time. You see, we decided that the only sensible thing was to get the marriage annulled. Or rather, I decided and he agreed."

Judge Hendricks looked at her thoughtfully. "How do you feel about that now?"

"Oh, I don't know." She turned away, wringing her hands. "I've just been so afraid."

"You've been afraid of what? Are you afraid of him?" he asked, no doubt desperately trying to keep up with the turns in the conversation.

"No! I was afraid I'd fall in love with him."

When she couldn't bear the silence between them any longer she turned to face the judge. He caught her hand and gently guided her back into the rocking chair. His voice was kind as he asked, "And have you, Kate? Have you fallen in love with this man?"

She buried her face in her hands.

His voice held tender amusement. "You have. You love him, don't you?"

She met his gaze and said with an air of desperation, "I'm afraid so. It took me a long time to admit it because of the mistakes I made with Andrew, but now I know. Nathan is God's will for me."

He laughed. "Then why are you so distraught?"

"I'm just not entirely sure I can trust God's will. I think a part of me is afraid that I'll end up…" She couldn't finish her statement.

"You're afraid you'll end up like your parents," the judge said knowingly. "Kate, it would be a wonderful thing if you did."

She stared at him in confused shock.

He smiled compassionately. "You've been focusing on your parents' deaths so much that you're allowing it to eclipse the way they had lived their lives. They were never afraid to love those around them or to act out that love. They were so intent on living each moment that their enthusiasm and joy for life infected those around them. Do you remember that, Kate?"

She nodded as tears filled her eyes.

"Think about how they lived. Let that be their legacy. Let that be what you carry with you, not the pain and sadness of their deaths." He took her hand and leaned forward earnestly. "They'd want you to move on, Kate. They'd want you to trust that they ultimately ended up right where they were supposed to be. They wouldn't want you to miss today for fear of tomorrow."

"You're right," she breathed, as she accepted the handkerchief he gave her. "I know you're right."

"Good." He smiled then shook his head in awe. "I must say, if this young man helped bring you to a place where you can move past that tragedy, then he is worth keeping around."

She gave him a watery smile then allowed him to pull her into a hug.

Chapter Twenty-One

Nathan leaned back in the courthouse's waiting room chair, bouncing his worn Stetson on his knee. He was more than willing to try his luck at charming the old snake the sheriff mentioned if he ever showed up. Nathan had been waiting for the judge for nearly an hour. Thirty minutes more and he just might have to give up this stakeout altogether.

When Nathan had arrived at the courthouse he'd been informed that Judge Hendricks had lit out of town only minutes earlier leaving no information regarding his return. For all Nathan knew, the judge could have set out on another one of his prolonged journeys. While he waited, he'd been able to get reacquainted with his old friend Mr. Potters. The man had offered his skilled assistance but Nathan had been more inclined to wait for the judge. At least, he had at the time.

He pulled the crisply folded letter from his pocket and reread his father's letter for the second time since he'd been at the courthouse. The offer was still there. He'd decided he was going to take it. He didn't have any other option. Now that the judge was back, all it would take was Kate's signature on a piece of paper to divorce him from her life forever.

He'd tried to have faith but it was time to face reality. Kate's decision had been made long ago. Despite his attempt to woo her, she'd given him no real indication that she felt anything more for him than friendship. She had declared him exactly that after the fire. "You are a good, honest Christian man and a very trustworthy friend," she'd said.

His jaw tightened. He would only be fooling himself by continuing to hope there could be anything more between them than what already existed. He swallowed against the sudden lump in his throat and carefully placed the letter back in his pocket. He bowed his head. *I tried, Lord. I really did. Now I'm giving it up to You. Do whatever You like with me.*

Suddenly a tall, dark-haired man breezed through the small courthouse's door. The man's boots rang confidently across the wooden floor as he strode toward the office door directly across from Nathan. Nathan grasped his Stetson and stood quickly to his feet, earning the appraising eye of the gentleman before him. "Sir, are you the judge?"

"That's what I've been told. Who are you?"

"Nathan Rutledge."

The man's eyes narrowed which couldn't be a good sign. "Nathan, you say? Well, come on in. There's no use jawing out here in the hallway. Does this have to do with that new criminal sitting in the town jail?"

Nathan followed him in but couldn't bring himself to sit down. "Not particularly."

The man set his hat on a wooden rack and settled into his chair before bothering to ask, "Well, what else would you like to discuss?"

He set his shoulders and met Judge Hendricks's gaze directly. "I need an annulment, sir."

"You *need* one?" he asked, then read a paper on his desk before placing it into a drawer. "Why is that?"

Nathan finally took a seat. "The young woman I married doesn't want to stay that way. It was all a misunderstanding. She never really wanted to marry me. She doesn't want to try to make the marriage work, which is completely understandable. I probably would have made the same choice if I were in her shoes…probably."

Judge Hendricks still didn't look up. "Who is the young woman?"

"Kate Rut—" He caught himself. "Kate O'Brien, sir."

The judge shuffled through his papers and read over another. "I see."

Nathan frowned at the man's obvious disinterest. "Listen, I'd like to get this done as soon as possible. Is there some paperwork we need to fill out?"

Finally, Judge Hendricks looked up and met his gaze. "No."

"What do you mean 'no'? There is no paperwork?"

The judge tossed his papers aside. "I mean, no. I will not give you the annulment."

Nathan shook his head. "I don't think you understand. The marriage was never consummated. It was a mistake from the start. Kate never agreed to marry me. Her siblings devised a scheme to marry the two of us by proxy with the help of Ms. Lettie. It all happened without Kate's knowledge. This marriage probably isn't even legal."

The judge nodded in agreement. "It might not be at that."

Relief filtered through Nathan. "Then you'll give us an annulment."

"Absolutely not."

Nathan sat back and stared at the man. "You can't be serious."

The judge tilted his head as he surveyed Nathan. "Tell me, do you want to make this a problem? Because we can make this a problem."

They glared at each other for a long tension-filled moment. Nathan dropped his gaze then leaned back into his chair. He tried to appear calm but his thoughts were racing. The judge's expression turned contemplative for a moment, then he tossed his pen back onto the desk. "All right, Rutledge, I'll give you one last chance to persuade me."

Taking a deep breath, he straightened. He began to speak then thought better of it. *What is the use anyway?* He met the judge's gaze. "Nothing I say will change your mind so let's not play games."

Judge Hendricks gave a slow nod. "All right then, no more games. Agreed?"

"Agreed."

The judge leaned forward then waited for Nathan to do the same before he spoke. "I want you to understand that I'm not worried about what's best for you. I couldn't care less. Kate's father was my best friend. We served in the war together, came out alive, took this fledgling town and made something of it. If her parents had died but a few months earlier, I would have been her legal guardian.

"Marrying you would be the best thing for her and those children. So the answer is no, Nathan. I will not authorize the annulment." Judge Hendricks leaned back and crossed his arms.

Nathan tapped his Stetson on his leg. "You're sure?"

"I'm sure."

"Then I reckon there's nothing I can do about it." Nathan stood, then placing his Stetson on his head, he moved toward the door.

"Nathan."

He turned toward the judge who gave him a wry look of amusement. "I expect you'll be making a visit to Reverend Sparks first thing."

Nathan grinned, realizing he hadn't fooled the man for a second. "Yes, sir, your judgeship," he said. Tipping his hat, he walked out the door.

Kate smiled as Doc snapped closed his black leather bag on the kitchen table and pronounced her healthy enough, considering the circumstances she'd been subjected to. She shot a glance toward where Ms. Lettie sat across the table. "I told you I was perfectly fine."

Doc frowned. "That is not entirely true, Kate. You are still dehydrated so you will need to drink plenty of fluids. I also want you to rest and give yourself time to recover."

"I understand your concern," she began, "but the barn—"

"The barn will wait until you are physically able to deal with it. Is that understood?"

Kate bristled at his tone. "Perfectly, Doctor."

Ms. Lettie sighed and exchanged a glance with her husband. "Now, Kate. Don't be upset. You have to take care of yourself. If you don't, you won't be able to take care of your family."

"I know that," she said. "There is just so much to catch up on. Now I have to decide how to move forward with the barn. Then I have to figure out something to tell the bank about all of this. We've just now caught up on the mortgage. I don't know how we'll get the money to rebuild."

Ms. Lettie caught her hand in hers. "Let us help you."

Kate glanced from Ms. Lettie to Doc. "How?"

"Leave that to me. In the meantime, Luke has some calls to make, but I would be more than happy to stay with you and prepare dinner."

"Then who will prepare yours?"

"We'll eat here."

"I don't know what we have in the pantry."

Doc smiled and with an uncustomary drawl proclaimed, "Well, now. It seems a certain woman we are all familiar with just happened to bring a few things in our buggy."

Kate laughed. "Then stay. You've worn out my resistance."

"That sounds like my constant state of mind," Doc said with a smile just for Ms. Lettie.

Kate watched in amusement as Ms. Lettie blushed then she teased, "Maybe you should attend to Ms. Lettie, Doc. She looks a little flushed. What medicine would you give her for that?"

Ms. Lettie frowned at her in exasperation and affection. "You are an impertinent young woman."

"Yes, I've been told that before," she said, then smiled at Doc. "I'm still waiting for your answer."

Doc met her smile with his own. "You've forgotten I don't want her to recover."

She laughed.

"Love can be both the affliction and the remedy." Doc met her gaze seriously. "You don't look surprised. Maybe you were already aware of that."

Kate held Doc's gaze though she felt her cheeks grow warm as she realized what he was implying.

"I wish she was," Ms. Lettie sighed then glanced at Kate. "My lands, I think she is. Don't worry, dear, it really is a wonderful affliction."

Nathan spent the afternoon at a workstation he'd created near the paddocks, that consisted of nothing more than an old table and a few borrowed tools. He figured he may as well try to do something productive while he waited for a chance to speak with Kate.

The day was beginning to try his patience. When he'd arrived home from town, he'd found Doc leaving and Ms. Lettie settling in for the day. There had been no chance for him to find a private moment with Kate.

The longer he waited, the longer he had to wonder about how things would end up. His initial relief at the judge giving him what amounted to a second chance had faded with the realization that he had to give Kate a choice. He wasn't going to go along with everyone else in her life by trying to decide her future for her. If she wanted him to stay, then he would be thrilled to do so. If not, he was resolved to leave and let her live her own life.

He'd managed to replace a few essential things the fire had taken and was just starting to build a new feeding trough for the horses when the children arrived home from school. They tied their horses to the paddock gate then rushed toward Nathan. Lawson made it to him first. "Nathan, the news is all over town. The judge is back."

Nathan didn't glance up from the groove he was trying to carve into the wood. "I know."

Ellie gasped. "You do?"

He glanced up to meet her panicked gaze. Sean placed a calming hand on Ellie's shoulder. "What are you going to do, Nathan?"

"The only thing I can do. I'm going to talk to Kate."

"You mean you haven't already?" Lawson asked.

Nathan smiled at the urgency in Lawson's voice that reflected his own. "She's been busy."

"She's not too busy for this," Ellie said. "I'll go get her."

Nathan caught her sleeve before she could get far. "Hold on, you three. This is something Kate and I have to figure out for ourselves. I'll talk to her when the time is right."

"When will that be?" Sean asked.

"Soon," he promised. "In the meantime—"

Ellie's eyes widened. "We won't say a word."

He grinned. "That wasn't what I was going to say, but that works, too."

She grimaced. "I'm sorry I interrupted."

"I was just going to remind you guys to take care of your horses." He let Sean and Ellie slip away but asked Lawson to stay for a moment. "How did you like staying with Doc and Ms. Lettie while I was gone?"

Lawson shrugged as his eyes became guarded. "It wasn't bad."

"Doc asked about you today."

"Why?"

"He wanted to know if you might consider settling with him and Ms. Lettie permanently."

Lawson stared at him as hopeful silence stretched between them like a thick blanket. "They did?"

He grinned. "They sure did."

"What did you tell them?"

"I told them they'd have to ask you about it," he said.

"That isn't your only option. You can always stay with me. You know that."

"You say that now, but what if things don't work out with Kate? Where will you go then?" he asked.

"Oklahoma. I told you my pa offered me a job there. You would be more than welcome to come."

"Oklahoma," Lawson echoed.

"Just think about it."

Lawson nodded thoughtfully. He began to turn away, then paused to glance back at Nathan seriously. "Either way, I think you should know that we're brothers now."

"Thanks, Lawson. I—"

"No, I mean we're really brothers. I prayed after Kate came home. Now we have the same spirit or Father or whatever you said."

"Oh. In that case." Nathan grinned then held out his hand. "Welcome to the family."

Lawson shook his hand then smiled teasingly. "Thanks. Now if you've got half the sense the Lord gave you, you won't waste any time in getting your own. You fit, remember?"

He nodded. "I hope you're right."

Yes, he hoped. He hoped but he had surrendered the situation to God. It was up to Him now. Nathan could only pray His will would be done.

Chapter Twenty-Two

Kate let out a quiet sigh. Her blue eyes lifted toward Nathan as she shifted in the rocking chair until she faced him more fully. The rhythmic cadence of his voice had drawn her attention. "Therefore, behold, I will allure her, and bring her into the wilderness, and speak comfortably unto her."

I don't remember reading that particular verse in Isaiah before, she thought absently. She dragged her gaze from his distractingly handsome features to stare at the arms of the rocker her father had made. Her mother had rocked her here when she was little, shushing her fears while offering love to replace them. She missed their guiding lights even now. Or was it especially now?

She wished she could ask her mother's advice about Nathan but she knew what the judge told her earlier was true. Her parents would want her to put aside her fears and live as they did. She thought of the way she had been living for the past two and a half years and couldn't find a starker contrast.

She had been so focused on protecting her heart, on being careful, on being sensible that she'd nearly forgotten everything they'd taught her about how to live. She'd even allowed the thing that least represented who they were—their death—to become a stumbling block between her and God. She wondered how her life would be different if she followed their example. How would she change if she really allowed herself to trust?

Her gaze lifted to trace the room and its inhabitants. A small kerosene lamp battled the dusk creeping in through the windows and touched the golden strands in Ellie's hair. The girl lay on her stomach close to the settee as she toyed absently with a piece of string. Flick lazed before her, halfheartedly lifting a dainty paw toward the twisting string, prompting a smile on Ellie's lips.

Lawson slumped in a wooden chair, his arms on the armrests while he stared in thoughtful consideration at the ceiling. Sean leaned against the cool brick of the fireplace with his brow knotted in deep concentration as he faithfully shaved at the chunk of wood in his hands.

More importantly, how would my family be different if I was able to restore some of what we lost when Ma and Pa died? She bit her lip, then glanced down at her rich green skirts. It would take a lot of courage for her to do so. The fears she'd allowed to distract her from God had become familiar and comfortable. She hadn't had to depend on anyone but herself—not a man and not even God.

Lord, I want to trust You with my heart. Free me from the distrust of You and this fear of the future. I want what You want for me.

She glanced up as the quiet timbre of Nathan's voice deepened. "I will betroth thee unto me forever."

He met her gaze. Her breath stilled as he continued, "Yea, I will betroth thee unto me in righteousness, and

in judgment, and in loving kindness, and in mercies."
A smile tugged at his lips as he regarded her. "I will
even betroth thee unto me in faithfulness, and thou shalt
know the Lord."

Their eyes held and Kate could not have looked away
if she'd wanted to. The intimacy of the firelight played
across his face, blurring the cozy scene surrounding
them. Somewhere a snicker sounded. The world was
suddenly in focus again. Kate's gaze flew toward the
sound yet snagged as it drifted past Ellie. The girl lay
perfectly still. A string dangled precariously from her
fingers with her mouth slightly open as her gaze darted
between Nathan and Kate.

Lawson was sitting up in his chair and, though his
gaze rested on the floor, a smile pulled at his lips.
Sean's green eyes watched them carefully. Feeling her
cheeks warm, Kate turned toward Nathan and lifted her
chin. "That was from Isaiah?"

He glanced down at the Bible. "Isaiah?"

"Yes, Isaiah forty-three, starting with verse two."
She watched him suspiciously as he scanned the page.

His warm brown eyes met hers. "My mistake."

"Thank you, Nathan," Kate said over Ellie's giggles.
"I think that's all for tonight."

Ellie sat up abruptly and placed her hands in her lap.
"I have a wonderful idea. Why don't we go watch the
stars?"

Kate stared at her sister in confusion. "The stars
won't be out for another thirty minutes. Besides, it's a
school night."

Sean set his carvings aside. "It won't take long this
time."

"Yeah, just long enough," Lawson added with a sly
half smile at Nathan.

Her gaze darted from Lawson to Nathan as she asked, "Long enough for what?"

"Long enough to catch a few fireflies before it gets completely dark," Nathan said as he closed the Bible and set it on the table. He turned toward Kate. "What do you say, Kate?"

"You want to catch fireflies with me?" she asked with a bemused smile. At his nod, she shifted her gaze to the children. Ellie widened her eyes then nodded adamantly. Sean and Lawson seemed to wait with baited breath. Kate finally understood.

"Oh." She bit her lip to keep from laughing then echoed Ellie's nod. "That sounds fine."

The children jumped up and rushed out the door with a few backward glances to make sure Kate and Nathan were following. Nathan held the door open then stepped back for her to precede him. The children dashed toward the corral fence. She and Nathan followed at a more sedate pace.

"I've wanted to talk to you all day," he admitted.

"You have?"

He glanced toward the corral fence and smiled. She followed his gaze to see Ellie waving them on toward the open land. Kate rolled her eyes then muttered, "Really, Ellie?"

Nathan laughed. "I can take a hint. Come on."

He caught her hand and led her toward the fields. The sun was sinking slowly behind the tree line to the west, leaving the meadow covered in deep blue dusk. A few early fireflies began lighting up around them as Nathan cleared his throat nervously. "Kate, I talked to the judge today."

Kate glanced up at him as anxiety filled her stomach. Surely Judge Hendricks hadn't told Nathan about their conversation. She braced herself. "What did he tell you?"

"He said he wouldn't give us an annulment."

"Oh," she breathed, then waited for him to continue. He didn't.

She bit her lip and glanced away. So Judge Hendricks hadn't betrayed her feelings to Nathan. He'd just closed Nathan's only way out of their marriage and left her to do the rest. She didn't know whether to be amused or alarmed.

"Is that all you have to say?"

"What do you want me to say?" she asked softly as she lifted her gaze to his.

He tightened his hold on her hand slightly to pull her to a stop. "I want you to tell me the truth. Do you want me to stay or not?"

She glanced down at their joined hands and swallowed. "I want you to stay."

"Why, Kate? Why do you want me to stay?"

She finally lifted her gaze to his. "I need you."

He shook his head. "That isn't enough. Why do you need me? Do you need me to build your barn and milk your cows and keep the bank from foreclosing? If I've learned anything about you in the past two months, it's that you don't need me for any of that. You can do it all on your own, but it's the only reason you've ever let me stay around. I need to know if you need me for the same reasons I need you.

"I need you because the world is better when I'm with you. I'm better when I'm with you. I need you because I don't want to imagine my future without you living in it. I need you because I can't imagine God creating me for anyone else. Is that how you need me, Kate?"

"I—" she began but fear weighed her tongue down. She was tired of questioning. She desperately wanted to trust Nathan with her heart but it wasn't really about him at all. It was about surrendering to God's will—the very thing she'd prayed for just minutes earlier. But was she truly ready?

"I love you, Kate. I love you so much that I don't want to settle for anything else." He stepped back. "It's your decision now. I'm going to the cabin and I'm leaving in the morning. There's only one reason I'll let you stop me. You know what that is."

He began to walk away. She watched him in disbelief, then panic set in. That's when it hit her. This was life outside of His will. This was life figuring things out on her own. She was so paralyzed by fear that she couldn't stop the man she loved from walking away from her. It had to change and it had to change now—before it was too late.

She glanced up and saw Nathan had made it a good distance across the field. She bit her lip. Pulling in a deep breath, she yelled, "Wait!"

Her voice traveled quickly across the quiet field. Nathan slowly turned to face her. He didn't move toward her so she ended up picking her way toward him through the high grass of the meadow, dispelling fireflies in her wake.

"You can't just tell a woman you love her then in the next sentence tell her you're leaving. It doesn't work that way," she said.

He stared at her in disbelief. "Do you have any idea how long you were silent after I said all of that?"

She stopped in front of him and lifted her chin. "I

was thinking. Besides, it wasn't that long. You're exaggerating."

"I don't know, Kate. It felt like a pretty long time," he said then stared down at her cautiously. "Why'd you stop me?"

"Why do you think?"

He caught her arm and guided her across the distance that separated them until only a few inches remained between them. "You mean—"

"I mean I need you for the same reasons you need me. I love you, Nathan Rutledge. Completely, irrepressibly, desperately," she said then smiled ruefully. "Lord knows I tried to fight it, but the funny thing is I don't think I was ever supposed to. You came into my life and helped God change it completely. I'm so grateful for that and for you."

A slow grin spread across his lips. "I wondered how long it would take you to figure that out. I was really hoping I wouldn't have to leave tomorrow. I'm not even packed."

"Well, you're staying so don't even think about it."

"In that case," he said, stepping back and kneeling on one knee, he reached into his pocket to pull out the wedding ring Ellie had been so curious about months earlier. "Kate O'Brien, will you marry me?"

She responded with one word. "Rutledge."

His brow furrowed in confusion. "I'm sorry, what?"

"My name is Kate O'Brien Rutledge."

He grinned then asked, "And what, Kate O'Brien Rutledge, is your answer?"

"My answer is yes." She smiled. "I would love to marry you."

He slid the ring onto her finger, then stood and took a slow step that erased most of the distance between them. She caught her breath as his arm slid slowly into place around her waist. The corners of her mouth lifted into a gentle smile as she watched those dangerous gold flecks in his eyes warm to lustrous amber. She closed her eyes as his thumb trailed softly over her lips and he lifted her chin.

Her lashes flew open at the last moment. "What about the children?"

"I don't think they'll mind," he murmured. Then softly, stirringly, sweetly his lips captured hers.

Epilogue

Kate sat patiently in a wooden chair in a small room in Peppin's church as Rachel and Ms. Lettie made a few last touches to her hair and endeavored to attach a veil to their wondrous creation. Ellie let out a less-than-patient sigh where she stared up at Kate from a nearby footstool with uneven legs.

The girl was so full of nervous energy that she rocked the footstool side to side at a nearly feverish pitch. After a moment of watching Ellie's ribbons quiver to and fro, Kate barely stopped herself from shaking her head and upsetting her curls. "Ellie, you're going to fall over if—"

She was scared speechless as the footstool tilted too far to one side sending Ellie perilously toward the floor. At the last moment Ellie shifted in the other direction to regain her balance and set the leg of the footstool down with a loud thump.

Ellie seemed to stop breathing for a second, then her wide green eyes lifted to Kate's. They stared at each other. Kate bit the inside of her cheek to keep from laughing. "Why don't you fetch Sean? It's nearly time to get started."

"Right." Ellie nodded and eagerly bounded from the room closing the door behind her a bit too loudly given the church service was going on just down the hall.

"Finished!" Rachel exclaimed. "Come, see yourself in the mirror."

Kate carefully stood and turned toward the mirror. Ms. Lettie smiled, then handed her a bouquet of wild-flowers in a riot of different colors before stepping aside. Kate caught her breath at her reflection in the mirror.

Her hair was pulled back into an elaborate chignon but it was the dress that made her eyes fill with tears. The wedding gown was trimmed with the Irish lace Ellie had mentioned in her letter to Nathan, given to Kate by her mother, and had been altered only slightly to bring it into style. It had also been tailored to fit Kate's figure perfectly. She shook her head in wonder. "I look…"

"Beautiful?" Rachel questioned.

"Enchanting," Ms. Lettie stated.

Kate laughed. "I was going to say, I look like a bride."

Rachel grinned. "An enchantingly beautiful bride."

She turned to hug each of them. "I can't thank you two enough for everything you've done to help me plan this in just two weeks."

Ms. Lettie hugged her in return. "I believe you just did."

A rap on the door sounded. Butterflies began to flutter in Kate's stomach. She pulled in a deep breath. "That must be Sean."

"We'll make sure everyone is ready." Rachel picked up her smaller bouquet of flowers, then opened the door for Sean to enter before she and Ms. Lettie stepped out.

Sean caught sight of her and his expression shifted to one of awe. "Wow."

She laughed. "Thank you."

"You look wonderful, Kate." He swallowed. "So much like Ma."

She reached out her arms to her younger brother who always seemed mature beyond his years. His gangly arms pulled her into a tight hug. She sighed. "I miss them, especially today."

"I wish they were here. Pa would know just what to say at a time like this. Even so, I'll try my best to say what he'd want me to." He stepped back to clear his throat and met her gaze seriously. "I couldn't be prouder to have a sister like you. You kept us together when everything around us was falling apart. I am so grateful for that, and even more grateful that now you've found a love like Ma and Pa had. I know they are happy for you, too."

A smile blossomed across her face even as tears slipped from her eyes. She quickly wiped them away. "Oh, Sean, I couldn't have been more blessed than to have you for my brother. Thank you for stepping up in Pa's stead and giving me away."

He presented her with his arm. "We'd better hurry up if you still want me to do that."

"Of course," she said. Slipping her arm through his, she let him lead her out the door to the where Ellie and Rachel stood waiting.

"Doc and Ms. Lettie already took the seats on the front row you designated for them next to Judge Hendricks," Rachel said.

She had asked them to sit in the front row to honor everything they'd done for her family both before and after her parents' deaths. "Good."

Rachel grinned at Sean. "Don't you look handsome?"

"Thanks," he said with a wry grin. "It isn't the most comfortable getup, but I guess it's all right."

Kate chuckled, then after receiving a curious look from the rest of the party she explained, "I just realized something. After me, Sean will probably be the next one in our family to get married."

The look on his face was a mix of confusion and horror that slowly faded into resignation. "I guess you're right."

Ellie giggled. Kate was going to question the mischief she read in her gaze but at that moment the music inside the chapel changed. "Get ready!"

They all stepped aside as Ellie took her position at the door with her basket of flowers in hand.

"Try to look the opposite of what you are. You know, sweet," Sean whispered.

Ellie shot him a glare. The door opened, signaling the beginning of the ceremony.

Nathan's heart beat rapidly in his throat as the doors to the chapel opened to reveal Ellie dressed in a spring green dress. The girl looked surprisingly innocent with her blond hair artfully arranged so that wisps of it purposely hung around her face. She glanced over the crowd then gave a demure smile. An "aw" escaped the crowd as one.

He knew Ellie too well not to notice the way her lips curved a bit too smugly in response. She was up to something, no doubt about it. She gaily prepared the way for her sister by tossing brightly covered flowers onto the aisle. As she neared the end of the aisle she glanced up from her task. Nathan met her gaze and grinned. Delight sprang into Ellie's eyes. She nearly took an unplanned side trip toward him but Ms. Lettie caught her hand and guided her to her seat.

Rachel was the next down the aisle. Finally, the music changed and Kate appeared in the doorway. His heart, which had been pounding in his chest moments earlier, seemed to still along with his breath. She was stunningly beautiful in the Irish lace dress he'd read so much about.

Most of her cinnamon-colored locks were pulled away from her face in an elaborate knot with a few escaping tendrils. A filmy veil covered most of her face, maddeningly so, for he desperately wanted to see her expression.

Lawson discreetly leaned forward to whisper, "Breathe."

Nathan shot him a grateful glance.

"Dearly beloved, we are gathered here today in the sight of God and this congregation to join together this man and this woman in holy matrimony," Pastor began. "Who gives this woman to this man?"

"Her family and friends do," Sean said. At the minister's affirmation, he lifted Kate's veil and handed her to Nathan before he moved to sit beside Lawson on the other side of Doc and Ms. Lettie.

Hand in hand, they turned toward the minister but Nathan could not keep his eyes off Kate. Her blue eyes met his. She smiled and suddenly it was as if everything in his world was put to rights.

As the ceremony progressed, he repeated the words he had said once before but this time with a new understanding of their importance and the depth of their meaning. He'd certainly never dreamed that the pledge he had made then would lead him to this time and place with a woman he loved so deeply. He had to admit. This was better than any dream he could have imagined on his own.

Kate had never felt more at home than she did at Nathan's side as they accepted congratulations from the stream of well-wishers. Even Mrs. Greene managed a courteous, if mumbled, expression of congratulations. It was long before the streams of parishioners and guests dwindled to just their closest circle of friends.

Kate smiled in greeting as Judge Hendricks stepped forward. She accepted his kiss on the cheek, then watched as he shook Nathan's hand. "Congratulations to you both. I'll be heading out soon but I wanted to give you this."

Kate took the piece of paper the judge held out to her and studied it carefully before an amused smile lifted her lips. She handed it to Nathan. "It's our marriage license."

"Your official marriage license," the judge interjected.

Nathan grinned. "I'll be sure to keep this in a safe place. We might even frame it."

"You do that." Judge Hendricks laughed, then said his goodbyes.

For the first time all day, Kate found herself in a moment alone with Nathan. She glanced up toward him. He took a step closer. Suddenly Ms. Lettie appeared at her side.

"Sorry to interrupt but I thought you might be interested in taking care of the gifts now so you'll be free to slip off when you please later."

Kate frowned. "We didn't need any gifts."

Rachel stepped forward. "Don't be silly. Everyone receives gifts at their wedding. It's only proper."

Deputy Stone nodded. "In this case, it might even be timely."

"What are you talking about?" Nathan asked suspiciously.

Doc handed Kate a sealed envelope. "This was entrusted to me to give to you. Go ahead and open it."

Kate broke the seal. Opening the envelope, she gasped. She'd never seen so much paper money in all her life.

"Practically everyone in town who had something to give contributed. Life's been a bit rough for you lately. The town has wanted to do something to support you for years. When your barn burned down they saw that as an opportunity. There's enough in there to purchase the lumber you need not only to replace your barn but to build a bigger one for the future."

She felt Nathan tense beside her and knew he was wondering if she'd accept such a gift. A few months ago she certainly wouldn't have. She'd learned a lot since then. She'd learned to trust. She'd learned to love. She'd also learned to accept help. Kate smiled tremulously. "I don't know what else to say besides thank you."

Deputy Stone grinned. "That isn't the only gift."

"I'm not sure if I can accept anything more."

"This one isn't for you, Kate. It's mostly for Nathan. As much as I'd like to say I thought this up and carried it out, I can't. This one came from someone named Davis Reynolds."

Nathan caught Kate's questioning gaze but shrugged. He was just as confused as she seemed to be. The entire party followed Deputy Stone down the steps of the church to where the few remaining horses and buggies stood. "Davis contacted the sheriff, who put me in charge of the covert operation. There he is."

Nathan followed his friend's gesture toward one of the finest and largest stallions Nathan had ever seen. He heard Kate gasp and realized that even though she hadn't had much exposure to horses, she was able tell the quality of the animal. He stepped toward the horse haltingly, not entirely sure if he should believe what his eyes were seeing or where his brain was leading him.

"Was there any message with the horse?" he asked.

"He said you'd understand."

Kate stepped up beside Nathan. "Does the horse have a name?"

Nathan shook his head incredulously. "Samson. The horse's name is Samson."

The deputy frowned. "How did you know?"

"I guessed." Nathan turned to Kate to explain. "Davis is an old friend of mine. He always said I should raise horses again."

Understanding lit her blue eyes. "That sounds perfect."

"What about the wheat?"

"I have no particular affinity for it except that it puts food on the table," she said. "We can always try doing both until you become established in this."

Incredible, Nathan thought to himself as he strode forward to inspect the animal more closely. As impressed as he was by it, his gaze kept straying toward where Kate stood talking with her siblings. He felt someone nudge his ribs and turned to find the deputy's eyes twinkling meaningfully. "It's about time for you two to be heading out, isn't it? Why don't you attend to your bride, Nathan? I'll take care of the horse."

Nathan grinned. "Thanks. I owe you one."

"Good." The deputy's gaze strayed toward Rachel. "Who knows, I may actually collect on that."

Kate closed her eyes as a last sultry breeze of summer danced across her cheek like a warm touch. She pulled the ridiculous pins from her hair and tucked them in her skirt pocket before peeking inside the picnic basket Ms. Lettie had sent along with them. Her stomach growled. Ms. Lettie was right when she said no one actually ate at their own wedding.

She'd succumbed to the temptation of one of Ms. Lettie's cookies before the door opened behind her and Nathan stepped out of the house in his regular clothes. They'd both been uncomfortable in their wedding finery. Kate took a deep breath just because she could as they set out for the creek. It wasn't long before she slipped her hand into Nathan's strong yet gentle grasp.

He lifted her hand to kiss the tips of her fingers. She met his warm brown gaze and smiled at the love she saw echoed there. The corners of his mouth lifted into an answering smile as he tugged her slightly closer to his side. She sighed. "The ceremony was beautiful, wasn't it?"

His gaze turned teasing. "Best I've ever been to, that's for sure."

She laughed even as she sent him an exasperated look. "I'm serious. What was your favorite part?"

"My favorite part," he echoed. He met her gaze seriously. "The wedding vows."

She angled her steps sideways so she could see his face. "Really?"

He nodded. "Without a doubt."

She turned to walk forward again, then hearing the

gentle roar of the waterfall, she smiled. "Dearly beloved, we are gathered here today—"

"In the presence of God and these witnesses," he interrupted. She laughed as he gestured to the empty woods around them before his deep voice continued. "To join—"

She placed a hand on his chest as she stepped in front of him, forcing him to stop. Lifting her gaze to his, she allowed her deepest feelings to show unrestrained as she said, "To join together this man..."

"And this woman," Nathan said slipping an arm around her waist. "In holy matrimony."

He would have kissed her but Kate shook her head and slipped out of his arms, teasing, "That doesn't come until later."

He grinned rakishly. "Well, I forgot what comes next so I thought we could just as well skip to the end."

She laughed. "No. The next part is very important."

"What's that?" he asked as he took the basket from her and set it on the ground in a dry spot.

"If anyone knows of a reason the two should not be joined together, speak now or forever hold your peace," she said over her shoulder as she slipped out of her boots. The water looked wonderful. She bet it was just the right temperature. She tiptoed through the mud near the bank of the creek to find out.

"You think that was an important part?" Nathan asked as he joined her to wade in the creek.

She lifted her chin to meet his gaze. "It's important because it leads to the most important question."

"What question would that be?" He reached out to slip his fingers through her cinnamon-colored curls.

"The question was, if you, Nathan Rutledge, would take me to be your lawfully wedded wife."

He stepped closer. "And I did."

A smile tilted her lips. "You do remember what came after that, don't you?"

Her lashes drifted closed as his lips covered hers in a loving kiss that was all the answer she needed.

* * * * *

Dear Reader,

I began writing this story at the tender age of sixteen. It all started with a simple question. What if you found out that, through no fault of your own, you were married to a stranger? I've lived a lot of life since I asked that question. Just like me, this story has grown and evolved in ways I never expected. I've had the most creative co-writer along the way—God. He is not only the Author and Perfecter of my faith, but also of this book.

He taught me that it all comes down to trust. I learned that life doesn't always make sense, it isn't always comfortable, and sometimes is downright painful. Yet, like Kate and Nathan, I also discovered that if I hold on long enough and allow God to lead me, then I will end up in a moment like this. A moment when my dreams have come true, my work is complete and His glory is revealed.

Thank you for stepping back in time with me to the fictional town of Peppin, Texas. I hope you enjoyed reading Kate and Nathan's story as much as I enjoyed writing it. Sean's story is next so look for more of the O'Briens' marriage mayhem soon. In the meantime, I would love to hear from you. Please contact me at www.NoelleMarchand.com or check out my Facebook page.

Blessings!

Noelle Marchand

Questions for Discussion

1. Kate believes she is proving to everyone that she doesn't need help taking care of the farm and her siblings. How do Sean and Ellie feel about this at the beginning of the story? Why do you think their perceptions differ?

2. Do you think Sean and Ellie were right to take matters into their own hands at the beginning of the story? Why or why not? Is there a different means by which they could have reached the same end?

3. What was Ms. Lettie's role in the story? In Kate and Nathan's relationship? How would you label her? Is she a busybody, motherly figure, friend?

4. In the events leading up to the story, Kate, Nathan and Jeremiah have all experienced the death of someone close to them. How do the three characters deal with their grief? What are the similarities? What are the differences?

5. Nathan chooses not to tell anyone about the events in his past that led up to him responding to the advertisement. What are his reasons for doing this? Do you think he was right to keep his past a secret? How does this impact the story? How does this impact his relationship with Kate?

6. Why is Nathan estranged from his family? Do you think he could have done something to prevent that

from happening? Why did Lawson urge Nathan to repair his relationship with his family? Why did Sean?

7. How do you feel about Lawson's desperate need for a family? The story hints that Lawson may decide to live with Doc and Ms. Lettie Williams. What do you think the future holds for him?

8. What was the turning point in Kate and Nathan's relationship? How did they reach it?

9. Kate struggles to discern and trust God's will at different points in the story. Have you ever had this problem? If so, what did you do to overcome it?

10. Nathan decides to pursue Kate and begins courting her. What brings him to this decision? Why is it important to his spiritual walk with God? How does it affect his relationship with Kate?

11. How does Nathan's presence change the O'Brien family? What does he teach them about living life? He emphasizes the importance of not only working hard, but also of enjoying life. How does this impact the O'Briens' relationships with him and each other?

12. What would you say are the overriding themes of the story? Why?

13. Were you expecting the judge's ruling about the annulment? What reasons did he give for his decision? Do you agree with him? Why or why not?

14. How do you think Kate and Nathan's marriage will affect the O'Brien family? What will change for them?

INSPIRATIONAL

Inspirational romances to warm your heart & soul.

Love Inspired.
HISTORICAL

TITLES AVAILABLE NEXT MONTH

Available November 8, 2011

SNOWFLAKE BRIDE
Buttons and Bobbins
Jillian Hart

THE RANCHER'S COURTSHIP
Brides of Simpson Creek
Laurie Kingery

AN HONORABLE GENTLEMAN
Regina Scott

THE DOCTOR'S MISSION|
Debbie Kaufman

REQUEST YOUR FREE BOOKS!

2 FREE INSPIRATIONAL NOVELS
PLUS 2
FREE
MYSTERY GIFTS

Love Inspired

HISTORICAL
INSPIRATIONAL HISTORICAL ROMANCE

YES! Please send me 2 FREE Love Inspired® Historical novels and my 2 FREE mystery gifts (gifts are worth about $10). After receiving them, if I don't wish to receive any more books, I can return the shipping statement marked "cancel". If I don't cancel, I will receive 4 brand-new novels every month and be billed just $4.49 per book in the U.S. or $4.99 per book in Canada. That's a saving of at least 22% off the cover price. It's quite a bargain! Shipping and handling is just 50¢ per book in the U.S. and 75¢ per book in Canada.* I understand that accepting the 2 free books and gifts places me under no obligation to buy anything. I can always return a shipment and cancel at any time. Even if I never buy another book, the two free books and gifts are mine to keep forever.

102/302 IDN FEHF

Name	(PLEASE PRINT)	
Address		Apt. #
City	State/Prov.	Zip/Postal Code

Signature (if under 18, a parent or guardian must sign)

Mail to the **Reader Service:**
IN U.S.A.: P.O. Box 1867, Buffalo, NY 14240-1867
IN CANADA: P.O. Box 609, Fort Erie, Ontario L2A 5X3
Not valid for current subscribers to Love Inspired Historical books.

Want to try two free books from another series?
Call 1-800-873-8635 or visit www.ReaderService.com.

* Terms and prices subject to change without notice. Prices do not include applicable taxes. Sales tax applicable in N.Y. Canadian residents will be charged applicable taxes. Offer not valid in Quebec. This offer is limited to one order per household. All orders subject to credit approval. Credit or debit balances in a customer's account(s) may be offset by any other outstanding balance owed by or to the customer. Please allow 4 to 6 weeks for delivery. Offer available while quantities last.

Your Privacy—The Reader Service is committed to protecting your privacy. Our Privacy Policy is available online at www.ReaderService.com or upon request from the Reader Service.

We make a portion of our mailing list available to reputable third parties that offer products we believe may interest you. If you prefer that we not exchange your name with third parties, or if you wish to clarify or modify your communication preferences, please visit us at www.ReaderService.com/consumerschoice or write to us at Reader Service Preference Service, P.O. Box 9062, Buffalo, NY 14269. Include your complete name and address.

UH11B